P9-EKY-183

"In the matter of the de Lagenays, I would advise you to employ extreme caution. Their whereabouts are largely uncertain and, as you may guess, rumor abounds in such a spot. The family is eccentric, and any claim they may assume in the property is, at best, hypothetical. I would, however, insist, in the strongest terms, that you do not venture outside the bounds of the chateau unaccompanied. My intention is not to alarm you, but to make provision against all circumstances, however remote."

Christian was not properly awake, and the nonsense of this fitted perfectly with his mental state. De Lagenay was a name he did not even vaguely recall. He lowered his lids till the fire became a fringe of golden grass. He laughed bitterly and fell once more asleep.

And dreamed of a fair-haired, lily-like girl, her arms flung crosswise over her throat, her eyes staring at him.

LYCANTHIA

or

The Children of Wolves

———◆———

TANITH LEE

———◆———

DAW Books, Inc.
Donald A. Wollheim, Publisher
1633 Broadway, New York, N.Y. 10019

COPYRIGHT ©, 1981, BY TANITH LEE

All Rights Reserved.

Cover art by Paul Chadwick.

FIRST PRINTING, APRIL 1981

1 2 3 4 5 6 7 8 9

 DAW TRADEMARK REGISTERED
U.S. PAT. OFF. MARCA
REGISTRADA. HECHO EN U.S.A.

PRINTED IN U.S.A.

TABLE OF CONTENTS

Dedication:

To
FREFF
Who can find sunlight
in the darkest forest.

PART ONE

LE PAYS INCONNU

Chapter 1

---◆◉◆---

The Arrival

The train, running north under its hammerhead of smoke and steam, had prematurely entered the land of winter, as if through a great, pure, silent door. How cold, how changed, the world was in the white morning, as the still, white light began to come. A world of wet woods, vague hills. And on the horizon's edge, the pines, blocking in the land with ink. An empty region, apparently. Nothing by the track or visible between the branches, none of those piled towns, sloping villages, none of those shacks, sheds, cottages, farms, that had been interminably visible all yesterday, as the locomotive unfurled itself from the city. Nothing now, till the station appeared, swirling up about the train as if tediously and pointlessly to detain it. There was a remnant of the fall huddled around the station; on a bush, the occasional sodden yellow leaf, on a bough a cherry-red one: refugees.

The air, as he stepped down, was keen as a knife. It immediately pierced to his lungs, and he coughed desultorily, not really noticing he did so. His box and bags were placed around him. He stood with them, a little island of dark in the albino morning, as the train drew away.

Half a mile along the track, it gave a lonely cry, calling farewell to him, heartlessly, over its shoulder.

The station was ramshackle and looked deserted.

When the train was gone, it seemed he had been marooned, shipwrecked in the midst of a wilderness. Christian looked at his baggage hopelessly. There was too much to carry. He did not want to carry it. He had been promised a meeting here, and a conveyance.

He did not want to make any decisions. The thought of doing so, of planning what should happen next, made him feel depressed, bored and exhausted. He sat down on the box. He had not been able to sleep in the train. Something about its eternity of motion, which had drugged him, had also kept him awake. Bareheaded, yet swathed otherwise in the dark astrakhan greatcoat, he imagined himself blending, dissolving into the landscape. Black and white like the winter morning, and the woods. Black hair, black coat; the white face. A young face, except for two fissures carved out under the eyes. The eyes . . . what color were they? Black and white mixed; a gray, luminous but leaden. Curious. (He was picturing himself, now.) Not even the little crimson touches of autumn about him. Till he thought of blood, and all the leaves left clinging on the bushes around the station wall pulsed and burned as if alive, and he felt the terrible mindless disbelieving fear, and then—

And then a man came out of the station building. He was tall and cloaked, a funereal top hat rising like a chimney from his head. He was all clothes, and did not seem to have a face.

"Monsieur?" he asked. "Monsieur Dorse?"

Christian rose, acknowledging his name.

"Yes."

"The car is below on the road, monsieur. Peton is coming for your luggage."

"Yes."

They stood indecisively, the young man, the newcomer in his top hat, like actors smitten with amnesia. What came next?

"I am Sarrette, monsieur."

The driver. There was nothing else to be done but walk away from his luggage, abandon it, move forward empty-handed into the void.

Sarrette held open two doors for him and then a gate. Steps went down between earth banks. Trees clouded on the far side of a narrow gravel road, where the big car rested like a jet-black, strangely elongated and roofed bath chair.

"It's very cold, monsieur," said Sarrette, as he opened the

door of the car. Another man had emerged from somewhere, gone into the station, and was now returning with the box. Peton. He was strong, bareheaded as was Christian, but without the young man's wealth of hair. Thin strands were combed over Peton's scalp like pencil drawings. He loaded the box at the rear of the car. Sarrette made gestures with a traveling rug, as Peton loped back up the steps and presently returned with the other bags. Peton did not glance, at any point, at Christian.

His task accomplished, an incoherent altercation broke out between Peton and Sarrette, conducted in the local dialect— virtually incomprehensible. The incomprehensibility removed it from Christian's sphere of concerns, and he was relieved. The freezing air had begun to intrude under his skin, hurting him.

Then Peton was suddenly making away. Sarrette started the car and climbed into the driver's seat. The car shuddered and slid forward.

"I am afraid, monsieur . . ." said Sarrette. There was a pause. "There are only the four of us at the chateau. As I believe Monsieur Hamel wrote you."

"Yes."

"It's a bad state of affairs. But to take on service at this time of year is impossible. Until the spring—"

"I understand."

"Out here, monsieur. The Styx. The desert."

The road curved away from the railway tracks, and now the pine forest flowed toward it. It was the forest of a childhood story. Nothing needed to be said or thought about it. Sometime or other, some romancer had thought and said it all. . . .

The feeling of a claw scratching in his throat increased, and Christian coughed again, lightly, not indulging the cough. Let it wait.

The driver said, "Wonderful country for the health, monsieur."

Christian watched the dark green and black pagodas of the trees. He was twenty-eight. Before the spring came, he might be dead. There was a thought, now.

He felt rather ill, drained, but it was not unpleasant while he could lie back in the plush of the seat. He wondered if Sarrette thought him handsome and wished, on a merely paternalistic level, to take care of him. This had happened quite often. Was Sarrette a local product? Christian was not really used to a tradition of retainers, the notion of serfs, which, however much blurred and euphemized by the epoch, would still be present here in this wild winter country. The servants of his childhood, and at the house of his cousin in the city, had been affectionate, unproud and insulting.

He wondered how long it would be before he saw the chateau, and how he would react to it. His mother had lived in this place, but only until her seventh or eighth year. His grandfather's debts had then lost them almost everything, and the house had been sold. The family had become city dwellers, and at eighteen, a good marriage to a provincial hôtelier of foreign extraction had snared his mother, and brought Christian. It was a freak of fortune and ancestral connivance which had returned the chateau, forty years after its sale, into Christian's possession. He had not thought to have it, nor ever thought to want it. Life had systematically taken away from him the things he had wished for most. The chateau was a kind of bright bauble flung to him as he lay stranded and crying with despair. Childishly distracted from pain and ruin, he had picked it up.

The landscape looked its age. The Romans had built their forts on it once.

The road ascended steeply between palisades and hanging curtains of trees. Periodic breaks revealed distant depths showering away, pine on pine, the occasional fir, bluish and smoldering, the attenuated counterpoint of larches. Above, slabs of hillside sometimes leaned like balconies from the forest. Once, a blush of smoke indicated some isolated dwelling, or charcoal burners, perhaps. The smell of the smoke, and dank, crushed, fallen leaves, permeated the car, chocolaty and immemorial. Such scents, like those of cooking meat, sap in a bud, a woman's hair, had existed since the beginnings—primeval, timeless, permanent.

(Of course, he would inevitably think in such a way.)

The village appeared almost without warning. A stone marker at the wayside, next a farm, piercing through the trees with its raw carpet of stubbled fields and long fence. Abruptly a church hung above them, angled almost horizontally as it perched sideways on the incline. Houses burgeoned. They looked very old. Iron crosses, hammered into the plaster, had lapsed drunkenly sideways, pots of brown soil cluttered windows and stairs. Roofs fell toward each other. Kept falling. Walls leaned. A situation du Moyen Âge. Women in black moved about, and tainted air rose from the forge. A child ran down the street toward the car, a dog barking at its heels, but Sarrette was driving very slowly.

Christian expected faces to open like flowers, staring at him, and he held himself together, braced. But these people barely glanced at the car. There was some kind of monument in the square, and there was a well, still in use, naturally.

They drove around the square, by the memorial and the well, past the church, and slowly back into more forest beyond.

Five minutes later, two stone animals manifested on either side of the road, heraldic dogs, rampant, with shields. Another minute and the wall reared up, the wall of the chateau, a huge rampart, partly crumbling. Two more stone dogs watched them through the open gates.

This ground had been cleared, partly landscaped at one time, probably. To Christian, the view had no format. It belonged to him, and some dim stirring in him tried briefly to assimilate, to recognize: an avenue of leafless limes, a cypress tree commanding a hillock, a cluster of stones that might have been part of some former building. . . . But no, the land about the chateau remained elusive and as indeterminate as anything he had witnessed from the windows of the train.

The road ran right over the estate, finally crossing a bridge, that looked as if it were constructed of gray marzipan, above a moat. If any water remained in the moat, Christian could not see. The chateau loomed on the other side. It was large. Like the cleared land, it defied acceptance.

He gazed at it wearily, let it have its way, too tired to fight with it. The little town houses and flats of his past, with their reassuring claustrophobia, the suite of rooms in his father's stucco hotel, facing forever out to sea as if from a becalmed liner—these homes and dwellings had nothing to do with the chateau. It did not seem inhabitable. Rock-like bastions, stained plastered walls, shutters, battlements, balustrades, all glued and grown together, an enormous petrified vegetable.

The road, and therefore the car, stopped under a tall gray terrace, by a staircase flanked with cement urns. Sarrette sounded the horn. They sat still in the quietly popping car, waiting.

A boy ran from the chateau suddenly, along the terrace, down the stair. He was about nineteen, red-cheeked. Christian experienced a terrible apathetic contempt for the boy's health and vigor.

Christian opened the car door, not waiting to be released. He got out and looked at the staircase, at the boy running down it.

The boy nodded anxiously to him, a bob of the head, a paragon of obsequiousness. He moved at once and began to unload Christian's box and the bags.

Sarrette emerged from the car.

"Renzo," said Sarrette, indicating the boy. "Madame Tienne will be in charge of the domestic arrangements, and of course there is the woman from the village, who will cook. And there's the girl who'll live in, to attend to the cleaning of the rooms. This is unsatisfactory, naturally, but until the spring—"

"Yes," said Christian. He observed the stairs, trying to count them. Forty, or was it forty-two?

"Much of the chateau is still shut up. Madame Tienne has opened the master suite on the first floor for your convenience, and the grande hall and salon are in good order. But if any other apartment—I believe the music room interested you, monsieur?"

"Not until the advent of a piano tuner."

"Oh yes, indeed. Monsieur Hamel engaged someone from the city. It was seen to last week. Didn't you receive the letter?"

Christian recalled the lawyer Hamel's unmistakable last envelope arriving at the house of his cousin just as Christian was leaving for the station. His cousin had been in tears, a taxicab stood at the door. Christian had thrust the letter into his coat, and, convinced of its pedantic unimportance, forgotten it.

He went on looking at the staircase. The boy, single-handed, like Peton, was lugging the box toward the terrace.

"Presumably I go up," said Christian.

"Yes, monsieur. Madame Tienne is waiting in the salon for your orders."

Christian negotiated the stairs slowly. On the twentieth, he paused. He looked back, as if taking in the vista, steadying himself casually against the pedestal of an urn.

Sarrette, who had not offered to help him at all, was leaning against the shiny car, watching. From the first, Christian received the impression of—what? Not exactly unfriendliness, more indifference.

I am an interloper, Christian thought. *They instinctively expect that I shall come and go, just like the nuisance of the impending winter. Arrival, and inevitable departure. And how right they are.*

Beyond the man and the car, the curve of road and bridge, the land rose modestly. A crippled lime tree looked for a moment impossibly familiar.

There were forty-five stairs. Renzo, the boy, passed him twice, returning for and then carrying the bags. Renzo was cheerful. He ignored Christian's slow ascent.

Christian actually felt the dry pallor of his face, as if it had been painted over, like the peeling facade of the chateau. He paused on the terrace, breathing. His legs were water, but he had Madame to deal with. He visualized a doll-like figure in a provincial white apron, knowing the image would be false.

He still heard his cousin's voice—"Don't go, don't leave us, my dear. You're not well, not fit—"

Mummified by frost, husks of flowers still lurked in the urns beside the door, which stood wide to receive the new master.

He heard the car driving away around the side of the house toward the antique stables, now reduced to a sprawling garage.

He coughed, and went through the door into his absurd ancestral home.

Chapter 2

─────◆◦◆◦◆─────

The Salon

Like the forest, the grande hall of the chateau was exactly
the product of a romance. Carved panels of wood alternated
with brocades. Velvet drapes packaged the views in the windows. Two enormous chandeliers dripped from the high ceiling. Two enormous fireplaces excavated the walls. A long
table of polished bloody mahogany waited to seat forty or
more.

An indoor stair swept toward heaven, with the bizarrely
curving banister erected to allow for the passage of birdcage
skirts. (Renzo moved up it with the bags.) Above a gallery, a
single high-up stained-glass porthole, sumptuously and frig-
idly blue, indicated heaven had already been attained.

The salon opened to the left through double doors, little
sister to the hall, with a similar display of long table, chandeliers and drapes. The solitary fireplace was fired, though the
room remained chilly.

Madame Tienne stood before the hearth. He had been
foolish to suppose she would not be just as he had predicted.
A figment of his imagination, she clasped her doll-like hands
over her white apron. The doll face was that of a stern ma-
tron made of ceramic. He wondered if she had been in
residence when the drunkard, the man who bought the
chateau from Christian's grandfather, had sipped and swallowed himself to death here.

She introduced herself with a stiff, very little bow, and the medieval cluster of keys at her waist jiggled and clanked. She spoke of the apartment upstairs, where his bags had been taken. Renzo would unpack for him. Renzo would act as steward, porter and valet, if Christian required it. She spoke of the fire in the grate. She inquired what Christian recommended in this instance. Would he take coffee? When would he wish luncheon? Would anyone else be arriving? Would he be content to leave the menus, and similar affairs, in her hands?

Sometimes his appetite was voracious, at others it did not exist. Today, it did not exist. He thanked her, and told her he would have coffee, and when she had gone he sat by the fire in a chair. He knew he would have to wait to be alone.

First Renzo came in to report on the fate of the bags. Then Madame herself returned with the coffee things. A slim vase of cognac and a glass had been added, and a little plate of cakes. When she had poured his coffee, she went away. Renzo came back to see to the fire. During this operation, Sarrette appeared. Shed of his coat and unorthodox undertaker's hat, he had become a soldier, gripping his hands behind him, thrusting out his chest. Would monsieur need the car again today?

When Renzo and Sarrette had departed, a girl evolved to clear the coffee tray, and finding him with the cup untouched, she emptied it, and poured afresh.

The heavy white light in the windows, the primrose-colored fire, did not seem to give much light. The room was dim, and he barely saw the girl. Wholesome and quite plain, her hair rolled like a sausage, she glanced at him under her lids, and he wondered idly if she would be the one who would decide to cosset and take care of him. Catching his eye, she blushed, but it was timidity rather than attraction.

As she was going out, he said, "Please tell Madame Tienne I don't require anything else. I can see to the fire, and the coffee. I don't want the car, or luncheon, or a single thing. If one more person comes into this room, I shall be forced to vacate it." He paused, and the girl balanced on her astonishment, or whatever it was. "Will you do that?"

"Yes, m'sieur," she said, and was gone.

He drank the fresh hot coffee, took a bite from one of the cakes and threw the rest of it wastefully into the fire with a sense of its betrayal.

Disturbed and without energy, he prowled the room, looking at ornaments, paintings, avoiding a mirror, but unable to
take in anything.

The room seemed to darken further. Probably the day was
growing overcast. Like the road, gas had been brought
uniquely to the chateau. Lily-shaped gas lamps branched
from the wood above the fire, and at intervals along the walls.
He need never be in the dark.

The servants—*his* servants—had brought him cognac either
because they deduced he was an invalid, or because they
remembered the drunkard. Perhaps they wished to insure
Christian's departure from the place. Slow murder via bottle
and glass. He pictured them plotting it in a stone kitchen
beneath his feet. He did not really believe in the servants.

Maybe he should go up to the music room and investigate
the piano. When he thought of it, a surge of pleasure went
through him, followed aptly and unavoidably by a surge of
weariness, a colorless desire not to move.

He sat down in the chair again. It must be about eleven
o'clock. He gazed at the fire; the room was warmer and he
grew drowsy. As with hunger, sleep frequently eluded him, or
else came overpoweringly.

He closed his eyes, and saw his pretty cousin. Thirty years
of age, Annelise, married and with three children, was nevertheless in love with Christian. Or in love with what he
represented. The aura of something dying could fascinate,
was immensely alluring to some, though for complex, subcon-
scious reasons.

He had unbuttoned his greatcoat, but not removed it. Now
it occurred to him to do so. In some odd way it had to do
with also removing the importune mind-apparition of Annelise. He rose, and as he drew off the astrakhan, Hamel's last
letter, somehow dislodged, dropped into his hand.

Christian sat down again. He watched the letter for some
while, not wishing to read it. This was a foolish procrastina-
tion to which he constantly fell prey. The letter, of course,
would contain merely a few fussy leftover lawyer's details.
And yet, there might be some onus on Christian to reply,
some new query or happening with which he must involve
himself. He felt a distinct dread at such a thought.

He sat, holding the letter, and let torpor overcome him.

His senses began to go, blissfully, the firelight, the warmth and the dimness melting them away.

A log barked on the hearth and woke him.

A year seemed to have passed, but the fire was still high, its yellow stars leaping to the chimney.

If anyone had come in to summon him, like a baby, to a noonday meal, he had not woken. Had they viewed him with pity? With scorn?

Hamel's letter crackled under his palm. Almost absently he lifted it and slit the envelope.

The dull window light made it almost illegible, and what was illegible need not be taken seriously. . . .

A paragraph of legal trivia. A paragraph on the piano tuner. A financial paragraph. A good wish. Christian's eyes could not keep a purchase on the paper. He leaned back in the chair and held the paper so the fire shone radiantly through it and the words danced.

—"In the matter of the de Lagenays, I would advise you to employ extreme caution. Their whereabouts are largely uncertain and, as you may guess, rumor abounds in such a spot. The family is eccentric, and any claim they may assume to the property is, at best, hypothetical. I would, however, insist, in the strongest terms, that you do not venture outside the bounds of the chateau unaccompanied. My intention is not to alarm you, but to make provision against all circumstances, however remote."

Christian was not properly awake, and the nonsense of this fitted perfectly and almost graciously with his mental state. De Lagenay was a name he did not even vaguely recall Hamel mentioning earlier, in the city office. A claim to the property? Neither did Christian remember such a point. But then, he had sat in Hamel's plush chair, looking alert and intelligent, nodding, grunting at the correct intervals, signing documents when they were placed before him, hearing little, understanding less. Christian had found it increasingly difficult to take such things seriously, and his powers of concentration, sometimes insanely formidable (the study of a moth poised on a shutter, a man at a street corner, a strain of music) were inadequate.

He lowered his lids till the fire became a fringe of golden grass. He saw the de Lagenays, ten or so burly peasant farmers, clustered amid the pine trees. They carried staves, knives, an ancient musket. He laughed bitterly, and fell once more asleep.

And dreamed of a fair-haired, lily-like girl, her arms flung crosswise over her throat, her eyes staring at him.

"Monsieur," someone was saying, hesitantly but repeatedly. "Monsieur, monsieur."

Christian raised himself from a grave of black velure and opium poppies. For a moment he saw Renzo standing apparently in space, lit by a bloom of shadowy light. But the light exuded from a window, and Renzo stood on the floor. The fire was nearly out. It was cold, the northern afternoon advancing toward a windy northern evening. Christian smiled at Renzo, and the boy faltered, transfixed by the stunning charm of the smile.

"I've come to light the lamps, monsieur," said Renzo. "Sylvie came in before, but you were asleep."

"I was still," said Christian, "asleep."

He found he could not breathe, and began to cough, rackingly.

The spasm went on and on, lifting him of itself first into an upright position, next bowing him forward. When it passed, the boy, carefully ignoring him, had coaxed a glint from the fire onto a taper, and was inserting it into one of the gas mantles. The blue hiss of gas ended in the expected pop. The greenish flame fluttered into life. Encouraged, the boy offered fire into the second lily cup.

"Madame says, will you have dinner served in the salon, or in the hall? Madame says, will you have English tea served at four o'clock? Madame says, it was the custom of your grandfather's time. The tea. China tea."

"I said," said Christian, his voice a soft clear rasp, "I said no one was to come into this room."

"But the lamps, Monsieur."

"No English China tea," said Christian. "No dinner."

Renzo gasped.

Christian got up from the chair and made a move toward the basket of logs beside the hearth. Renzo hastily forestalled him. Wood plunged on the dying embers with a crash.

"Madame," said Renzo, "says to inform you dinner has usually been served at eight o'clock."

"Then serve it," said Christian. "I shan't eat any of it, but I don't want to spoil anything for Madame Tienne."

He stood, leaning by the hearth, shivering, watching the light crawl under the wood. Across the long room, the girl called Sylvie had entered like a ghost and was drawing the drapes. The grounds of the chateau were lost in a coalescence of silver gloom, and might no longer have existed.

Renzo, passing Sylvie to ignite a new branch of lamps, muttered something in the dialect. Christian tensed to detect the phrases of illness or insanity.

"Tell me," he said to the fire, "about a family named Lagenay."

Renzo's muttering had broken off. There began to be silence. Christian listened for the hiss and pop of the gas mantles. When it did not come, he turned his head and looked at the two servants. Sylvie stood before the drawn curtains, solid and immovable, eyes lowered. Renzo was in the act of untidily crossing himself.

"So bad?" Christian said.

"No, monsieur. I only—"

"M'sieur," said Sylvie briskly, not glancing at him, "there's a local family, de Lagenay. But not in the village."

"In the forest."

"Oh *no*, m'sieur."

Renzo looked frightened. He darted a wild glance at Sylvie. The taper flickered in his grasp.

"My lawyer, Hamel, implies the de Lagenays reside in the forest, and warns me to be careful of them. What connection do they have with the chateau?"

The taper lit Renzo's face hellishly from beneath.

"They've got no connection with anything, or with anyone, those de Lagenays haven't."

"Shush!" said Sylvie sharply.

They stood in a line, Renzo hypnotized by the taper, Sylvie by the Persian rug, and carried on their dialogue fiercely.

"I'll speak," said Renzo. "It has to come out. It can't be stopped."

"*Shush!* He doesn't want to know."

"He asked me, didn't he? I'll tell him."

"Don't you say a word. I'll go to Madame."

Christian realized that for them he was simply a figment of their personal awarenesses, as they were for him. He might not have been present. Intrigued, he watched as they bit their lips, sizzled, lapsing into dialect again, as he lost the meaning, but never the spirit of their interchange.

When Madame Tienne spoke crisply from the doorway, he, too, flinched.

"What is this?" A significant pause. The two naughty children trembled before the white-aproned schoolmistress. "And in front of monsieur. Get out, the pair of you." They hurried to obey her, Renzo still clutching the taper, which died in the wind of their passage. "Please excuse them, monsieur," Madame Tienne said to Christian. "They're very young, typical parochial adolescents. And they have much to learn of service to the house."

In the half-lit salon, she looked sinister and cruel. He beheld Sylvie and Renzo, naked as plucked fowls strung from a rafter, while the woman lashed them with a bundle of knotted twigs.

"It's after four," she said. "Will you take tea?"

"No, Madame."

"Your luncheon was served, and brought away untouched."

So, they had crept about him while he slept. Her face had perhaps been peering down at him. When he slept with women, sometimes their kisses, pressed irresistibly to his cheeks, eyelids, had woken him. ("My angel. . . .") But not Madame. Not a trace, either of pity or appetite.

"I'm too tired to eat, Madame."

Ah, he had made his first excuse to her.

"I think you're unwell, monsieur."

"Do you? How interesting."

"Do you wish dinner?"

"No, Madame, thank you. But I gather the cellars are well-stocked. A bottle of wine. Upstairs. I leave the choice to you. Something," he hesitated, watching her, "dry."

The smallest spark went off in her eyes. The antagonism pleased her. She and the drunkard had probably often fought, in subtle, sullen ways.

He took up his coat. Hamel's letter was yet in his hand, and he replaced it in the coat pocket. He went toward the door, and Madame Tienne stood aside to let him pass.

"Oh, Madame. These de Lagenays. Who are they?"

She did not respond with any emotion. Naturally, he had left her a long interval in which to ready herself for reply.

"Please don't pay too much attention to gossip, Monsieur Dorse. The village people are excellent in their way, and will serve you well. But uneducated, ignorant. The de Lagenays? Well, they're social outcasts, monsieur. Their family will have done something in the distant past which the villagers condemn, or fear. Such people don't forget. So, for generation after generation, the Lagenays are treated as lepers."

"And why," he said, "should I be warned against them?"

"Who warned you?"

That was very quick, very alert.

"My lawyer, Madame. Monsieur Hamel."

"They will be rough folk. Perhaps—"

"Yes, Madame?"

"There's the story of a blood link, monsieur, with the chateau, years ago. A girl was forced. An illegitimate birth resulted. But there'll always be stories in such a feudal place."

She said it boldly, and her eyes glittered.

He thanked her, and passed himself in the mirror as he walked out into the grande hall.

The stained-glass porthole near the ceiling had turned to indigo. Gas lamps illumined the walls, and the curving staircase.

She had followed him from the salon and observed him as he began to climb. The steps were shallow; it was not unbearable. He recollected, from the plan Hamel had sent him, where the master suite was situated, along the gallery, a passage.

When he was almost at the top of the stair, a chittering of crystals made him turn and look at the nearer of the two chandeliers. Some draft must have caught it, for it rippled superficially all over, like disturbed water.

Madame Tienne stood in the hall, a strangely fixed and threatening figure in her immaculate apron.

Chapter 3

————●◉●————

The Dog

The wine was a dry red, good, yet with a resonant heaviness uncommon to dry vintages. The vineyard was not twenty kilometers away, and had at one time been in the possession of the chateau. The name on the label was curious, too: *sang-de-seigneur*.

He drank two glasses as he took in the master suite. It comprised five rooms, one of them a gigantic glacial bathing chamber, to which, nevertheless, hot water must be lugged from the kitchen copper. The bedroom contained a tapestry, two meters by three. The bed was also huge and inevitably canopied. Conceptions, births and deaths without number had likely taken place there.

Christian stood and regarded himself at last in the great mirror that dominated the mahogany dressing table. Like others, he was not immune to his own appearance. He considered himself with an objective sensuality and dismay. The clarity of skin and eyes, the rich expression of hair, the elegant counterbalance of purely masculine slenderness. To himself he was a source of wretched fascination, for he was artist enough to acknowledge human physical perfection, and to lament its loss. All this was to be wasted. Perhaps more terrible than anything was the fact that the disease, which riddled him like a rotted piece of meat, had so far only heightened his glamour. What use was it all? A kind of self-protective lure, maybe, a dying plant beautifying itself in order to snare

24

and feed upon the creatures thereby helplessly drawn into its orbit.

There had always been those who would care for him. He had had little need of them, and had striven to escape rapacious parents, hungry friends and lovers. Then, the illness had found him (he imagined it seeking him through all the narrow city streets and the broad boulevards, knocking on doors: "Is Christian here? No? Then I must go on." And at last, gliding soundlessly through the corridors of the conservatoire, bypassing student after student. Eventually hearing the notes which ran over from his piano like a rising lake. Yes. It had *found* him). He had been grateful initially to be housed by Annelise, and by her husband. He had even indulged an impersonal sentimental concern for their children. And then he had acknowledged that the thing which had found him would not leave him. All unknowing, somewhere in the night, sickness had married him. He seemed to cross instantly into another dimension, a country where no truth remained true, no symbol or fact was as it had been. As if he had gone blind, or deaf; it was like that.

He had debated about Annelise scarcely at all. He had been glad at her goodness to him, not surprised, of course, but glad. But it was also in the nature of the thing that had come to him that it stimulated, perversely, a demanding concupiscence. As if life strove to drive out death, the sexual urge, piercing sweet as a nerve wounded in a tooth, would race through his flesh. A sort of torture, that evoked unpleasantly erotic fantasies of crucifixion, the body reared and bent backward like a bow, the line between ecstasy and agony no longer calculable, the blazing nails that thrust through palms and feet, and the ultimate nail, pulsing with its liquors, hammered outward from the juncture of the thighs.

The husband had been away, the sick young man, too weak to cause anyone any harm, stretched out on a sofa, the pretty cousin moving about her seemingly innocent tasks. Quite abruptly he had seen her eyes, and all that was in them. Without a word, he had pulled her down, and in a matter of instants, perhaps less than a minute on the face of the clock, they had been struggling against the barriers of each other's musculature, as if up a steep hill, screaming their lust, oblivious to anything else.

When the husband returned, Annelise, in the throes of an

awful guilt, tended to him like a slave. Her eyes were bleak with shame, but also with anticipation. Her eyes now said to Christian with every look, "Our vileness is terrible because we shall continue to sin. Tomorrow, mon amour, and tomorrow."

She loved his death. So it seemed to Christian. Worse than adultery, necrophilia. At the first opportunity, which happened to be the chateau, he ran away.

In the master suite, all the gas lamps were alight, and fires burned in each grate. The plan of the suite was straightforward. A drawing room opened into a bedroom, which in turn opened into a dressing room and a bathroom. On the left hand, the drawing room also opened into a private library of some distinction.

The library gave additional access out of the suite. Beyond it, a corridor recessed into the fourteenth-century stone bastions that had gone up in the days even before La Mort had ridden over Europe on her thin pale horse.

At an angle of the passage, a door opened. Three steps, a second door. Secretive, locked into a space between two walls, one medieval and one of modern construction, a room shaped like a wedge of gateau: the music room.

The walls were of a pale golden wood, glimmering, for even here Madame's prediction had sent a lamplighter ahead of him. There were sad neglected beings all about, three or four mandolins and guitars suspended from pegs, a tall harp with broken strings. But the piano was massive and alive. Not only tuned, but polished. It stood beside a narrow, uncurtained and embrasured window, a shining black monster, waiting to devour whatever prey chanced to come near. For the piano was the ablest of all predatory beasts. It enticed by aloofness; it offered itself only to those who would toil to master it. And when they came to it, clad in the spicery of their learning, it would magnetize their fingers to its ivory fangs, and suck the soul out through the naked feverish skin. In short, a vampire.

He drained the glass of its wine (known as Blood-of-Christ. Why not?) and set it on a table. Seating himself before the flat steps of the keys, he felt a familiar excitement. The leap from the precipice.

He began to play a transcription he had made the year before, from a piano concerto of Rachmaninov. For a second he was afraid, before his hands found their purchase on the keyboard, afraid of getting lost in a labyrinth. Then the strength came back into joints and wrists and spine. Somber chords from the lower, white beads tumbling out from the higher octaves, a succession of melodic developments which opened from each other in extraordinary fans. Within the labyrinth, knowing the way.

At first the sense of being watched did not distract him. A year before, he would have been used to it, for he was then often watched, at practice or composition. There had even been a coterie who were prepared to sit for an hour at a time while he executed the variation of scales.

But no one was present in the room.

Someone listened, then, at the door. Renzo, or one of the women from the village, Sylvie or the cook. Surely not. And surely not Madame Tienne. As his thoughts intruded, became fragmented, he grew disoriented and next dizzy. The dizziness was very fearful to him, since it had been the prelude to his illness, and to its most horrible aspect. One gargantuan chord seemed to smite straight through his skull. He stopped playing immediately, and, in a ghastly silence, pressed his arms and his forehead to the upright face of the piano, where the music would have rested.

Christian, sweating icily, remained in this position some minutes. All solidity, all gravitational center, seemed to have gone from him. The piano had eaten it.

Finally he moved, not because he felt able to, but because there was nothing else to be done.

He staggered up, and to the door and flung it wide. Nobody was there. He no longer really expected anyone to be.

He left the door, and went aimlessly back to the piano, now as inaccessible to him as if he had never learned to play. Beyond the piano, the window.

Christian leaned into the embrasure. There were no shutters, and the pane of glass rose effortlessly on its sash frame. A pane of sheer coldness replaced it. Branches of a great bare tree, which must be growing only a few inches from the wall, caught the room's light and were embroidered over the sky. Scrolls of stars were visible, the shrunken, hard, brilliant stars of winter, flashing on and off. A vague garden seemed to descend below. Topiary, the hip of an urn, presented unsure milky outlines.

Something moved, appearing and disappearing between the gaps of the boughs of the tree. A few specks of light trickled on its long back. In a lacuna of the branches it halted, and raised its head as if out of a pool.

The eyes dazzled, leaping ridiculously from perspective, two flat green flames, seeming only inches from the window, while the dog remained twenty meters down, on the terrace.

Something changed direction inside Christian's head. He drew away from the window, touching the back of his hand to his face. From the left nostril had issued a single flawless jewel of blood.

He waited in the music room till the feeble bleeding eased, then shut the window, picked up the wineglass and went away.

He dreamed the dog was in the bedroom. It walked back and forth between the dressing table and the long windows, slowly lashing its tail like a lion. Obviously, it was not a dog at all. Nor was he alone in the bed. A human figure lay close against his right side; its long hair spread over the pillow, under his cheek. There was a scent of roses. As he caught the perfume, he also caught the slight breathing of another sleeper, on his left.

Christian woke at about two in the morning, familiarly and ravenously hungry. Not a healthful hunger, but nauseous and imperative.

He knew the location of the kitchen precisely from Hamel's map, but was unwilling to seek it—the room, even the bed, were freezing. Besides, he might encounter Madame on the stairs, like a child who refused his meals and was apprehended gobbling sweets. He considered this possibility idly, the strung fowl images of Sylvie and Renzo augmented by his own.

Finally he got up, put on the dressing gown of exotic velvet panels his cousin had awarded him (a prize? a bribe?) and went to the door of the suite. An oil lamp stood on a little table, matches beside it. Christian lit the lamp, and walked out into the dark waters of the house.

Nowhere had a solitary gas fixture been left alight.

The corridor, the gallery, the grande hall, everything was sightlessly black. Like a sentient thing, or pack of things, the furry dark swarmed close, held back by the bars of the lamp.

The memento mori of this was intolerably banal to him. Irritated him, even.

A passage ran out of the hall, steps descended. In the lower regions of the chateau an extra detail of dead sound prevailed.

Quite suddenly, he grew confused, and the geography of the remembered map deserted him. He came to a standstill. The invalid's hunger was already dying fitfully in his intestines. The wine would doubtless have sufficiently anesthetized it, if he had stopped to think. There was also the anesthetic of the book he had left lying on the bed.

Christian leaned on the wall. He might as well return. But the futility of further movement oppressed him. He lowered the lamp to the ground, straightened, turned, and rested his forehead on the clammy plaster of the wall.

Anomalous thoughts drifted through his brain, and in the midst of them, a girl's smoky voice, between laughter and malice.

But the girl's voice did not belong in his mind, neither a phantasm nor a memory. Somehow, the girl's voice came along the passage, buzzed through the wall, disembodied. He could not hear any words, only the tone, that odd murmuring, almost invitation, almost some other contrary thing.

Christian smiled. A servant, perhaps one of the two village women; presumably Sylvie; for the other, the cook whom he had not seen but who was undoubtedly older. This was a young voice. And there was, too, something unmistakably sexual in it. It was this quality which had reached to him from the darkness, above all others. And even to the voice he was responding somewhat, rather bemusedly, his pulse escalating, the inertia leaving him. He had had a dream in the salon, something like this—no, not like this at all.

Christian pushed himself away from the wall.

The intimation of a hidden act stimulated him. It was unsavory, yet enticing. He had no inclination to uncover it, merely to share with it in the gloom. Sylvie and Renzo, maybe. He felt a slight fastidious scorn at the notion. And yet, he had heard no other voice, and that tone of hers, though provocative, was not quite a lover's.

He left the oil lamp in the passage and moved on, following the inclination of the wall, treading noiselessly. He had a picture of himself as he did so, unpleasant and alien, but for a long while he had not particularly cared anymore what became of him. Parasite, voyeur. It was all one.

The black was nearly tangible, pressing deeply into his eyes. Then a bend in the passage revealed the entrance to the big kitchen. A soft erratic light, that of an unshielded flame, made a silent earthquake of doorway, walls, floor and ceiling.

The girl spoke again, inside the kitchen. Husky, playful, tantalizing. She used the dialect, but either Christian was growing accustomed to it or his senses, stirred, were more acute, for he followed.

"Wouldn't thee care to," she said, "wouldn't thee? Nice, so nice . . . So juicy and so tender. And all for thee . . . thee would, would thee? Shall I like it for thee, too, to give thee?"

Christian came to the edge of the wall, and faced the doorway.

The oblong stone chamber appeared in a sort of pastiche, whitewashed, scrubbed, dressed with ghostly shallots and garlic, pots and knives, the squat copper, the fireplace, with its immobile spits. A fat candle put forth its bud of fire over a long table. The room galloped with the alternations of the light, but he beheld the girl almost at once, and stepped into the doorframe, openly, aware she would not notice him.

It was Sylvie indeed, but not as he had seen her last. Unbound from its prim butcher's roll, her hair lay over her shoulder blades; coarse, dun peasant hair, but strong and galvanic. Her nightdress was a translucent yellowish batiste, too fine for the village, inherited or sent away for, worn meticulously at the chateau. The whalebone buttons were undone, and as she swayed herself to and fro, glimpses came and went of her smooth body, her pointing breasts, the turgid white-amber of her skin.

"Thee would like to," she said. She said it to the cold black blind of night beyond the window, to the nothing beyond the opened shutter and the raised pane. "See," she said. "See me." And she shook her breasts, their weight gloriously heavy as the tide of hair down her back, and she laughed, picking at the bone buttons with one hand, while in the other she lifted the final incongruous item: a chunk of redly dripping meat.

Christian felt the impulse, almost undeniable, to laugh. He began to move across the kitchen toward her, toward the radius of the powerful sensuality which she exuded like a musk.

Since the window was raised, she need not even see his reflection in the glass, and her own shadow, slithering and shifting before her, would eclipse his own. She did not seem to feel the cold, yet he could imagine how chill her body must be to the touch, like soft and slippery winter marble, and her hair like grass tasting of frost.

The bloody joint puzzled him, as did her words, her ritual. This puzzled, but did not perturb, until he had come close enough to her to see beyond her into the night.

A freakish architecture had set the kitchen one story above the courtyard below. A flight of steps could just be seen, leading obliquely along the wall from some invisible door, but clear of the window by several meters.

Where the bottom step met the court, two peridot sparks hung motionless on the blank page of the night.

"Am I bad to thee?" said the girl, leaning to the open window.

The two green lights seemed polarized, by some occult geometric thread, to the two oval tips of her breasts. Then the lights winked out, and on again, and Christian molded, like a sculptor, from the clay of the darkness, the shape which must accompany the eyes of the dog.

The dog moved a fraction, but its gaze not one iota. And Sylvie tickled the buttons of her nightdress, the juices of the meat running down her arm.

Christian began to choke, but even as he did so, he seized the piece of carcass from the girl's hand and hurled it far out into the court below. In half a minute he had pulled closed the shutter and dragged down the window, before folding himself against the table as if to cough loose his very soul.

Chapter 4

———◦———

The Bedroom

In the tapestry which hung opposite the bed, two tarnished knights were tilting, on horses the color of a lily and a bone. As they came into focus, they brought with them a rouge-faced boy snoring in a chair. It was light, and Renzo was collapsed asleep under the silver hoofs. Christian lay and watched him for a while, with a poisonous amusement. The boy had been put in as guard or nursemaid or a combination of both, failing lamentably on all counts. Christian moved a little, his body cramped, the skin unpleasantly sensitive. The real pain came arbitrarily, slicing through his ribcage at uncertain intervals like a striking cobra.

After a few minutes, observing Renzo lost its savor. Christian reached out carefully, and deliberately knocked the book he had left lying on the bed onto the floor.

At the plummy thud, the boy jerked into consciousness. He came to his feet, glaring at Christian in distress.

"Monsieur, am I to go for the doctor?" he blurted.

"Why should you want to do that? Are you ill?"

Christian's own humor entertained him. He laughed, but it hurt him and he left off. The boy floundered.

"Last night, I was to go to the village for Monsieur Claut, but you wouldn't have it, monsieur."

"Wouldn't I? I don't remember."

" 'No doctor,' you said, monsieur, over and over. 'No doctor, no doctor.' "

"It seems I don't like doctors, Renzo."

"You fainted, monsieur. Sylvie heard you moving about in the kitchen, monsieur, and came to see what you needed, but she found you lying against the table, monsieur, and ran to Madame for help."

Christian looked at the tapestry, but only saw himself carried or hauled up the chateau stairs. It was a muddled sequence. He recollected very little after the girl had rushed away between the shallots. He had been—occupied. Surreptitiously he glanced about him, but the pillows, the sheets, were scrupulous.

"I wonder what I was doing in the kitchen," he said. "How fortunate that Sylvie happened to hear me. Perhaps she was concerned about the dog."

Renzo blinked.

"Dog, monsieur?"

"Yes. The large dog that I saw outside last night. Whose is it, by the way? Sarrette's?"

"No, monsieur," Renzo began to sidle toward the door. "I'll go to tell Madame you're awake."

"Is it Madame's dog, perhaps?" said Christian.

Renzo stood by the door, twisting the knob nervously.

"There isn't any dog, monsieur."

"Yes, there is. It had also stolen some meat, I think, or been given some."

"No, monsieur."

"Oh yes, monsieur."

Renzo opened the door and said quickly, "The de Lagenays have a couple of rabbit hounds. It might be one of those."

"Then it shouldn't be on my land, should it?"

"Your . . . no, monsieur. I'll tell Madame."

Christian lifted himself farther up against the pillows, ignoring the irrelevant pain. "Tell Sylvie to bring the coffee."

Renzo nodded and vanished.

Christian lay almost perfectly still, watching the knights in the tapestry, or the fire-dogs guarding the fire, until he heard the faint footfall on the carpet of the drawing room, and the knock. The door widened, but Madame Tienne came through, the tray of coffee and rolls held like Salome's salver in her hands.

"I'm glad to see," she said, "monsieur is feeling better. But

I would nevertheless advise a visit from Monsieur Doctor Claut. A provincial, but of sound good sense. Reliable. Thorough."

"Madame," Christian said, "apparently last night I was dragged up here yelling that I would, on no account, be visited by any doctor. Nothing has changed. Please put down the tray, go and find Sylvie, and send her in as I asked."

"Sylvie has her work to do, monsieur."

The woman's eyes were like black glass. It would be easy, perhaps restful, to give in. He had now a transparent scene in his mind's eye, Sarrette carrying the body, Madame Tienne preceding, straight-backed, enamel-lipped.

"Do as I say, Madame," Christian said. "I don't intend to discuss it with you."

"Very well, monsieur."

She went, and he poured the coffee. His throat was raw, to drink an exquisite misery that brought its own relief in cessation.

The girl did not knock for almost twenty minutes.

When she entered, it was the original Sylvie back again. The stolid plainness, a figure compressed by corsets and servile frock, its hair restrained, its eyes down. She even flushed faintly, as she had earlier in his presence.

He had expected some ghost of the previous night's horrid excitement to come in with her, but it did not. Cool and scarcely interested, he found himself saying to her, "Whatever lies you've been telling make hardly any difference to me. I just thought you'd like to know that."

"I don't know what you mean," she said.

"You know exactly what I mean."

"I do not."

And, because she was prepared to resist, a distant note sounded somewhere on the broken reef of his libido.

"If I ask you," he said, "to come up here tonight, what will you say?"

She raised her eyes slowly.

"What if I won't?"

"I could tell the awesome Madame Tienne how you otherwise spend your evenings."

She flushed more deeply, but this time with fear.

"I was doing nothing. I remembered the bit of meat left out and not in the cold larder."

"Whose dog is it?" he said.

"No one's."

"Why play games with it?"

"I was never playing no game with they," she said, in the dialect.

"Why," he said, "are the de Lagenays hated, and why is their dog on chateau land?"

Her eyes were very bright, he saw, feverishly bright, like his own.

"I'll come up to your room, monsieur," she said. And he realized the brightness in her eyes was tears.

She was afraid, and he did not, after all, want her. Last night he had wanted her, and she had not been afraid. For himself, he felt a kind of fear. A kind of electric, primeval terror. If it was terror, or had nothing much happened at all? Had his perceptions grown so warped, so colored, that the most innocuous and mundane events, seen through his eyes, deciphered by his reason, became grotesque?

"Don't trouble," he said. "I apologize for asking you."

"M'sieur," she said, turned quickly and went out.

He lay all day in the bedroom of the master suite. He looked at the sundial shift of daylight across the ceiling beyond the canopy. Beyond the windows, balcony rails, a suggestion of the murk of the ambient ring of forest, diluted black vistas of pine trees far away.

Later, rain came, tossed against the panes like handfuls of sugar.

Renzo cleared the uneaten rolls, unfinished coffee, left the unfinished wine. Christian contemplated what he should do about them, these servants. He had cast himself like a pebble into the luminous puddle of their quietude. He should send them away, must do so. Someone would arrive, by magic, who would care for him. His glance fell sometimes on the locked box which contained his books, his sheafs of music, and, at its ultimate depth, the tiny pellet of easy death which waited to usurp the merciless prerogative of nature.

Night. He dreamed Sylvie was in the bed with him, but the dog was in the bedroom again, too. Sylvie rose on her elbow, pointing at the dog. She smiled, and the gleam of her teeth filled the darkness.

"It isn't a dog," she said. "Thee can see it is no dog."
Yes, he thought, *I can see it isn't.*

Spasms of coughing shook him awake once, twice, three
times, four times. He drank a little of the lifeless uncorked
wine to moisten his throat. But he woke a fifth time, and a
sixth. At length he could no longer sleep. He lay alone in the
unknown bed, in the unknown house. Unknown forces were
everywhere about him. They pulsed in the room. He had not
really studied any part of the house, and so had given it
power.

He wondered if the dog was beneath his window, pondered
the idea calmly and rationally, and finally got up to look.

A creeper had netted the balcony and was rooting in the
brickwork beyond the bedroom window; he had not noted it
before, this beautiful evidence of decay.

Distance had dispersed in night. Perspective ended about
forty yards from the wall. But looking down, he could see
into a corner of the topiary garden, the garden where the dog
had stood, as if listening to Rachmaninov.

But the dog was not there. Instead, a phantom was wandering up and down.

She was like a billow of smoke, coming and going through
the dark blots of the yew trees, but a statue, perhaps, when
she paused. Sylvie. Who else but Sylvie.

He watched her a very long time. Periodically he would
lose her in a shadow, or around the bulk of the grim tower
which swelled out into the garden, concealing most of its avenues and pergolas. But she was paler than the weather-
blotched urns, and reappeared as inevitably as a mechanized
figure on a clock.

The night, about to turn to morning, was cold enough to
have given off the peerless chime a wineglass utters when
lightly struck. Yet Sylvie, clad merely in batiste and skin and
grassy hair, circled through it, danced with it. A sense of su-
perstition and panic filled Christian as he witnessed her.

She was a dream of his fever, and he would send her
away. He would send them all away.

Chapter 5

—◦◦◦—

The Excursion

Christian stood in his greatcoat before one of the empty firepits in the hall. Something was scratched just under the huge mantel, on the stone cliff that fell down into the grate. He could not make it out. Sarrette came through the open door of the chateau. The chimney of top hat was firmly in place on the man's head. Failure to remove it was patently no particular mark of disrespect. The stiff formal nod was rendered. Sarrette, when not adopting the military stance, leaned slightly forward, giving a bizarre impression of teetering height, which, upon acquaintance, was found to be false.

"The car is ready, monsieur."

As they walked across the terrace, Sarrette moving ahead to arrive first at the vehicle, the face of Madame Tienne appeared at the window of the salon. She watched Christian go down the forty-five steps toward the car, and he felt her eyes upon him. The servants were everywhere in his chateau (did he not own it, the whole sprawling, crumbling mass?). Like dolls in a dollhouse, they infested his rooms, stairways, passages. Sylvie with her rags and waxes, Renzo with a broom or on some mysterious, hurrying errand. The unseen cook lurked in the kitchen like a spider, laboring at the iron-grated range, sulking that the newcomer did not eat her dishes. And Madame patrolled the floors, knocked with her white acorn knuckles on door panels, and was omnipresent even in absence.

The car was throbbing, alert with its aroma of gasoline and leather, as Christian got into it.

Sarrette drove away from the chateau, across the moat bridge, and the moat empty or not of fluid, into the chateau grounds.

In the afternoon it was all the same. The crippled lime, the piled stones on the grass, the cypress dominating its rise. Even the thick white light. Time might not have moved since the morning of his arrival. Christian glanced at a patch of disharmonious color, and saw what seemed to be the remains of a mangled and partly eaten hare. A small dull shock passed through him, and he thought at once of the de Lagenay dog. But as the car slid on, he decided he might only have seen a rusted fern, rotting approximately in the suggestive pattern of a dead animal.

"You wish me to drive you to Claut's house, monsieur?" asked Sarrette abruptly.

"No. The village square will do."

"The square?"

"Some auberge will be open for business, no doubt. You can wait there, if you're sure it's safe to leave the car."

"Quite sure, monsieur. Chateau property is respected."

"Go to the inn, then. Take this."

Sarrette, driving slowly, neither turned to look at the money nor moved to accept it.

"That isn't necessary, monsieur."

"You'll want a glass or two of wine, won't you, while you're hanging about waiting for me?"

"Perhaps, Monsieur Dorse, but I have already received adequate wages from your agent."

Christian relaxed back into the seat. His father's frisky servants at the hotel, the concierges, waiters, maids and chauffeurs of the city had all been ready, actually prone, to be tipped. Annelise would frequently resort perforce to bribing her maid into visiting the market for fresh vegetables with enough coins for chocolate or cheap face powder.

Of course, it would be a mistake to treat the retainers of the chateau like the domestic itinerants of city cafés or flats. Christian became absorbed in why he had made such a mistake. He was frankly curious at himself. Had he intended to offend Sarrette?

"I've offended you," Christian eventually said, with a half-hearted but by now conscious desire to provoke further.

"Not at all, monsieur."

Christian closed his eyes. He was tired to death, and they had not even arrived.

"There was a part-eaten hare on the grass about three quarters of a kilometer back," he said.

"Foxes, monsieur."

"Or dogs."

"As you say, monsieur. We must be more careful of shutting the main gates. Renzo does not like to go out that way after sunset."

"In the village," Christian said, "who is the best person to ask about the de Lagenays?"

They had entered the avenue of limes, and between their unclad skeletons the high gates and heraldic hounds came into view.

Sarrette, as if intent on negotiating the car beyond the margin of the estate into the forest, did not reply.

Christian smiled, knowing the man might see him.

"How strange they've incurred such a taboo," said Christian. He touched the hidden breast pocket of his coat. "But I've written to Hamel on the subject. He warned me about these people in the first place; he might as well answer my questions. Since you won't."

The forest climbed up about the car. Christian stared out at it, aware only of Sarrette's obstinate silence. The letter was, in fact, a fabrication. The local mail service, a plunging of sacks to and from the occasionally passing trains, was in the charge of the carrier, Peton. When the snow came the mail frequently did not. In no circumstances had Christian considered writing any letters.

The distant trees were like spires. Along the road they grew generally close together, resembling a hedge, and virtually impenetrable. Doubtless there were paths and tracks inside the wood, but to be lost there seemed as equivalently natural as to be drowned in the deep of the sea. The sudden breaks and chasms made him giddy today, as if the floor of the car were dissolving.

Presently the road coiled and the fantastically balanced church appeared.

Sarrette pulled up in the square, which was deserted. Shutting off the engine, he jumped swiftly from the car, ran around and pulled wide Christian's door. As Christian got out, Sarrette said, "You'll need me, perhaps, Monsieur Dorse, as a guide."

"No," Christian said. He stood, feeling the world settling about him after the motion of the vehicle, like sand in a bottle. "Go to the inn. Or sit in the car."

He began to walk off, and Sarrette said, "Be cautious, monsieur."

Christian looked around and grinned at Sarrette. As Renzo had been taken aback by the magnetism of the young man's smile, so now Sarrette was plainly unnerved by the satanic quality of the grin. There was something decidedly malevolent about Christian Dorse in that moment, as if, like a mirror, he had begun to reflect some quality in the air. But the picture of Sarrette beside the black car, in his top hat, like an undertaker beside his hearse, was much too perfect. Christian turned and moved away.

The square was steep, like the church, set almost on its side. He went by the well, the memorial—an obscure obelisk of pitted stone with eccentric carving. Around, sheer and falling streets of cobbles and packed earth poured downhill, a line of roofs, several active chimneys. He glimpsed the auberge, trapped in a bending alley, a smoky woodcut; you might expect men of chain mail to step out of it. Somewhere sheep bells clanked solemnly. No human creature was visible.

As he came level, he glanced at the church. It was coated in the whitish pastry of plaster that covered so many of the adjacent dwellings, but it seemed far more recent than anything else, its riotous lines cleaner and more prosaic. First the forest had been there, then maybe the forerunner of the road, arm of some other highway. Then the chateau, to which eventually the road had been suborned. Next, under the patronage of the castle, the inn, the village attaching like barnacles to everything. Lastly, two hundred years ago—it looked no older—the church. An afterthought.

The bell was discernible in the head of the tower. The white lead sky washed the windows, bleeding them of possible tintings.

Previously, some other buildings must have dominated the village and inspired the ancient square which now contained the church.

Ignoring the main gravel road, he walked out of the square into one of the narrower streets, little more than a lane between impacted walls.

He did not really know why he had come here. An experiment, possibly. To see what would happen. Or merely to escape his servants. Yet he felt so exhausted; his limbs seemed filled with sawdust. There was no one in the lane. He approached an antique wooden door, shut fast as a coffin lid.

He could no longer hear even the sheep bells.

The blacksmith's forge, seen suddenly across a low wall, was silent and shut as the door, the parasol of fumes absent from its roof.

The narrow lane ended uncompromisingly in a midden, the stench suppressed only by the freezing temperature.

City life had distilled him; he did not quite credit the archaic dung heap, and retraced his steps hurriedly.

When Christian reached the square once more, Sarrette had disappeared, possibly to seek the inn, as Christian had proposed. Alone, the car, a symbol of shelter, had acquired a blackness too black for the blurred winter tones of the village, and now appeared two-dimensional.

With Sarrette gone, the whole area seemed quite vacant, despite the smoke from certain chimneys, the vague scattered clues to occupation—a brown broken bottle lying on the cobbles, a hoe propped against the shuttered window of a house.

All the windows were shuttered.

The weather, obviously, necessitated such a measure. Out here in the waste, perhaps, they even lacked window glass. . . .

(He imagined Renzo running into the village in the youth of the morning. As Christian shaved before the mirror, Renzo whispered harshly to the village. As Sarrette drove the car, warm and purring, to the foot of the terrace, the doors and shutters of the village slammed in a cacophony of drawn bolts.)

The door of the church was also secured, by a padlock, an unusual sight in such a spot.

Christian coughed. He pressed his hand across his lips to hold the coughing inside himself. When it subsided, he strolled back up the slope of the square to the monument. He would examine that, then go leisurely to the auberge. He would drink a glass of rough local vinegar, and study Sarrette's demeanor, discomforting him.

Tomorrow, Christian would have Sarrette drive him to the ramshackle station, and raise the marker which informed the train it was required to halt. He need send none of them away. He could go himself.

I can return to the city. None of this matters. I have no reason to remain. I've seen my property, investigated it. I could sell it. I could travel to Switzerland. They say Switzerland is the place. Its frigid snow cones packed into the optic nerves and heart, like ice, stopping the hemorrhage. Almost as cold as this damned countryside will be in the gut of winter when the snow comes.

He could make nothing of the monument, distorted shapes, something like a gargoyle craning out higher up. His eyes swam and burned and he turned from the incongruity of the stone to the incongruity of the uninhabited village, and started toward the slanted alley with the inn.

A door banged.

Christian looked behind him.

At first he saw no one, then he perceived a figure, composed of the soft charcoal shadow manufactured by the winter day, posed in contrast against the pallor of the church facade. If it had come from the church out of some side exit, Christian could not be sure. Its garment of loose cloth reached almost to the ground, and might be a priest's soutane, or the long skirt of a parochial woman—the sex of the figure was indeterminate.

He could go over to the church and accost this apparition—if he could make himself understandable to it, floundering through the verbal mud of the dialect. Christian felt no inclination to do so. The game of interrogation was played out. He did not even care about the de Lagenays anymore, the momentary interest they had afforded him had been talked to death.

He turned once more in the direction of the auberge, and checked. The same stifled little shock went off in his chest as he had felt when he beheld the rotting fern like a mangled hare. Another figure had arrived as suddenly as the first, as if conjured, in the door recess of a house three meters from him. A woman for sure, this time, her black provincial shawl drawn over her head and bound about her, giving the impression that she had no arms. And again, that immobile charcoal darkness, as if she had been blocked in on the paper street while his head was averted.

"Good day," Christian said to her.

He searched for her eyes, but only the demilune of the jaw was visible, carved out from the shadow of her heavy wrap.

"Let me introduce myself," said Christian. "I am the present owner of the chateau."

On this occasion, the movement caught his eyes, he responded quickly, and saw a man come from the house where the hoe was propped on the shutter. The man advanced a couple of steps before he, too, became a stationary drawing.

Needles probed Christian's eyes. Water formed in them, making everything on the square waver as if beneath a pool. Christian pivoted, bowed to the woman in the door.

"Enchanted, madame."

He strode into the curving alley that contained the inn, and, following the inclination, seemed to walk straight into a post with a black sign daubed on it. The sign, huge and oddly disquieting, was of two disembodied hands, the tilted index finger of the right, the thumb of the left awkwardly adhered to make the sigil of the cross.

A symbol of ultimate good, it had acquired, in this form, an unmistakable menace. Yet the most disturbing thing about it was its newness. It seemed to have been done no later than . . . this morning.

Preposterously, Christian acknowledged a silly, inexplicable impulse to run. But the door of the inn was just thirty paces away. He walked to it, and put his palm on the timber, realizing only a second before he did so, that he would find this, also, locked.

He struck the locked door once with his fist, in infantile pique more than anything else. Presently he rested against the wood, staring up stupidly at the inn's plaque, which hung motionless above him. This sign was almost as odd as the other, a somehow monstrous lily, surely unsuitable for a drinking house, even one so securely shut.

The church bell began to toll, leadenly. The bell of plagues, strife and burials.

Libera me, Domine.

A gnawing desire came on him for one of the Egyptian cigarettes he had ceased to smoke in the city the day after he left the conservatoire. Not so much the drug of the tobacco, but its unassailable *modernity*.

What was happening? The sky had dimmed, the alley was a gully of shade, swirling with the notes of the bell, the psychic fumes of lilies. The light was going out.

Christian's heart beat emulatively, in hard adagio pulses.

This was what dying would be like. It was not uncomfortable. There was no pain, and no longer any true sense of fear.

A clot of charcoal pencil shading was creeping down the alley toward him, like a soft black snowball, gathering depth as it came. . . . Christian's eyes were almost closed. The inn door seemed to tremble. He was slipping down years or centuries into a morass of bottomless time, and the snowball of darkness rolled over him, catching him by one arm. A balding medieval knight gawped from his armor, the bulbous lips struggling to convey clarity.

"Sarrette says thee wish a letter sent to the city, monsieur."

Christian widened his eyes, and tears caused by cold and surprise gushed down his face. Peton, the carrier who collected the mail, stood before him, holding out his hand for the nonexistent letter to Hamel.

Chapter 6

———•◦•———

The Forest

"There isn't any letter."

"Pardon, monsieur?"

"No letter. An invention. A joke I had with Sarrette. But apparently he took it seriously."

Peton folded his lips. "Ah." He did not comprehend, only that Christian was withholding the letter. "I am authorized," Peton said at last. "The train tomorrow will take the letter."

Christian shuddered abruptly. What he had seen for a fraction of an instant as a link-shirt were the ring-like loops of Peton's woolen coat. When Christian had arrived at the station, three mornings ago, Peton had not looked at him. Not once. Now, his thin threads of hair disarranged, his breath acid with wine (some other inn?), he levered himself toward Christian, unblinking.

Christian considered haphazardly that the cold-formed tears which had sprung from his eyes might have led Peton to believe he was weeping. Should he assume some overmastering sorow? Clap his hand to his forehead, reel, declaim upon an unfair fate?

"Tell me," he said to Peton, speaking carefully, "the sign on the post there. What does it mean? The finger and thumb forming a crucifix so clumsily?"

Peton glanced at the post. He mumbled. "The Lysinthe—it's nothing. Are mad here, monsieur," he said. "Superstitious."

"A sign against the evil eye?"

Peton nodded uncertainly.

Christian sighed, letting his head rest on the inn door. Peton's head lurched forward, as if joined to his by a string. Aware of the subject's staleness, Christian said, "I deduce the Lagenays have the evil eye."

Peton threw back his head and laughed.

"Yes, monsieur. Thee has the right of it. Evil eye twice over."

"And where would I find them?"

Peton subsided. He licked his mouth. "The forest."

"I know that. Where?"

"Thee wants to visit they?"

Christian stood and watched him. Christian's eyes were luminous, almost silver, and Peton seemed gradually to become glamourized, as if falling slowly in love.

"Thee is not strong enough, monsieur," said Peton sluggishly, "to walk the distance."

"What makes you think that?" said Christian softly. "I can outwalk you any day of the year, you drunken sot."

Peton started, then he chuckled. "Come, monsieur. I show the track."

To be in the forest, as he had half fancied before, was like being on the bed of some great water. A saw-toothed wind had risen, and everything was in motion—the tall slim pine tops, their boughs, the heavy tiers of their spines, the light therefore, which swayed back and forth between each tree, and the shade. The sound also was of water, of the sea, that same rushing, sighing bombast as of waves and tides.

The cold did not totally numb the sharp scent of balsam, just as the shadows of the wood did not quite bury the track, though it was largely overgrown, an ancient footpath that feet seemed not to have disturbed for many months.

They had been walking about ten minutes. Peton slightly and obsequiously moving in the lead, now and then lifting obstacles—a stone, a fallen branch—off the way, clearing it for Christian as if for some delicate and dangerous princely child. They had come initially up through the village, now empty once more of all figures, and past the black car—still abandoned—until, following the gravel road back in the direction of the chateau, they moved out between the bastions of the pines.

But, after some half a kilometer or so, Peton stepped abruptly off the gravel, and inserted himself between the close-knit stems of the trees, the surge of underbrush, with scarcely a rustle to mark his progress. Christian, altogether more slender and more gainly, made by far the greater disturbance and difficulty, the needles and the crab-clawed bushes tearing at him, trying to restrain him. A minute more was lost in negotiating the enormous boles of ancient trees, which seemed to form a rear-guard action just off the road. Then they had broken into the sea of the forest, and were beneath its windblown currents.

The track burst suddenly from the earth, indenting it, like a rill or spring, which possibly it had at one time been. And, for a few steps, it had a scar-like nakedness, but farther on the overgrowth encroached almost, though never quite, obscuring the blond and powdery soil of which the path was composed.

Now Peton had hesitated again, for there was something else in the way that seemed to need removal. However, he did not bend to the work, and coming up, Christian saw that the fresh obstruction on the track was two long yellow bones, each large enough to have been taken from a bull or horse. These were laid awkwardly and lopsidedly crossways, and the implication, however makeshift, was blunt.

"Well, monsieur," said Peton.

"Well?"

"Well, thee go on alone from here."

"You were to be the guide, I thought."

"Thee need no guide from here. Follow the track. Follow her to return. She lead thee."

"Where?"

"Where thee asked to go."

"The de Lagenays live beside the track."

"Do they?" said Peton. He looked down at the crossed bones.

"You won't go any farther with me? I thought you were brave, Peton. Is the wine wearing off? Come on. Come with me. When we get back to the village, I'll buy you another bottle."

"Thee go on alone. Thee was meant. Not up to me."

Peton, still looking at the bones, backed away from them ceremoniously, passing Christian, putting each foot behind him cautiously, never straying off the path.

Christian turned from the carrier, exasperated by these antics, yet stimulated in an unpleasant way he could not name. As he walked over the bones, he brought the heel of one boot down savagely. Neither bone cracked nor even shifted at the pressure.

"Monsieur," Peton called suddenly. He sounded already far away. Christian did not look around, but paused, waiting. "Monsieur," called Peton, "the sky's bright. But thee have less than one hour, monsieur."

Christian waited a little longer, but nothing else was shouted at him. He walked on.

Less than one hour? To sunset, presumably. Certainly, the forest after dusk, darkening on its darkness, closing on its closeness, an intensity of land, trees and night, would be most inimical. Unless to a native.

Why am I here? What am I doing? Pursuing some tribe of subhuman rubbish, too obnoxious even for the obnoxious indigents to accept.

He had a recurrence of the previous vision, which had amused him bitterly—rough snarling fools with staves, knives, a solitary musket.

No, it was nothing to do with that. The overhanging rock balconies of the rising forest, its sudden valleys, were not visible from the track. The enclosing trees rocked and bowed, and chiaroscuro scintillated over the landscape. All the country seemed in quake, and he remembered the candle causing the same effect in the wide kitchen, when Sylvie, in her unbuttoned nightgown, crooned to the dog below the window. The de Lagenay dog.

I'm alone in the forest. Exactly what Hamel warned me, in his melodramatic note, to avoid.

Mischance must be luring him. Like the little pellet in the box. A need to anticipate—

But as he went on, keeping as faithfully to the track as Peton had done (of course, it was sorcerous; to stray meant to be confounded forever), something made him reach into his coat pocket and draw out Hamel's letter, thrust back there as if to be ready for this moment.

Walking, he spread the paper. The waves of dark and

bright flowed over it. He scanned the paragraphs under the flickering pines.

Just as before: The legality. The piano tuner. The financial aspect. The good wish.

Christian came to the final lines. He read.

He stopped, one more stone on the track. He put up the other hand involuntarily to help hold the weightless page. He read a second time.

—"In the matter of the boundaries of the chateau lands, it is a melancholy fact that few of the documents agree or would be likely to be sustained in a court of law. That all surrounding countryside was, in the medieval era, the property of the Seigneur, there is small doubt, but by now there is neither the proper jurisdiction nor, I am sure, the desire on your part to enforce such a ruling on the local inhabitants. Although, to any shooting you yourself might wish to indulge in, or any game you might wish to have trapped in the woods, there could, naturally, be no objection. My intention in relaying this state of affairs to you is not to cause unnecessary confusion on your side, but to make provision against any mistaken claims being unwittingly made."

Christian stared at the paper. A thought darted across his brain: the servants at the chateau had stolen the letter and copied it, purposely omitting the original warning against the de Lagenays. But no, too fantastic. Where would they come on Hamel's notepaper, his typewriter with the tiny break in the "e" which Christian had noted before, the curlicued signature behind which Monsieur Hamel concealed himself and his true person, as if behind a bramble hedge?

No, not a copy. The one and only letter.

Where then were those words which had inevitably brought Christian onto this sorcerous path in the wood? The words which, perused in the firelight crepuscule that first day, had said:

—"The de Lagenays—any claim they may assume to the property—hypothetical—do not venture outside the bounds of the chateau unaccompanied."

It seemed that, improperly awake in the salon, a stranger in his own unfamiliar house, he had dreamed, hallucinated, imagined it all.

The derangements of illness.

Yet where had he obtained the name de Lagenay, to fit so

crudely, but so aptly, in the pattern? A servant's muttering unconsciously overheard? Some chance remark of Hamel's to which he had paid no heed in the city, but which, once here, had roused to haunt him? Or merely some other word misinterpreted by a mind drowsy and depressed—an uncanny coincidence. He felt all at once smitten beyond endurance. It was not sufficient that his talent be bled from him, his life torn in two pieces and thrown away, but he must go insane, too. No scrap of dignity or self-reliance or amour propre must he be allowed to keep.

He could not think what to do, whether to go on or to return, or simply to lie down on the ground.

As he stood in this nebulous state, the awareness of being watched came over him in fragments. His skin stiffened as if brushed by a feather, his muscles tensed and his eyes, which had ceased to trouble him, began again to water. Bewildered, he glanced up, and the small clamor of shock which he had felt twice before that day went through him a third time.

A ragged giant hemlock rose from among the pines near the path. Against this primeval tree leaned a masculine presence. It had not been there when Christian halted, and coming since, it had made no slightest noise. It—he.

Not more than twenty-five or -six, which was discernible mostly from build and physical articulation, there was something much more youthful, something of adolescence in him. His complete stillness, perhaps, suggested a second contradictory element, of age. A stillness that had absolutely nothing to do with his immobility, that had rather to do with the impression he gave of growing from the soil, along with the towering tree.

At first, in those swells of sky and shadow, which blanched out the color reflex of the sight, he was monochrome. Cool gray, coolest brown, pallor and dark.

Christian, having transferred his stare from the letter to the apparition, was dissatisfied. It was necessary that something replace the limbo of his thoughts, and so, with a kind of anger, he stepped off the path, and walked straight toward the creature. Which neither moved to meet him nor in retreat, did not even rearrange itself, in the automatic way of one who is being approached, the nervous shift of limbs, or head. It—*he*.

When Christian was two meters away, he stopped. Colors

and textures had evolved by then. The gray-brown clothing had faded and deepened against a white winter face. The hair, which hung to the shoulders, suddenly sprang into a swarthy auburn, the shade of the autumn's burned fruits and leaves, a color that otherwise no longer existed in the evergreen forest. The eyes were large, the ghost-blue of smoke, and there was something curious about them. . . .

These light eyes were the only part of him which seemed to move, and they executed a peculiar contemptuous little bow, the eyelids drooping, then lifting, like two white shutters—the left lid was a fraction longer than its fellow, which perhaps accounted for the indecipherable oddity—

"Which way," Christian said, "to the de Lagenay house?"

It was a formality, a challenge. There could be no error admitted in such a situation.

"De Lagenay?" said the young man. His eyebrows raised themselves as his mouth opened to speak. His voice was dry and without accent of any sort. "Nobody visits the de Lagenays."

"So I hear at the chateau. What did you do to incite such hatred?"

"*I?*" The beautiful face began to smile. The mouth widened and a thin line of glinting teeth was revealed. The eyes were lazy. "Am *I* a de Lagenay?"

"Are you? But yes, I think you are."

"Oh, you're very clever. What gave me away, I wonder?"

The confrontation was producing in Christian the bizarre excitement he had somehow known it would. Self-doubt had perished. The air was no longer cold against him, but tingled. An electric vibration seemed to run into his bones from the earth. What was it? Only the aura of unsafety, maybe, which the being in front of him seemed to exemplify beyond all mortal probability. A bastard branch of the chateau, very likely. The pigments, the features, the demeanor were not the village's, nor the precise language and diction. This one had had a tutor from the city, perhaps. And now it wandered the woods in garments of fox and rabbit skin, like something from a child's storybook. And it was drawing off a glove, revealing a hand, short from the wrist to the first knuckles, long in the fingers. The spatulate nails of the hand were dramatic, the dull thick red of terra-cotta, dimming as they cleared the skin as any other human nail would have done. Patently natural, if such a word could be applied to them. And with this hand, the de Lagenay reached up and began to pluck at the collar of his coat. By no means an uneasy gesture. It was obviously specifically designed to show off the type of the hand to its full effect.

Christian looked at the rusty nails, then back into the smiling, hazardous face.

And he felt the excitement permeating him, driving everything else away. Like wine. Almost like the demand of hunger, or of sex.

"You have a couple of dogs, I believe," Christian said.

"Dogs? Is that what they told you? At your chateau?"

"If you're wise, you'll keep them off my land."

"*Your* land?"

"Unless you'd like them shot."

The de Lagenay laughed, a soft and husky growl.

Something astonishing happened. He seemed not to move, yet he moved; was in a different place, closer. He put out his ungloved hand and rested it gently on the shoulder of Christian's coat.

"Oh," he said. "I should like you to try to shoot them. My two dogs."

He was Christian's height, their eyes abruptly level and mere inches away. It was like looking into something which glowed, one thing, not two, each iris no longer separate, but socket spilling into socket, straight across the bridge of the nose.

"Incidentally," said the de Lagenay, "I was most entertained the other evening. Out here in the Styx, one seldom hears Rachmaninov so powerfully rendered."

The hand on Christian's shoulder squeezed, an intimation of strength, and then the creature was gone, three or four meters off. It was the leap a large animal might be capable of.

Christian quietly and insultingly brushed the shoulder of his coat. He stared after the young man, but the black portions of the forest were beginning to win their perpetual battle with the bright. Forms were vanishing, or metamorphosing.

"I trust you'll remember my warning," Christian said to the wood, cordially.

"I trust you'll remember mine," said the dry voice out of

the wood. "You'd better go back, my seigneur. Before the sun sets. Before it gets dark."

The shapes of the pine trees had seemed to unravel, allowing him to pour through them like vapor. Till he was gone.

Christian was alone in the forest. And at once he was chilled, dulled. He turned to look about for the track he had left, and the claw scratched in his throat.

He had walked some way before he accepted he should by now have regained his objective. Due to the failing of the light, or some fault in his awareness, the sorcerous path had disappeared.

Chapter 7

———◦◉◦———

The Devil

The sun did not seem to sink, but the whole sky appeared to lower itself to touch the points of the trees. An impending gloom soaked through the forest. The remaining panes and interstices of light became lavender, and then went out. With a vast, inaudible sigh, the world went black.

Christian had been unable to find any trace of the path. He was not alarmed, but the futility and idiocy of the situation made his hands tremble.

His prior excitement had gone. Coughing intermittently, and vilely tired, he had begun to trudge in the direction the path should have been, looking for any break in the trees that might indicate a way back to the gravel road.

It was not amazing that the rush of twilight had blotted out the incoherent track. Not at all. But as he waded through the blackness, gripping his shaking arms around his body against the cold, he grinned to himself with a hatred of it all, the dark, the wood, the boy he had spoken to, himself.

It was icy. Each breath was a form of torture.

And inevitably it came to him that, if he had hallucinated the paragraph of warning in the letter, why not the path? Why not Peton, leading him on it? Why not the being under the hemlock tree?

He hung on a bough, coughing until he retched. When he could breathe, he crouched there, amid the branches, the scent of somber resin that reminded him, child of civilization

54

that he was, of far-off Christmases, and the green wonders of pines torn up and brought in to die, upon fires and in garlands.

Good God, what am I doing here? Get up. The road is that way. Probably.

He could force an exit through all these soaring, naked, living yule trees. Master them, as Peton had done. It was only night which made the forest seem impassable, a maze from which, once lost therein, you never could escape.

Or had he been led altogether away from the course of the gravel road? (He must beware of those chasmic drops he had seen from the car.)

Did he now stumble in circles? A sightless wall on all sides, the trees gave no clue. No longer did they possess even a shape. They were merely *darkness*.

Something crackled through the undergrowth on his right. He envied it its assurance, the uncomplexity of its mission and its hopes.

Then he had blundered into some kind of thicket. He thrust against a bristled mass, spikes, talons, adamant stalks like pillars. And it was as this nonvocal struggle took place between him and the trees that there came out of the depth of the forest, as if from the bottom of an abysmal well, the awesome, long-drawn howl of a dog.

It was a truly dreadful sound. Some distortion of distance or acoustic had made it both larger and less tenable than any such cry he had ever before heard.

Caught in the thicket, like the sacrificial beast, Christian stopped still, hung there, letting the sound fade through his ears and mind, waiting for a repetition, which presently came.

One of the de Lagenay hounds giving tongue? But could such a noise issue from the throat of a dog?

Diable chasse avec des chiens.

The proverb, dredged up into his consciousness, vaguely startled him, for it was released by some primitive nerve ending, his reaction to the howl of the dog.

Christian smiled with painful disgust, and resumed his duel with the thicket. Another idea was coming to him, macabrely absurd. He visualized the boy he had met in the half hour before sunset, throwing back his strong throat, his terra-cotta hair gone to ebony in the blackness, parting his pale mouth, paler teeth, ululating through the choirs and galleries of the wood.

Something in the barrier gave way across the breadth of Christian's body. He had broken through one of the forest's tangled skins, half falling, but netted before he hit the ground. Suspended, clutching at the brittle tines with his hands, he expected to find an abyss before him, but instead, he beheld a faint eerie glow beyond the trunks and boughs now in front of him, like a bank of mist hanging above some river. As he struggled upright, he realized, with a sudden shift of perception, that the luminous mist bank was the blanched gravel of the road.

Realization was enough to set him lashing out with renewed violence, a desperate swimmer making for shore. In a few moments he had smashed free of the pines. Standing on the gravel, he discovered himself breathing in harsh and drinking gasps, as if he had been a long while running.

A meager fruiting of stars had lit the road. It represented landfall, yet cut the nocturnal scene with a lonely and desolate barrenness. It had no particular welcome for travelers.

The thing had not cried again in the forest.

Christian took in the length of the road. An awareness of direction came back to him. Here, he was some distance above the village, well on the way to the chateau gates. Sarrette might be awaiting him in the square. But Sarrette had previously abandoned the car, concealed himself in some phantom auberge—let him wait.

To walk in the opposite direction, toward the chateau, should not be unduly lengthy. A matter, perhaps, of fifteen minutes, although uphill. . . . At the notion of it, Christian felt a familiar strengthlessness. It seemed to him he could go no farther, but he was used to such drainings of energy and spirit. He ignored his misgivings and started to walk up the road under the frugal stars.

His footsteps were loud.

Partly, he did not care for this loudness. He was vulnerable, a moving entity on the bleached road surface, without camouflage or cover. Presumably, then, he anticipated assault.

Whom might he meet that would offer a threat? Another de Lagenay? Or the original model? If Christian had dreamed the former warning, the second personal one had been implicit. Curiously the boy had called him by the archaic title: *Seigneur*. There had been a wealth of malevolence in that term of obeisant respect.

The forest, on either hand, was blacker than the sky. The forest was still now, for the wind had died with the sun. As still as if restrained itself from motion, holding its breath in check, and with it some colossal unimaginable power. Though now and then, over his own too-loud footfalls, he would catch a small arid rattling from the underbrush, or the scrape of the fringed pinnacles overhead—some creature stirring, or some remote passage of the air.

At first, there was nothing to disturb him in these noises. Only the stillness itself was somehow unlikable, as if it offered itself, an empty vessel, for some more displeasing sound to fill. But then, after he had walked the road for five minutes or a little more, a certain recurrence seemed to establish itself. With all the quiet variation of sounds, one even quieter did not seem to vary. It was a sort of delicate ticking, like the tiny soft strokes of a brush, not on trees or bushes, but on the road behind him.

With an appalled sense of nightmare that was almost amusing, Christian halted and looked back.

The first time he did this, he saw nothing, though the miniature sounds left off, as if on cue.

The road curved back under a billow of forest, sliding out of sight toward the unseen village. The gravel was blank. But the moonless night seemed to gather in the eyes, dimming them in the way in which vision will cloud over before a faint.

Christian hesitated only an instant, then faced toward his equally unseen goal once more and proceeded.

But the dappling of little brush strokes returned.

Diable chasse avec des chiens.

The imbecility of his plight came to him forcefully. But he had all the while been at a disadvantage, for he had never really, even having witnessed it, believed in the dog. Even after it had shattered the wood with its voice. And not even now—

He swung about. The gravel behind him was level for a stretch, but no longer unoccupied. It was there.

It seemed the center of the night, all the flat black of night poured into it, the lean line of it and the long head. And then the eyes came on like two green gas jets.

It was some forty paces away. Which would be nothing to it.

It would be savage, and probably kept two-thirds starved. Here in the wilds it might, besides, be infected with madness.

He was alone with it, between the forest and the sky. Weaponless. Without shelter.

"Damn you to Christ, you foul and stinking thing," he whispered.

Yet he could not have told if he was afraid. He itched with an intolerable urge to attack the dog, or to fly from it, calling out. But if these impulses were of terror, or of some extraordinary primitive sub-emotion, nameless in the current world, was unsure.

Then the dog took a slow, almost courteous step toward him, and Christian thought of how he might climb one of the trees if he could only reach one, if he could only be swift. And a wave of unlaughing, laughless laughter came over him, and sheer horror washed through in its wake.

He did not run, since to run would be to incite the creature to run after. But as soon as he moved, it broke into a ghastly bounding gallop. It launched itself toward him, and then he did run a dozen steps, before flinging himself irresistibly about again to confront it.

And he saw it as it went up into its spring, as if in flight, and he heard himself cry out, far away, beyond all help.

The beast came down on him, as if from the sky, a ton weight, a bolt driven through his chest. He felt himself fall, the weight on top of him. The gravel crashed against his back, his skull. The beautiful face of something entirely beyond evil was poised close to his. A mouth wider than vision glittered twelve or thirteen centimeters above him. Terror came. Christian knew terror. Terror was sensuous. It demanded surrender in a thrashing of limbs, wordless screaming. Paroxysm. An orgasm of agonized death beneath the warm body of this relentless lover.

Christian realized he had thrown his left arm across his own neck. He struck out with his right arm. The blow burst against the animal's mask, jerking its whole head aside.

Christian struck again, and a boiling of the primordial emotion—exceeding fear or rage—lifted him bodily, his teeth clenched and his eyes starting. And as both his hands grabbed now for the shaggy throat he made out a noise that belonged many hundreds of centuries in the future.

A yellow lightning spread across Christian's eyes, blinding him, and stayed frozen there. The thing he had gripped forcefully tore itself from him. The heat and pressure of its body was gone like a hot wind.

Christian lay stranded, his arm across his eyes.

"Monsieur—monsieur—come quickly to the car and get in."

Sarrette bent over him in his ludicrous top hat, framed by the headlamps of the car, which had pulled up less than a meter away.

Christian sat. He could do nothing else.

"Help me," he ordered Sarrette, and Sarrette complied, half lifting him onto his feet, to the car and into it. Sarrette pushed hurriedly into the driver's seat, and urged the chugging engine into motion. The vehicle lurched forward.

"It ran off," said Christian. "The car must have frightened it."

"Yes, monsieur. I drove as near as I could. I was searching for you along the road."

Christian coughed. It was a formality. His body had no solidity, his muscles were fluid. Yet such a blade of life had lodged in him; he burned, fidgeting, unable to keep still, too weak to support the display, shivering, the blows of his heart rocking him.

"You weren't hurt, monsieur?"

"No."

"It was a dog, monsieur. Some of the farms have such brutes. It's unwise to travel on foot by night."

Christian began to swear, clearly, nicely; obscenities, almost a prayer. And as he prayed in this manner the weakness left him.

Sarrette said nothing else.

The lamps splashed over stone dogs by the road, and next across the disheveled outer wall of the chateau.

Chapter 8

❖

The Feast ·

Madame Tienne stood in the firelight, her hands folded on her apron.

"The woman has returned to the village," she said.

She was speaking of the hireling cook. The implications: monsieur had eaten so very little for the three days of his presence at the chateau, sending back what dishes had been prepared with only the tiniest omission from them, ignoring completely the custom of dining as if it had not been invented.

"Then, Madame, you yourself had better see to it."

The sparks glimmered in her eyes, as before.

Christian lounged in the chair, watching her, the brandy goblet tilted slightly, negligently, in his hand—his property, both liquor and goblet, to spill or to break. But his hand was perfectly steady.

"Monsieur will be satisfied to dine at nine o'clock? It would be impossible, otherwise, to prepare as you wish."

"Oh, quite satisfied. That will allow me a couple of hours, won't it, to look at this place. I haven't seen it yet. Perhaps you'd give me the keys? And send Renzo with an oil lamp. I gather the gas doesn't extend to every room."

Her face, a smooth peeled almond, the thin lips that seemed to have been appliquéed on, the eyes, stilled now and made of serpentine—nothing altered. She looked embalmed.

"Parts of the chateau are very old, monsieur. There are

60

narrow stairs, passages, and the old court is in poor repair. Even with a lamp, at night it's unsafe."

"An unsafe evening. Didn't Sarrette tell you about my adventure with the dog?"

"Yes, monsieur."

"Should I prosecute, do you think, Madame?"

"It would be difficult, monsieur, to prove the owner. There are three or four farms in the area, cleared from the forest. All have dogs."

"All right," Christian said. He smiled at her, and with that brilliant razor's edge of charm, which, whenever he used it, excited him as much as those he practiced on. "I have no jurisdiction outside the chateau gates. But within, Madame, you'll do what I say, won't you? Arrangements for dinner to be served in the grand hall. Renzo with the lamp. The keys."

"Very well, monsieur." (You cannot charm *me*, monsieur.)

He rose and took the keys out of her fingers when she had detached the ring. When she was gone, he turned gradually, gazing at the room as if he had not seen it before. Perhaps he had not. Everything seemed subtly changed. His reaction to the forest had left him; only the surge of life in him remained: hunger, thirst, the alert curiosity of someone he had once been, no longer was.

Indeed, who are you?

He had glanced toward one of the mirrors, which glanced back at him from its gilded socket, presenting him with himself. As ever, it had arrested him, this slim, glowing glove of flesh. He went across to it, slowly. Almost puzzled by himself, but not, at this moment, dismayed. How strange he was, how strange to live inside this case of cells. (Entertaining the wish to contact himself through the medium of the glass, he spread his palm against the palm of the reflection.) And how curious the illness was, which, as it killed him, seemed to banish all impurities from skin and hair, giving him a burnish, the high-gloss of fine enamel and satin. And the clear eyes, like two separate living things which had taken up residence in his head. He leaned his forehead against the forehead in the mirror as he had sometimes done as a child. In this position, he mentally reviewed Hamel's letter and the hallucinatory paragraph, and did not care about it anymore. And when he thought of the beast lying hard and heavily against him, was neither disconcerted nor astonished, that the sting of sex went gliding upward through his body, like a water level in a jar.

After a minute or so, he heard Renzo come into the room behind him, and a new note shot across the mirror—the light of the oil lamp.

Christian turned, and let the lamp rinse his face with gold.

The boy did not meet his eyes.

"I'm to go with you, monsieur?"

"No."

No. This feast was also to be devoured without companions. He had not been inclined to look, to taste of it, earlier. He had been indifferent. And now what prompted him? The long head poised above his own, the two fistfuls he had grasped of sinew and hair?

He carried the lamp in one hand, the brimming glass in the other. Hamel's elaborate floor plan, Christian's passport to the alternative country of the house, stared from his waistcoat pocket, occasionally plucked out and referred to, then reinserted like a wafer.

Historical dates were scribbled all over this map, but dates did not interest Christian. Nor really any individual item of the complex of the house. What he encountered, what he traversed, remained an amalgam. Comprising: huge cavities of rooms, stacked with furnishings robbed of all personality beneath their dust sheets; carven stairways; carven beams overhead submerged in a deep water of height. The elder portions of the chateau cascaded back in time. The towers, graftings of stone and demolished earthworks. Thin windows buried alive in their embrasures, one with the bones upon its sill of a small bird, blown in by some wind, unable to get free, dead of battering itself on the thick gray vitreous of the pane. Ropes of cobwebs, laces of wax descended from spider-like candelabra, pendant on cords from the roof. Winding steps went down to the dark hells of cellars, ascended into blank walls where ancient walks had perished and plastered rooms accrued.

Even where dissolution was not obvious, it had a neglected air, for it had often been neglected—shut up altogether, or when open, ignored its staff of servants pared, its depth unsounded by voices or human traffic.

From a gallery of windows, he found himself able to look

over into the old court. Far smaller than the yard below the kitchen, it lay like a cistern of darkness at the bottom of four stone walls. In the farthest of these, a wrought-iron gate, bound shut by creepers, led to another ghostly corner of the topiary garden, the humped contortions of its yew trees just visible beyond. An ancient well held the center of the court, with a tall cowl and broad-stepped rim where once the buckets and pots would have lined up in a row. But the well was long disused, the spring beneath having been diverted to pass through the tanks of the house, a piece of engineering decided and brought about in his grandfather's time.

As he looked down into the courtyard, Christian, feeling no connection with its past or its present, still became aware of a very faint outrageous urge to enter it. It would be easy enough to locate an outlet and wrench one of the keys around in the lock. He let himself play with this fancy for a while, the picture of himself idling in the court, tearing the creeper and passing through the iron gate into that mysterious and unvisited garden, where last night he had seen Sylvie fluttering about like a dark white crow. And the dog, the dog from the forest, trotting in at the wide-open entrance to the estate, trotting over the black vistas of the ground, its green eyes preceding it—

Yes, the thought of the dog stimulated him. The dog, which was, or might be, sudden death. Was it the same strange lust which had prompted the girl?

The golden cognac in the glass made him wonder, with a solemn tenderness, if the dog, or even death, was real. Presently, he looked away from the courtyard, and having again consulted Hamel's plan, began to circle back toward the humanized areas of the chateau.

He acknowledged the tour had not made him cognizant of ownership, let alone of ancestry, or those much spoken-of things, roots. He could recall long ago mentioning the chateau, years before he had ever thought to see it, and of referring to his grandfather—"My grandfather"—as if to some irrelevant historical figure, nothing to do with him at all. Of course, he had never seen him, either. And now, there were his feelings about this house, for the house, too, was like the forest—wooden thickets, chasms of stairways, beams like boughs, ceilings of overcast night. And to return toward the parts of the house which had been opened—cleared and tamed—was like returning to a firelit bivouac in the midst of the wood. Protected by the glow of brandy and a lamp, the stranger could demonstrably traverse the spot without threat, for nothing had followed him, on this occasion. But safety and comfort were only illusions.

And so it did not matter that still he did not know if there was water in the moat, or the structure of anything indoors or out, its landmarks, its secrets. He could laugh off the task of discovery with relief as quite hopeless. It meant nothing to him, for he was not the heir to any of it. But an orphan in an unknown country.

Reemerging from archaic to modern via one of the worm-like passages, he passed the entry to the music room and hesitated. A piano stranded in the forest, melody like shot hitting the shadows between their eyes. But he was ferociously hungry, felt the insane hunger that sometimes came over him. He moved away.

In the master suite the fires were all alight, waving to him from the grates. And when he went down between the ballerina gyrations of the grand staircase, the two vast hearths of the hall were now also in bloom. Their lights spangled across the red mahogany table with its elaborate setting of crystal and silver, dotted the chandeliers and hit the porthole of stained glass above, finding and refinding in it one singing ray of an almost unbearable blue.

Renzo was already attending to the wine, nervously, having doubtless been instructed by Madame.

The dishes began to come in promptly on the stroke of nine.

Christian had pondered what La Tienne would manage, imposed upon and with only the girl to assist her. Yet it appeared certain provisions had been made before the invisible cook was sent away. A soup and a pâté, a ragout, a roast of chicken and a joint, both with three or four side dishes, a marble pyramid of cheeses, marzipan and cold green fruits imported from the city out of season.

More even than his hunger could accommodate. Scarcely noted by his hunger. A medley of scents and flavors and textures merely heartlessly and unaesthetically devoured.

He ate like a boy of ten or eleven who all day has been running, riding, boxing, brawling, foodless, on some broad street of earliest adolescence. In this form, when it woke, his appetite presented itself to him.

Renzo came and went with the wine, or went out and reentered with the dishes, a stand-in. Sylvie also came with dishes, setting them down among the candles and the crystal, and the motion of her hands, the bending and unbending of her snake-like neck, began to hypnotize Christian.

As the hunger, appeased, died down, he watched her more and more as she slunk about, for slink she did. He watched her neck, her fingers, the turning planes of her face, and the coarse sausage of her hair on which the light slid and slithered as if wet. The dog was something they shared between them, this peasant bitch and he. He had wanted her to tell him about the dog.

Every motion of her body, which was in itself not particularly graceful, became provocative because it hinted at this obscured revelation. She was like an animated doll, behind which some creature hid, skilfully darting, always just out of view, yet always on the brink of showing itself. Something about this caused him to remember that brief dream he had had, on the first day, in the salon. The fair girl, with her arms crossed protectively over her white throat. There was something perversely erotic about the memory. Just as about Sylvie.

Two empty wine bottles had gone away, and the brandy had come back.

He did not really know himself at such times. That was the joy of them.

Madame had not reappeared, and Renzo had hurried out. The girl leaned to replace a dying candle in the silver branch. Her lips were slightly parted, as if to inhale the waxy smoke.

"Sylvie."

She straightened, eyes fixed on nothing.

"Turn this way, Sylvie."

She complied slowly. More slowly still, her eyes floated up to his face. Half-moon eyes, for the lids drooped as if she were tired. They reminded him infallibly of the white lids of the youth in the forest, the de Lagenay. Perhaps Christian imagined that she set out now, deliberately, to provoke; the tilt of her head, her parted lips, sleepy gaze.

He indicated the decanter of brandy. "Do you see that?"

"Yes, monsieur."

"In a quarter of an hour," he said, "bring it to the bed-room in the master suite."

There was a pause.

"I suppose you heard me," he said.

"Yes, m'sieur."

Leaving all the intervening doors open, he went into the music room, to the vampire there, running one hand along its black bestial carapace, the other over its bone-colored teeth.

He was very far from being drunk. He seated himself and began to scatter bolts of Liszt from the piano across the room, the dark corridor beyond, bright shards, pitiless arpeggios, music to be eaten in hunger as the feast of food had been. And when these fireworks, having exploded in lights and noise, fell down, he resorted to Chopin with a deadly rapturous irony. The desperation of the twenty-fourth prelude thrust itself through the walls. He could feel its rumors and murmurings driven between every stone. And soon the glorious horror of death lay over everything, the ultimate license. Swimming up through the last exhalations of the prelude, he pictured the silly lumpish little girl, on the stair, in the bed-chamber, growing rare, exotic, magical in her robe of life.

He struck a last development from the piano, an improvisation, as if striking the dead Chopin in the face. (The vampire had had that man's blood long ago.) Then got up and walked away from the instrument, out of the room and along the corridor, into the master suite.

The gas burned low in the bedroom.

Sylvie was standing by the small table where she had set the decanter and the glass. The firelight fingered their facets, and fingered the girl less selectively. Yet, she was idealized, like one of those Flemish paintings of feminine skin bathed by fire or lamp or candle, which had posed forever on the walls of his father's hotel. Her eyes, too, had that same polished quality. No more tears in them apparently, no quivering of the wrists or limbs.

He went to the decanter and filled the glass from it. She did not register his nearness or his actions.

"Did you hear about the de Lagenay dog?" he asked. No answer. "Which attacked me," he said. Her eyelids moved. "Aren't you sorry for me?" he said. He reached out one hand

and drew her face around. "Aren't you sorry to hear I was attacked by the dog?"

She stared straight down and said distinctly, "No, monsieur."

He gently pushed her head back into its original position, and drank from the glass.

"You ought to be sorry for me. In a few months, when you're cozily married to some local farmer, or wearing pink stockings in the city, I shall be dead."

She laughed. It was a short, solitary yap of derision, and interested him. He picked up her hand and put the brandy glass into it.

"Drink that."

"To get me foolish won't make of no difference," she said. But she raised the brandy, and drained it. Probably they had all been helping themselves from the cellars for years. "You said to me," she said, "it wouldn't be necessary. That thee wouldn't require it of me."

"I've changed my mind. I do require it."

She said, smiling with a sort of anger, still at nothing, "Thy blood requires it." And she poured for herself a second brandy, very large, and drank it down like milk.

Chapter 9

---•◉•---

The Seduction

He liked this. It eluded him, was a kind of game. Women came to him generally, eager, saying sophisticated and theatrical things. This one, slippery, evading, all the while slipping closer. Drinking the fine brandy like medicine against him. Slavish and resentful. Electric.

"Take down your hair," he said, and moved a foot or so from her, watching her, and when she began to obey him, her hard plain face vivid with its sullenness, each motion of her fingers, her arms, her torso, echoed through his own body.

The hair came loose in a spitting torrent; he heard the static sizzle in it as the last pin was plucked away. Then, without being told to, she unfastened her servant's dress, wriggled out of it, and next started to remove the unimaginative undergarments beneath, peeling layer upon layer, like wrapping paper, from herself. But the performance was functional only, something to be done, merely. The ugly stays had left their usual ribbing behind in the flesh, but unlike those other women, emerging from their froths of lace and ribbon, she presented even these marks to him with a matter-of-fact effrontery.

Naked, she was the heavy white of curds. The fire licked and sipped at her, describing her to him, over and over. He was snared in a vast pounding lethargy, unable to move, mesmerized. He did not have to tell her to come to him, for she began to walk across the short distance, momentarily doubled

68

as she passed the mirror of the dressing table. Now she looked at him. She smiled now. No friendship in it, no allure or wish to gratify. She came toward him as if to harm him with the opaque lambency of her body and the myrrh of her hair and the shadows that ran like leaves up and down the length of her with the reflected fire.

"Thee like me," she said. "Shall I like it for thee too, to give thee?"

They were the very words she had spoken to the dog. A surging thrill of pleasure rushed through him, almost intolerable. Her hands reached him first, and the first touch of them informed him that she was knowing enough for her denials to have been lies. His own hands were filled by her. The curious struggle had commenced, to fuse or force a way in through each other's atoms.

When he pierced her, she was lying spread on the rug beneath him, her head thrown back, already wordlessly crying, and straining with her arms to drag him down to cover her.

Initially, her violence bore him with her, the upheaval of her loins, and the two frantic arms clutching and grasping at him, and her face rolling back and forth across the mat of her hair. Desire had made her hideous, beautifully so. As if possessed by devils. Initially each stroke, each clash of movement ground him farther and farther into the soil of her body, closer and closer to the succession of instants when all reason ceased.

And then, like an inexorable floodtide, reason began to return. It came in low icy waves, pouring up over him, out of the floor, the sensation of the rug, her flesh, the thunder of his own pulse, which suddenly, like a broken clock, began to falter. He found he was observing her as she thrashed and shrieked under him. Noting, and inwardly appraising the long spasms; dissecting her. Uninvolved. A scientist, his experiment: Sylvie, who was being tortured to death.

When she lay abruptly quiet and stupefied, he found himself there on the crest of nothing, his spine still foolishly arched to suffer an ecstasy no longer credible or attainable.

A just reprisal, perhaps. Some native curse.

It was quite diverting.

He lay face down, the heat of the fire brimming and fading on his shoulders, listening as, without a word, she rose and dressed herself.

Yes. A joke. The seigneur eager and the girl reluctant, a rape. Ending with the girl appeased and the man cheated by his own body. The culmination of the succession of feasts— of terror, of stone, of food, of music—the feast of lust—a fallen tower. Perhaps it would always fail him now, that last febrile demand of his sickness. Perhaps the dark forest had put on him the bane of impotence. Always to desire, never to fulfill. Just as in some arcane story.

He heard the door thud softly shut. He imagined her face, washed of all expression, almost of all its features, by the uproar of paroxysm. He fell asleep on the floor, pressed to the floor's muscular ungivingness.

In the dream, it was Annelise who clung to him, her petticoats crushed between them; they had been in too much hurry to allow time to undress. And as he thrust himself blindly forward, as if trying to shatter the bones of her pelvis, she too screamed again and again, yet her cries were far away, out in some frozen garden under the shrill winter stars.

In the morning, Renzo did not come up with the hot water for the bath. No tray of rolls, preserves and coffee arrived. The elegant hotel was out of gear.

The sky was swollen up against the windows. Landward distances were gray; the edging of forest smoldered. Not a twig on the yew trees moved, not a whisper of wind or sound. Sarrette, hatless, in military stance, patrolled around the bulge of the old tower, and vanished among the black and unraveling hillocks of topiary.

The rap of Madame's acorn knuckles on the drawing-room door was unmistakable.

Christian went to the door and opened it, and stood looking at her. He was naked under the velvet dressing gown, but she, under all her garments, might not be naked at all.

"Forgive me, monsieur, for troubling you. I've taken the liberty of summoning Monsieur Doctor Claut. Sarrette will go in the car. There has been—some trouble."

"What trouble?"

"You'd better see for yourself, monsieur."

She stepped aside, and he went out into the passage. She followed him to the stair, herding him. When he hesitated, looking down into the hall, she came and pointed so he would not miss the bundle that lay on the long table, where, at nine o'clock the previous evening, he had dined.

"What is it?"

"There's been a dreadful accident of sorts, monsieur."

He walked down the stairs, and Madame Tienne walked just behind him. At each step, he heard Annelise scream in ecstasy. He thought of the well-known anecdote of the child woken in terror by such cries from the parental bed, these noises of pleasure that were identical to those of pain.

The bundle on the table was a dingy white. A sheet, maybe, taken hastily from one of the linen chests. Contours were obscure.

Christian was aware that the woman behind him intended him to inspect the sheet. On the bottom step he halted.

"Please look at it, monsieur."

Annelise screaming, rhythmically, in some garden.

"You mean the sheet?"

"Yes, monsieur."

"Tell me what's in it?"

"I had rather you'd look, monsieur."

He walked off the bottom step. He moved toward the bundle with a grim, calculated stride, already reaching to pull the folds apart. He had seen blood before, one day at the conservatoire. A hot day of summer, when there had been an argument, and playing the piano in rage, the cough which had begun to plague him, with no warning at all, dashed the fan of the keys with red. He had not been able to believe it then. He had leaned and touched the blood, his handkerchief pressed to his mouth. The metallic taste, but hardly any hurt, accompanied this relevation; it was so facile, he might scarcely have noticed.

Christian pulled the folds of the sheet apart.

A liquid glare splashed up at him, the blue morning light through the stained-glass porthole, dazzling on a pride of silver dishes.

He swung around, and Madame said to him, "Sylvie, monsieur. She'd taken it into her head, I'm afraid, to make off with these plates and bowls, all she could get at without disturbance in the night."

"A thief?" he said.

Sylvie, writhing as his own flesh slackened. Sylvie, the thief, or the whore.

"Regrettably, monsieur. A ridiculous plan. Where she would have taken it. . . . But, of course, she didn't get much farther than the kitchen yard. It's a terrible thing, monsieur. The animal must be found and shot."

"The animal?"

"The wild dog, monsieur."

The air pushed coldly against Christian and he turned again, this time to confront the opened door which gave onto the terrace.

Renzo stood in the doorway. He held one of Sylvie's shoes, proudly.

"Sarrette found it," he said, "under the trees."

"Go back to the kitchen," said Madame brusquely. She glided toward Renzo. "How dared you come in at this door."

Renzo's face, a sallow red and deranged, sank inwards.

"I'm sorry, Madame."

He clutched the shoe, in which shreds of a torn stocking still lingered. From the leather, and from his clutching hand, large pieces of dried caked blood flaked off and showered on the flags of the floor.

PART TWO

ENFANTS PERDUS

Chapter 10

—◦—

The Funeral

As sometimes happened, a student at the conservatoire had
taken his own life, and Christian, though he had known the
suicide scarcely at all, had been asked to attend the funeral.
Standing in the spring rain, the fashionable black, plumed
horses off to one side, the umbrellas steaming and streaming,
he had vowed with some solemnity that the next funeral he
would attend would be his own. A joke, it had turned out extremely unhappy; a prediction. And yet, here he was, following a second box, not his own, to its hole in the earth.
Though there was no rain. It was another dry, pallid winter
day, of low-slung sky and abrupt sweeping winds. Nor was
there anything fashionable about the cortège. Nor had he,
seigneur though he was, been invited.

He had meant to leave the chateau instantly. Truly, this
time he had decided. The doctor—unseen, like the cook—had
come and gone. The law was not in any way represented.
Some men had arrived, by the kitchen entrance, coming up
the stairs from the yard. He had reckoned them merely porters, for they had brought a cart and a wooden coffin. Then a
chance remark of Renzo's self-important hysteria, overheard
behind a door, had established that two of the men were rela-
tives of the corpse. It shocked Christian, at this late stage, to
learn she had had a father and a brother living in the village.
Like many of the children, she had been sent to the town to
be schooled, then brought home ready to be sent to the

chateau instead. The drunkard had drunk his way out of residence. The new owner arrived. Sylvie was sixteen when she lay under him on the rug. Sixteen when the fangs of a beast had shut together in her throat. Presently Sarrette, in military mood, had strutted in like a pigeon, and thanked Christian, on behalf of Sylvie's relations, for permitting them to collect her remains. They were, apparently, too timid to approach him themselves.

After the body had been carted away, the huge house settled, as if sinking back onto a sofa, utterly indifferent.

"When is the burial to be?" Christian asked Sarrette.

"Tomorrow, monsieur."

"Is that usual—so quick?"

"Sometimes."

There would have been very little left to go into the coffin. Christian had heard Renzo's babblings, though he had not seen the body himself. Except, of course, in his mind's eye, which had been sufficient to cause him to vomit. There would not be an embalmer in such a place. Nobody to repair or substitute. The coffin would be kept closed and shoved swiftly from sight into the ground. Presumably some record of her death would be awarded whatever office of the law obtained hereabouts. Probably some official in the town would peruse and dismiss it, for who would travel to such a place to investigate? Claut's word, whatever it had been, would be deemed enough. Or, the matter would be set aside for the future, and conveniently forgotten.

"Her father, the brother," Christian said. "What do they mean to do?"

"To do, monsieur?"

"About the damned dog."

"What can they do, monsieur?"

"My God," Christian said. "Is it as bad as that here? Why, shoot the bloody thing before it does more harm." But as he spoke, he beheld Sylvie, dancing at the night window, through the night garden. A seducer. What else? Something made him shiver. The same thing which produced the anger in him at the village's apathy. Which made him think of remaining somewhat longer. Perhaps his *guilt*. "These Lagenays," said Christian, "must be got hold of and hauled before a magistrate. If not here, then in town. And the two dogs have to be dispensed with. They could be rabid. For heaven's sake."

"Yes, monsieur." Sarrette stood politely, then said: "Will you be needing the car, Monsieur Dorse?"

"Tomorrow I shall," Christian said, "when I attend the funeral."

Sarrette reacted. Something of a face protruded through his attitude. A flat, resisting face.

"I don't think you'd care for it, monsieur. Uncultured people, monsieur."

"I know. The Styx."

Out here in the Styx, the youth under the hemlock had said to him, *one seldom hears Rachmaninov so powerfully rendered.*

"And their ways of going about such things—"

"They cut the neck of a fowl, I suppose, and pour it over the grave."

"Not exactly, monsieur. But—you are a stranger."

"And might not be welcome? I'm sure I won't be. They made that abundantly clear yesterday. With your assistance. However, I own this pile of stones. If the seigneur takes it into his head to grace the burying of one of his servants, they can't very well stop me. Put it this way. They're medieval enough to forgo the police. That makes me the only law."

Sarrette looked dubious, but his eyes were frozen over, as if he recognized something and disliked it very much. He was acquainted with the village, if not a native born. He did not approve of kings who meddled in the workaday rites of their kingdoms.

"Well," he began, "I would say—"

Christian was white with a half-pretended fury, acting, either to enhance or dispel his own uncertain feelings. He smashed his fist, which once he would have taken more care of, on a table, whose ornaments duly rattled and tottered.

"You won't say another word. Have the car ready for me in time tomorrow. Which is?"

"The service commences at eleven o'clock, monsieur."

"At twenty minutes to eleven. Oh, and Sarrette—"

"Yes, monsieur."

"Presumably there's a gun room somewhere in this sprawl. I don't remember seeing it, but I could have missed the door.

If any of the guns works, you or Renzo get a couple of them in order for me. And load them."

Sarrette gazed at him. Unfriend indeed.

"There are guns. I'll see to it."

Christian grimaced as he turned from Sarrette. Christian had never used a gun in his life, despite his father's energetic efforts to teach him. Blue-gray or brown birds dangling, or deer ripped open along red seams, had provided no inspiration. Yet, when he visualized the beast leaping on him in the darkness, the hot press of its body, he could feel the slender stem of a gun between his hands, and the concussion of the bullet as it left the barrel. Perverse, phallic, vengeful, whatever the images were, they coexisted. And Sarrette's unliking face, and loathing, repressed eyes, revealed that for the chauffeur, too, such symbols sprang from each other.

But poor demented Sylvie, where was she in this morass of impulses? Where had she ever been?

The bell was tolling through the dull air as they approached, but Sarrette had driven more slowly than ever; they were late. Christian did not urge the driver to make speed. A last-minute dread had come over Christian. The thought of the stuffy, icy church, the smoking breath of the mourners, the rituals of soil and incense around the wound in the earth appalled him.

The bell stopped just as they came into the square. The backdrop was exactly as before, soft blacks and muted whites, but on this occasion populated. Figures were pressing in through the open door of the church.

The car pulled up and Christian got out of it, and went toward the church with a premonition of claustrophobia. An enormous silence issued from the doorway. As he stepped into it, with the unavoidable sense of fluid closing over his head, he became aware of the mass of persons inside, all of them apparently standing up. The entire village, it seemed, was there, come to celebrate its lost child.

The windows, which had shown no color on the outside, let down sharp-edged ladders within. But their tints were sickly, the rich carmines, emeralds and sapphires for which ancient stained glass was noted, were notably absent. These patinas came from an era when the secret of color had been lost, or denied. Their pictures were similarly anemic and confused, all but one near to the altar, of the Virgin Mary, shrouded in veils, her arms overflowing with lilies.

Despite the windows, the church was dark, as if filled indeed by water. The candles burned in isolated beads. The watch fire, like the prow lamp of some sinking ship, seemed to recede.

He had an impression of thick stone pillars, and of a roof preparing to come down and crush pillars and men alike beneath its lid.

Since most of the crowd were standing, the benches must be limited and to the front. Christian, having placed himself at the rear, prepared to stand out the ceremony, also, reconciled by proximity to the exit point.

But the door was shut behind him with a tremendous thud, and a deeper atmosphere of shadow enveloped the church. Who could get out of such a trap?

A pale shine of something swimming on the rim of his eye informed him that a head had turned to gaze back at him out of the crowd. When he looked, there was nothing singular in it. It was like a face in a drawing, unfinished, merely a suggestion of light and shade. And then many of these unfinished faces began to turn, one by one, as if at some telepathic signal. Like leaves blowing over to show a gray underside. Leaf on unfinished leaf.

At first he had been ignored by the village, then avoided. Now he was stared at. Something clutched inside him, at heart or ribs. The vague guilt, maybe. He had acted the rape of the girl, and she, driven by obscure motives, had stolen silver from the house and run out to collide with death in the night. On certain unreasonable levels, his fault. And the blowing over of the gray unfinished faces seemed to indicate knowledge, even judgment.

He would turn and walk directly out of the church. The door would open, naturally, it would not have been locked.

He did not move, however. And after a moment the crowd itself began to alter its formation. It took him several long seconds to comprehend that they were giving way, making a path for him. He did not want to use it, of course, but now the route seemed unavoidable. They were courteously providing a gangway, as if in a theater, for him to walk to the seating area at the front of the church, adjacent to the altar and the coffin.

This is stupid. But he started to go forward.

Surely every bench would have been filled. It seemed not. The crowd continued to give way, and the smoldering watch-light to blossom nearer. He had reached the front of the church. Involuntarily, his head jerked up, for there were no benches at all. Merely one tall, heavy chair of wood, most probably four centuries old.

The seigneur's chair, no doubt of it. A quaint custom. Offensively so.

He felt their waiting, like a kind of void. When he did what they waited to see if he would do, he would drop into that void. He began to become dizzy with incipient panic. He glared at the coffin, the altar. The candle flames strung a necklace across his eyes.

Very well.

He walked over to the chair, and sat down in it. It was at once a relief and an oppression. He sighed slowly, hearing the breath tremble as it left him. There was no other sound. The aroma of the incense was very strong. His head swam, but he did not dare lose hold of himself in such a situation, and he gripped the old arms of the chair, blinking repeatedly to clear his eyes. As he did so, the lily Virgin in the window solidified and distorted: the chair was set head on to face her.

The priest came in, only one, and a single child with the censer.

What happened after this, supposedly the burial service, Christian could barely take in. His concentration was centered on holding himself together in the teeth of some extraordinarily nervous onslaught, some terror too ridiculous to identify, too large to be dismissed. And therefore, if what he actually noticed, in random snatches, of the service, seemed bizarre, no doubt that was due to the wandering of his mind, the strange tensions that came and went through his muscles.

There was an abundance of incense. It rose like clouds of ether, shaken over book and candles and coffin—erroneously, it seemed to him, in such a mass, where the office of the censer was surely differently spaced. . . . But then, again, he had rarely been in a church since his childhood. Yet the Latin, spoken by the priest, clotted over by the local accent, muttered by the populace in the church—he could not bring himself to join in, even where he recollected the words—incidentally, in places, seemed quite wrong.

Hostias, quaesumus, Domine, quas tibi pro animabus famulorum famularumque tuarum offerimus. . . . Look mercifully upon this sacrifice. . . .

He was becoming obsessed by the Mary figure in the window. Her face was only a wisp in the bled-out glass. Her eyes were like sockets, her long mouth had no gentleness, rather it was cruel, peculiarly unhuman. Now and then it seemed to smile a hideous smile at him as the spasms of vapor distorted it. The lilies spilling over her hands were also wrong. Hairy, fleshy flowers, impure and ugly—

Hostias, quaesumus, Domine. . . .

There was a coming and going at the altar rail. The priest—what was he like? Ah, yes. A little gray mouse. Men and women moved. Light splattered in blotches on the closed coffin. It was a play they were putting on for the individual audiences—one in his carven chair, one in her sickly window.

I'll always remember this. Yet not remember any of it well. Why is it slightly obscene?

Their fear, possibly. Their ghastly antique fear.

Or mine.

He saw a black casket delivered at the hotel. A package for you, monsieur. His father, whom he had not seen for ten years, seeing him packed in satin. Yes, the money, the rents, investments, and weird little business ventures that had come with the chateau, they would pay for it.

What was happening now? They were lifting the box. Six men, one of them the girl's brother, recognizable because he had been described, a nose smashed in some fight.

The door opened once more at the back of the church and a block of white glare fell into the nave.

The bearers moved forward, Sylvie on their shoulders.

The priest was ahead of them, the light shooting arrows through the lace surplice that shawled his soutane. Even the surplice was wrong.

The church was in motion, the congregation gushing after the box, now the plug had been pulled from the doormouth.

Christian rose slowly. The incense burned his throat, and he coughed savagely in the silence, as the last mourners trickled through the door. Nobody looked round. He went after them, but paused on the threshold. He glanced back. The Virgin had become a needle of dull light, without personality of any sort.

The somber procession wound across the square, and down the gravel road toward the lower end of the village. The graveyard was obviously outside urban limits. Somewhere off the road, too, for he did not recall glimpsing it on his arrival. In the forest, then.

Sarrette stood by the car, and had removed his top hat out of respect.

The bell began to clank again.

All this for Sylvie. When alive, who would have paid her any heed? Christian's guilt resolved itself in sentiment. His eyes filled with tears, but he knew he only wept for himself.

He went to the car.

"Give me the bag," he said to Sarrette.

"Monsieur," said Sarrette.

"Be cautious, it isn't wise. Yes, you told me."

"What happened in the church, monsieur?"

Christian leaned against the car a moment. "They put me, very politely, in the feudal lord's chair. I haven't felt so many eyes on me since the recital at Brach's. And then—no more interest in me. I'm intrigued. Give me the damned bag out of the car."

Sarrette did as he was told. The bag was heavy. Sarrette averted his eyes.

"I assume," Christian said, "if I asked you to accompany me now, you'd refuse."

"Monsieur pays my wages, I am at his disposal."

"Hamel pays your wages, out of the revenues of the estate. Which I own through a posthumous trick of my grandfather's."

"Do you want me to follow you, monsieur, with one of the guns?"

"That would look pretty by her grave. No, stay with the car. I expect you, this time, to *be* here when I come back."

He was able to pursue the last mourner, at a suitable distance, down the gravel road and off it some way below the village. It was the spot just beyond, and on the opposite side to, the farm, where the stone marker came out of the ground. A dirt track, a couple of meters wide, broke between the trees; he had not taken it in from the car, on the previous occasion. At the end of the track, a walk of about twenty meters, a lichen-plastered stone cross rose like a monstrous weed. It guarded the entrance to a large clearing, walled in all about by larches and seedling pines. Rotted stumps of trees rose from the tangled grass, and mingled with the leaning headstones, which the elements had leaded in, across shoulders and sides, with a dense black outline. Another drawing.

Christian watched the burial from beside the cross. Even now, out in the air, his head clearing, the rites about the grave appeared distorted. There the priest, pointing to the four quarters of the compass, or so it seemed. And now an emission of white crumbs scattering from his hand over the box, as it went down. Sanctification by the Host?

They were far enough away, he caught no word, only indeterminate hummings, fitfully lost in the sudden noisy soughings of the trees.

Even the wind was strange. Isolated rushings, separated by minutes at a time. As if great-winged and invisible beings passed, hurrying all the same way, and from the same starting place.

Chapter 11

—◦—

The Gun

The funeral disbanded without obvious subtlety, as two fellows advanced with spades and began to dig. The boy with the censer, the mouse priest, the villagers instantly started to ramble back over the clearing. Christian identified Sylvie's brother again with no trouble. An adolescent lout, it might be risky to confront him. But there was the one who must be the father, hanging on the son, with an old man's countenance collapsed in misery, yet dry-eyed, almost indifferent to its own despair.

The first two or three villagers arrived at the cross, and hurried past it, ignoring the slim young man in the dark greatcoat. After the alarming act of deference in the church, this was perfectly ludicrous. Conscious of his own foolishness, Christian reached out, and caught one of the next group to come up by the arm. The man peered under his brows, struggling to get free, yet somehow not able to detach himself from Christian's grasp. The jaw worked, the mouth tried to form a phrase. The eyes, forehead and nostrils tried to help it. Whether the words were of resentment or pleading or mere noncomprehension Christian did not learn. This struggling disturbed him. He let go, and the man floundered on.

The next to approach the track was none other than the little priest. The priest looked actually afraid; there was in his case no attempt to mask or excuse. He nodded to Christian, as if paying homage to the school bully, and scurried by. At a loss, Christian let this one, also, go.

When the father and son arrived, Christian stepped into their way.

The boy's head rose, the crushed nose like a warning beacon. He scowled. The father did nothing, did not change.

"Do you know me?" Christian said to the boy.

"Yes."

"Please accept my condolences on your sister's death."

This would be the trigger, if the boy was inclined to berate or attack him. Christian wondered what he would do in such an event. But the boy made no belligerent move. He lowered his eyes in the familiar fashion, and shuffled his feet, as Christian had foreseen.

"In this bag," said Christian, extending it, "are a few of the valuables your sister was bringing you from the chateau. At least, I think she was bringing them to you."

The other looked up again, startled. Christian thrust the bag against the boy's arms, and he took hold of it, unwillingly.

"Some silver," Christian said. "Look and see."

The lout clumsily undid the bag, looked inside, and was transfixed. The father hung on him, all this while, incapable, or undesirous, of understanding.

"I'd like you to have it," Christian said malignly. "It's no use to me. If, on the other hand, you don't want it, give it to your priest." Christian smiled. He put out his hand and rested it gently on the lout's bulky shoulder, and as he did so, realized whose gesture was the model. "I suppose I can't interest you in a shooting party? I can loan you a gun. For the de Lagenay dogs."

But the boy reacted definitely now. He jumped away, leaving both Christian and the decrepit father standing. The bag plunged clattering as both the boy's hands flew up in the air and came together in that sign Christian had formerly seen daubed on the post before the inn. Thumb and index finger rammed lopsidedly into the sigil of the cross. What did they call it? The lys-something. The *lily*?

"All right," Christian said.

He turned and strode away up the track, muffling the cough in his ungloved palm.

Sarrette stood waiting by the car in the square.

Christian got in, not speaking, and sat inspecting one of the guns. He remembered just enough of his earnest father's tuition to be able to fire it. Probably.

Sarrette drove sedately around the grotesque monument, under the gargoyle-like creature which hunched forward as if to inspect the weather, out of the square, into the forest.

"Just you and me, then," Christian said. "I'm positive you're a better shot than I am. I shall certainly make a mess of it. My hands are too strong, you see, and trained to do other things."

"Yes, monsieur."

"How odd of you, Sarrette, not to be afraid of going into the forest. I thought at first that you were. Afraid of aiming a gun at a de Lagenay cur, for example. Or are you?"

"No, monsieur."

"Why not?"

"Monsieur?"

"Everyone else is terrified. Of Sylvie's poor little corpse. Of the wood, the land by night, the dogs, the Lagenays. Of me. Why aren't you?"

"But it isn't night, monsieur."

"Of course, I see. And I shan't find the dogs, shall I, by day?"

Sarrette said nothing.

"Stop here," said Christian. "This is where Peton led me off the road. Do you know the path? With the two bones lying crossed on it?"

"I've heard of it, monsieur."

Christian coughed, and the convulsed tube which plumbed his chest began to burn and tear. His head ached, a bonfire was smothered in his throat. He got out of the car, held the gun inaccurately and dissolutely, contemplating Sarrette as he prepared to follow.

"But if I shan't find the dogs," said Christian, "I shan't need you. Shall I?"

Sarrette stopped moving about. He looked down at the wheel.

"My grandfather," said Christian, "insisted on having a clause inserted, during the sale of the chateau. If the buyer died without progeny, the chateau reverted to the original inheriting line. And he did die without progeny, didn't he, that drunkard? Did you know him, Sarrette?"

"Briefly, Monsieur Dorse. My father served at the chateau, and until last year I was in service in the town."

"Did you know why the drunkard drank?"

"No."

"The drunkard drank because his two sons and his daughter were drowned in a ferryboat disaster, in England. Thirty years after he bought the house from my grandfather. I recall my mother telling me. I would have been about eighteen. Drive the car back to the chateau."

"Monsieur?"

"The car. Drive it back. It's daylight, only about one o'clock. And I've learned the local method of making *la croix écartée*. I should be quite safe."

"Monsieur—"

"Go to hell."

The car started with a bang, and blue exhaust exploded from the pipe as it pushed itself away over the gravel.

Christian walked off the road, and directly between the trees. It seemed simpler this time, and the penetration was more elegant. Curious, perhaps, that he had recognized the spot so unerringly, for nothing appeared to specify it on the road.

The ancient growth of pines did not seem prepared to offer battle, either, as formerly. He got through the undergrowth as if through cords of silk rather than claws. The blond soil of the path, indented like a spring, was immediately obvious. But there was plenty of illumination at this hour, and generally it was static, swung down in broad lattices between the trees to the earth. The shadows similarly stayed quiescent, in their allotted pools or strips. Only when those sudden gigantic winds dashed by did the picture shift kaleidoscopically.

And yet. The forest was still a great water, and he, a diver with a gun, prowling the floor of it.

He did not feel excited now. He felt ill, but aggressively so. His debility angered him. He would have been glad to kill something in hot blood.

Christian walked onto the path. About ten minutes later, he inadvertently stepped over the two insane bones. Pine cones lay here and there, unseasonably. It was, all of it, out of joint. This place. These emotions and drives.

Having reached the area where Peton had left him, his pulse quickened.

Some minutes after, he approached the hemlock tree, which seemed to lift itself from the forest like a colony of ragged birds, flying on rent wings, one above the other. He checked at once. Here he had reread Hamel's letter, finding the imagined warning absent from it. And here the youth had appeared, with his dark red hair, flawless on his cue.

How quiet the forest was, between the journeys of the winds. As if dead a thousand years.

Christian raised the gun, touched the catch, lowered the gun.

He took several steps, enough to bring him level with the hemlock. He stopped and glanced away, permitting the manifestation to occur unseen. But looking back, no one was there.

One of the winds came by then. It was very cold, and ridiculously his teeth began to chatter, and he could not control them.

He perceived himself, a hunter not knowing what he hunted, or if it was there. Or if he wanted it, or feared it. Or if he had merely lost his mind.

The only reality was the gun. He himself was quite unreal. It would be easy to weep. To strike out at the boles of the trees, to shout at God, to demand why he should be cast off with nothing but a macabre legend and a loaded gun to cling to. He, who had had so much.

He stood on the floor of the forest, gripping the gun like a plank in the sea, holding down this awful desolation by main force.

After a few moments, he strode by the tree, no longer looking at it or expecting anything of it.

But the stride escalated. He was running. He ran and he cried out.

He was dimly conscious of one of those breaks somewhere ahead of him, a gap in the trees revealing an interval of descent, and beyond that, one of the balconied rock faces, waterfalls of pines and firs combed down over it. But he halted because the path itself came to an end against a heap of stones. What they had been part of he was unsure, but, losing his balance, he half fell against them. From this vantage, shaken back into external awareness, he found himself gazing into the shuttered window of a shack-like dwelling no more than a couple of meters ahead.

For almost a minute he stared at it. It crouched between the pines, partly strangulated and partly maintained by branches, the extension of roots, the tides of grass and undergrowth that thrust against it. A wild vine, apparently lush in summer but now a skeleton, clothed all the upper portion of the hut, encroaching even on the shutter. Being itself botched together from wood, unplastered, with a roof entirely seeded into moss and creeper, save for the extrusion of a crooked stovepipe, the small edifice was adequately disguised. From a slightly broader distance, it might have been missed altogether, lost against the impact of the rocky gap that fell and rose almost directly beyond.

Save that the sorcerous blond path, which ten minutes along its length was marked by two cruciform bones, finished virtually at the foot of this shelter.

Christian straightened up from the chaos of stonework. He looked at the hut a moment longer, and once more he raised the gun.

When he maneuvered around the stones, another side of the hut became visible, complete with a wooden door, firmly closed.

The house de Lagenay. It could be no other.

Christian crossed the few remaining paces to the door. It, like everything beside, seemed in poor repair. He glanced at the canyon beyond the house. A glint of water where the land went over into it, and bars of hard light piercing a group of smoke-blue firs, dividing them. . . . The beauty was lost on him, or merely added to his frustration. Nothing moved out here that he could identify as man or animal. He placed his hand ready against the catch of the gun, and kicked out at the hut door, one powerful vicious blow. And at that blow, the obstacle gave, hurling itself inward, and the lights of the daytime forest behind it.

He poised there, the lethal weapon in his grasp, the mysterious interior before him. It was very dark, very little was discernible. Even the light seemed only to rouse a swarm of shattered dusts and shadows. But gradually, there came a smoothing of textures, superseded by impressions. Christian made out, one by one, exotic curiosities, a cumbersome metal bath, a painted molded ewer on a stand, several staircases of books careering from the floor, a swath of curtain, once ecstatic with embroideries. Behind the curtain, the angle of a bed, a carved wooden bedpost, a portion of headboard, a cascade of sheet—

Christian walked into the hut, releasing the safety catch on the gun as he went.

Pushing by the curtain, he came against the bed frame. The banner of sheeting issued from under a pile of fur, pelts and rugs of all types. It was hard, at first glance, to be certain if the bed was occupied or not, so much lay over it, and of such variety. But his eye was hungry and alert. It eventually deciphered the landscaping one human body could produce under even so diverse a welter of coverings.

One human body.

Irresistibly, Christian visualized the extraordinary boy, so arrogant and assured beneath the hemlock, now vulnerably unconscious in this vulpine nest of fur. Indeed, so deeply asleep, even the crash of the door had failed to rouse him.

Employing the lip of the gun, Christian made a most careful insertion among the covers. Then swept barrel and bedclothes together upwards, and cast the latter away.

Not discovering what he expected was unnerving. The truth, rather more so. For in the center of the bed lay stretched a naked woman, regarding him with two luminous, uncanny, devilish eyes, both of which were wide awake.

Chapter 12

◆●◆

The Interview

"Excuse me," he said. But he did not move or turn away.

Nor did she stir. If his scrutiny offended or pleased her he could not tell. All he could ascertain was that, demonstrably, her nudity meant nothing indecent or embarrassing to her. She seemed used to it, relaxed. Clothed.

It was a beautiful body, the color of cream, full of delicately imperfect lines and cadences, lush, receptive, as if inviting possession. But the face, of a white slightly darker, like mature ivory, was built up on peculiar fragile bones, growing rather fleshy about the mouth, turning feline at the chin. And the eyes were two separate eyes set into that face, alike only in their color, the left eye wide and debonair, the right a fraction narrower, placed a fraction higher, a slim, gleaming and treacherous eye, containing secrets. Their shade was a gray more somber than his own, but the fine streamers of hair that sprayed over the pillow were like gilded smoke.

Sylvie had been sixteen, this one was twice Sylvie's age and somewhat to spare. It was not so much her body, or the dainty tracery of lines that the light touched in beside eyes and lips, which informed him of this. In repose, or movement, she looked, would look, far younger than the thirty-four or -five that was her due. It was her spirit which gave her away, the inner life under velvet flesh, relaxed forehead. Yet she was like a girl. Girl's hands and feet, girl's nipples, girl's lashes. And then, too, she was older, much older. Old as

91

the hemlock tree. She looked up at him from the well of time. No wonder she was not afraid.

She moved as the young man, her kindred, had done, before Christian could see it. Abruptly, she was kneeling, the smoke of her hair wafting up and drifting down, covering her shoulders, her breasts, but transparently. As she moved, he saw that these breasts, like her eyes, were uneven, the breasts of two lovely different women, linked only by the likeness of their buds, their marvelous flesh, as the eyes were linked only by their color. But the nails of her hands were the translucent red the young man's had been.

"Well," she said, "you have seen me."

And she was off the bed, and one of the big pelts had swirled up to cover her. For warmth, not modesty. Or to exacerbate him.

"Well, I've seen you." What else was he to say? But it was an echo.

The room was cold, and she had gone over to the corroded black stove, and busied herself with lighting it. Her actions were continued mater-of-factly, as if she were alone. Presently she seated herself in a chair before the stove, a chair with no pretensions, and which was obliterated by her personality, so that it seemed to disappear. One narrow foot protruded lazily from the fur wrap toward the heating stove. The nails of the foot were also reddish in color, and the second toe extended perhaps eight millimeters beyond the great one. The malformation was not unattractive; like all those other discrepancies, oddly exciting. And then she startled him by reaching behind her into some alcove or niche and producing a little pewter case and a cigarette from within it. Lighting it by a taper, she began to smoke this thing of male civilization, which seemed as remote from her as day from night. For she, like the other, had grown from the forest.

He thought, watching the smoke rise up into the smoke of her hair, how he had considered Egyptian tobacco as a talisman against the centuries of the village. Patently, it would not have been.

But she went on looking at him, and he at her. At length, something else must be said.

"I should like to sit down," he murmured, somewhat amused at his choice.

"Maybe," she said. "Are you asking my permission, after you broke in the door without apology?"

"I beg your pardon. There's a young man who hangs about in these woods. I thought I'd find him here."

"Asleep?"

"Perhaps."

"Another time," she said, "you might have."

Christian looked around him for a second chair, and seeing none, sat on the disheveled bed. Cognizant of the gun, he reset the catch and lowered the stem to lean against his knee.

"Do you," she said, "think it proper to be here, sitting on a woman's unmade bed?"

"Quite proper, I should guess." He smiled and looked down. Let her think he supposed her the local trull. But she did not respond, while his own response, even to the mere words, coupled with what he had seen, was definite.

After all, the forest had not put a spell on him. Or not the spell he had thought.

"Do you know who I am?" he said at last.

"A stranger," she said. "No one else would visit this spot, even by day."

"Oh, yes. Of course. I've given myself away, haven't I?"

"The accent, too," she said, "and the fine clothes." Her voice was light, itself without accent, but of unequal tones, some musical, some flat. Here and there a word was swallowed, as if she did not wish him to be sure of anything, even in the matter of speech. Yet, when she mentioned his clothes, did he detect a tinge of jealousy? And he pictured for an instant, irresistibly, an evening gown of the city splashed iridescently over her whiteness.

She finished her cigarette and tossed the stub onto the floor, pressing her bare foot over the glowing ember to crush it. How hard the soles of her feet must be that she could do that without scorching herself. She must often walk and run in the forest without shoes.

She absorbed him. Her relaxation, her movements. Her unconscionable eyes.

He remembered Sylvie, but that, too, was an echo. His excitement did not abate. The fit of despair had burned up in it. He could not envisage despair at this moment.

A legend. A contradiction. Two brats who had been lessoned in city speech but went on dwelling in sloth and a forest, subsisting on the superstitions of others. Because of the setting of the eyes, the length of a toe, a freakish tincture of the nails. . . .

"The chateau," he said. "My property."

Her throat, strong, smooth, and so white, tilted her head backwards.

"Ah," she said. And in a mimicry of the patois: "Thine, seigneur."

"I suppose the boy's your brother," Christian said.

She sighed. The pelt slipped off her shoulders.

"Why suppose that?"

"There's a similarity in your looks. And your way of going on."

"Oh, really?"

"And where is he? Out with the dogs?"

"Oh, come now," she said. Her glorious neck brought her face down to confront him again. "*Dogs*, monsieur?"

"I intend," he said, "to see both of them shot."

She smiled. Her eyes flared together, shining. There was green in them somewhere.

"Thee would require, monsieur, silver bullets."

"For two mangy rabbit hounds?"

"For my brother, and myself."

His heart pounded. It seemed to him he could see her heart, also, tumbling in the membrane of her throat, her temple.

"You believe it yourselves? Surely you're too clever for that."

"Much too clever. Of course."

"Where do you keep your dogs, then?"

"Here," she said. And she pointed into her open mouth, between the parted lips.

He got up and walked over to her slowly. Her lifted her hand, which was well-shaped and small in his. She did not resist, merely observed, as if the hand were not her own.

"You must have been very unhappy," he said, "as a child. The forlorn hopes of illegitimacy. This physical accident of manicure, for which the village hated you. Belonging nowhere. Poor little girl."

"No longer," she said. She seemed to flow up the air, fluid, reforming. She stood only a few centimeters from him, again her head tilted back to look at him. The absolute stillness of her eyes, one wide and mocking, one reserved, sensual and sly.

"No longer," he said. He let go of her hand, sliding his own hands around her waist. The fur seemed part of her. "Do I insult you again," he said, "by asking your price?"

"Oh," she said, "monsieur is used to women who give freely, for his looks, and his grace, and out of pity. Women love to pity you. Women who are afraid of you."

"Not you."

"I? I'd couple with you in the daylight. When the night came, I'd tear out your throat. You should be afraid, not I."

"You terrify me," he said.

"That's so," she said.

She moved her hands and caught his head lightly, and the touch of her fingertips snaking deeply through his hair, against his scalp, was exquisite. At the last second, she turned her long mouth from his. Her lips brushed his jaw, the lobe of his ear. And then she had caught that lobe in her teeth. It was so quick, he had no time to prevent it. A pain lanced through his ear, through his very jawbone and molars, a maddening, blinding pain. He thrust her from him, or would have, for she was already gone.

Putting his fingers to the side of his head, they came away with blood on them. It made him sick, the actual pain; that she had done it. He stared at her.

"The first time a woman ever harmed you, monsieur? But then, I'm not a woman entirely."

"You bloody bitch."

"Much, much worse."

"I'd advise you to give up this pretense," he shouted, pain making him shout. "Yes, I know the supposed marks of a werewolf. Ill luck cursed the pair of you with them. You terrorize the village. You don't play the trick on me."

He touched again at the lobe of his ear. It seemed she had bitten it through. If she had contracted the venom of the dogs, this wound might be infected. It should be cauterized, and where, in this Godforsaken waste, would he find a doctor capable of performing such a task accurately? (He felt the white-hot iron sear his cheek.) Nauseated and faint, an overpowering desire to harm her in return was mostly what kept him sensible, if not particularly sane.

But she, who had gnawed his flesh, who had darted from

him like lightning, now stood beside the stove, calmly smoking another of the cigarettes from the pewter case.

He turned about and seized the gun, knocking off the catch as he did so, and leveled the weapon at her. A month before—less—if such a vision of himself had been described to him, he would have burst out laughing. But now. Oh, not now. Now he was in earnest.

"Why, monsieur," she said, "you look so much more the beast than I."

He was not, even so, totally convinced, or his rationale was not, that he would next instant have blown out her brains. But in fact, he would have done precisely that. For when the fantastic concussion, like a hurricane, dashed against his body, throwing him forward and to the ground, the gun, swiveling aside, exploded. The shot ripped through the air and lodged somewhere in the wooden wall.

Christian lay on his face. He had not heard anyone come in, naturally. Now the unheard arrival had him securely pinned. This sensation was reminiscent, until the weight was withdrawn.

"Get up," said a dry young masculine voice. "Gabrielle won't hurt you. Don't be afraid."

Christian crawled to his knees, humiliated, the amalgam of hatred and aversion within him too intense to be controlled, or even expressed. When he rose to his feet, his ears buzzing as if from a dose of opium, the two creatures stood together in front of him, both immaculate and cool, auburn and fair, their glacial eyes discriminating. He, his head hanging, shaking like—what else?—some wretched beaten dog, stared back at them.

"I don't beg your pardon for knocking you down," said the red-haired young man. "I owed you that, at least, for those couple of blows in the face the other evening. Besides, if she'd got her hands on you after you fired at her, nothing on earth could have saved you. Gabrielle's a fiend, monsieur. Even after sunrise."

Christian coughed, and choked the coughing down. The four pitiless eyes observed him.

"Monsieur le seigneur is sick," said the young man.

"Which protected him," said the woman. "Or didn't you know that, monsieur, the other evening when Luc followed you along the road?"

"There was something else to tempt me that night," said the young man. "She was determined on it. So insistent. Running about so noisily in the dark with the silver clinking."

"Wasteful," said the woman. "A young girl. So much meat, and you didn't share it with me."

"She was mine," he said. "She wanted me to take her. This one's yours, I think. What a pity his flesh has a disease in it."

"You said he played the Rachmaninov with genius, cher Luc."

"So? You'd only have eaten his hands, chère Gabrielle."

Christian picked up the gun, and walked out of the hut by its open door. When he got to the amorphous heap of stones, he partly fell. But his sickness had become too permanent to be expelled. His whole body, the whole forest, seemed bilious, a kind of hideous universal mal de terre.

After a moment he dragged himself up again, and lunged onto the path. Which did not hide this time, but seemed to breathe at him out of the undergrowth.

As he went on he saw himself, a clownish, disgusting sight. He did not properly know what had occurred, what had been done to him. At some inexplicable level of consciousness or self, he had been wounded. Beside this damage, the torn ear was nothing, though it screamed shrilly in the cold.

Some awful awareness of horror staggered along with him. He did not believe in them, it was not so simple as that. It seemed to him dreadful that they had named themselves. Gabrielle. Luc. As if the civilizing properties inherent in naming had only made their ghastliness more abject. But he was not afraid. It was the fear which had excited him, perhaps. What then? What was this frightful horror which they, who had not come after him, had sent with him in their stead?

When he broke through into the gravel road, the cough came in short demanding rhythms.

He did not think for a minute that he would reach the chateau, but he did reach it. He came on the stone dogs, which were really wolves of stone, and on the gates, thrown back extravagantly. The gravel here, he noticed incongruously, was disturbed, perhaps by the entry and exit of the cart and the doctor's carriage yesterday. He entered the avenue of lime trees, and between their wind-frayed branches he saw Renzo, who ran a couple of steps toward him, then paused, then ran away.

Christian laughed at that, and raising his hand to his lips, suddenly he beheld a gem of red blood in his palm.

The terror which was greater than all others whirled up over him. The terror made of nightmare, of the white sheet with the scarlet flecks upon it, the fist squeezing in the throat, the drowned lungs. The terror of some hospital ward by night, and the ropes stretched fast into the earth.

He tried to deny the gem of blood. He shook it off like an insect. But he coughed and the gem was there again, and the copper taste.

Like an old man hurrying to refuge under inclement weather, so he hurried, eyes wide, hand pressed to his mouth, but toward no refuge at all.

Chapter 13

The Servants

Christian remembered everything that he did thereafter with the utmost clarity, as if he had scribbled notes on his own performance. The flight over the estate, the terrace invested by its cement urns, the outer stair and the entry into the chateau. Renzo had vanished, and the house door had gaped. The grande hall. The ascent of the inner stair. And halfway up, over the rippling sound the chandeliers were making, the voice of La Tienne: Did he require anything? Turning to her, guiltily concealing the piece of blood-stained linen in his hand, he had shaken his head peremptorily, and made on. (His second excuse to Madame.) The gallery, the passage. His drawing room.

To turn the key in the lock was automatic. To proceed into the bathing chamber also automatic. He had had some practice.

The last stage, reached perhaps a quarter of an hour after entering the chateau, was, however, new. He went to the traveling box, which all this while had sat unopened in a corner of the bedroom. Unlocking it, he removed the sheets of manuscript, the parceled books, until he found the little pouch of fawn suede, and inside the pouch the Louis V comfit box. Releasing the spring, he tipped into his hand the gray-brown pellet of quick death.

But having sped so far, he now sat down, the pellet between his fingers.

The fire had, as usual, been relit. Its reflection danced hellishly over walls, floor and ceiling, igniting the carved furnishings. (He had lain across the girl just there. But it might not have happened.) The tumbler of water stood ready.

He gazed at death between his fingers.

Was this really all it amounted to?

(He recalled the sinister ease with which he had been able to obtain the poison, in a back street of the city recommended by some acquaintance; a story told about a sick dog to be released painlessly from its misery—a sick *large* dog, in order that the dose be sufficient.)

And now, surely the time had come to finish. And he, who had so gladly and willingly fled to this Ultima Thule in order to be alone and unhampered, shuddered at his aloneness and all it symbolized.

And he, who had constructed such a neat dramatic plan of escape—

And he, who had moved so efficiently in preparation—

And he—

At this ultimate moment, was too terrified to take the last inevitable step. Terrified of a small gray-brown pill. Of a single gulp. Instead he would sit here in the fireglare, revolving the medicine in his hand, like an interesting bug, and think of Hamlet's: If it be now, 'tis not to come. . . . If it be not now, yet it *will* come. . . .

A sudden knocking on the drawing-room door made his heart leap and stumble agonizingly. For here was a reprieve, if only for a second.

"What is it?" he called to the door.

Outside, Madame Tienne answered: "You must let me come in, if you please, monsieur."

"Must I? What do you want?"

No further reply came through the panels, only two or three further sharp acorn-knuckle taps. He heard them out. When they ceased, he got to his feet, and waited there for more. None came. Presumably, she had gone away.

And now he must, he really must—

Like bracing oneself before a tub of icy water. A visit to the dentist. A naked space dressed only by an unoccupied piano. (His nervousness before a recital had become quite comic. To cross the room was an ordeal. And yet, once his hands met with the keyboard— But all that had been stripped from him.)

And it was a poor analogy. From the cold water, the antiseptic torture chair, the recital, one returned. Alive.

Somewhere far off he thought he heard a muffled outcry. He should hasten.

He walked over to the window, and looked out on the edge of the topiary garden. How heavy the sky was, sinking, wishing to obliterate the land. The dark, sulking, superstitious, bewitched land.

Those two children out in the wood (yes, even the woman, six or seven years older than he, was a child, carnal and lawless) he was almost positive that they would believe in God. Or in some great gust of faith, some power which had made them what they supposed they were. Or maybe, which they were . . . werewolves. The beautiful silliness of it made him rage. It implied a world where magic might triumph over fact. Where a Christ might stroll about working miracles. Where the sick might be healed.

He truly must do it now.

As he put his hand on the glass, a door slammed open. Accustomed to less complex apartments, he had forgotten that locking one entrance did not secure the suite. Someone had gone around and into the passage that connected with the old chateau, come by the music room and directly to the library, which was still accessible. Now they had penetrated the drawing room. And now the bedroom door was pushed wide.

Madame Tienne entered, and stared at him. He stared back, and directly she rendered her stiff and minuscule bow.

"Forgive me, monsieur."

"No, I don't," he said. "I don't forgive you. How dare you force your way in on me?" His hand shook so much that water slopped onto the rug. As this was happening, a man walked into the bedroom.

"Very well, madame," he said, as he passed her. "You'd better introduce me."

The impression was of a dark upholstery from which the stuffing was in the process of being expelled in tufts, tufts of gray side whiskers, tufts of pure raggedness and slovenliness of dress. But the cliché of the bag was true. There was no need for an introduction.

"Monsieur le Seigneur knows me," said the doctor. His yellow face was like a wizened fruit, some neglected apple, trapped in a grass of hair. But the eyes were those of a tame monkey, untrustworthy and too bright. "My name is Claut. The village physician. At your service."

"Get out," Christian said.

"Oh yes, presently," said Monsieur Doctor Claut. The trace of accent was minor, yet persistent, the words grammatical but gabbled. He smiled an evil smile, and came mincing over. His rate of progress was deceptive. Quite suddenly he had reached out and plucked the pellet of death from Christian's grasp. "And what is this? A sweet? Shall I eat it?" Christian stood shivering, arrogantly staring, incapable of thought. "Maybe not," said Claut, chuckling. With a flick of the wrist, common generally only to waiters or fishermen, he tossed the pellet into the fire.

"You're very fortunate in your servants, monsieur," said Claut. Madame Tienne had gone, the doors were closed, the lamps above the mantel had been lit. A strange medical examination was taking place, in which Christian seemed to have no real part, certainly no say. He was reminded of cadavers on whose chalk-white frames various points of interest were demonstrated to students. "Take off your coat, please. Your waistcoat. Unbutton the shirt. Turn your head, so. Look here. Look there." Why he submitted, Christian could not explain to himself. The old man's fingers were thorough, too much so. Christian's youth and body were a source of pleasure. *Ridiculous old lecher, fumbling with carrion.* "Your arm, please, monsieur. Thank you. I take it a razor is responsible for the cut to the lobe of your ear? You should be more careful. Get Renzo to shave you. As I say, you're fortunate. But then, such retainers are a tradition of the chateau. And now I'll examine your throat, monsieur."

"Don't trouble. I can tell you what you'll find."

"Indeed?"

Seated in the chair—he could not quite recollect when he had sat down again—Christian looked away from the monkey's eyes into the fire which had consumed his salvation.

"I'd like to know," Christian said, "how you come to be here."

"After the death of the girl. . . ."

"Madame Tienne suggested you call on me."

"I was already in the house on your return. Which was reportedly rather dramatic. Guns, bloody handkerchiefs. And then, a locked door. You invited interruption, monsieur."

"You've thrown the only hope I had into the fire."

"But then," said Claut, "you weren't about to resort to it."

"Wasn't I?"

"You had ample time, monsieur, I think. Such bonbons are quite abrupt, once consumed. And now, your throat if you please."

The nasty, clever, wiry hands fastened on Christian's jaw. The beastly little spoon employed in such an operation was swiftly inserted, and while he gagged on it, the black eyes, which looked as though probably dilated by the use of some drug, probed and winked at him.

When the filthy exercise was over, he sat huddled like a sick cat, while the doctor scrabbled among his paraphernalia. The nadir of wretchedness had been achieved. It had needed only this.

"How far has the disease advanced?" he asked eventually, in a conversational tone.

Monsieur Doctor Claut squeezed his ochre face juicelessly together.

"Disease, monsieur?"

"You know what I mean, well enough."

"Perhaps not, monsieur. There's some small congestion of the lungs, not uncommon among a people that forgets how to breathe. A slight weakness in the throat. But since you're not engaged to sing with the opera, that hardly seems a tragedy. And this will strengthen, given time. The tiny vessel which gives way and causes the bleeding will be soothed by a preparation I can have made up for you and sent from the town. As to your nervous state, it's lamentable. It seems something has been preying on your mind, monsieur."

Christian stood beside one of the fires that had been set in the grande hall. The brandy he was drinking dulled the metallic ache in his throat. The brown bottle of obscure linctus, laid on the table upstairs, he had flung across the bedroom. It had struck the mirror of the dressing table and cracked it. He had then looked at himself, poised there in the unbuttoned shirt, his handsome face and two demented eyes also cracked in two. When he came down the ballerina stair into the hall, the three servants who remained to him had already gathered. The doctor's murky dog cart had rattled out of the stable yard and away into the deepening enclosure of the afternoon. Left to their own devices, the faithful retainers watched their seigneur in varying attitudes of suspense—Renzo biting his red mouth, Sarrette hatless, chest thrust forward, frowning at an elaborate cornice. Madame Tienne with the hint of pyrotechnics in her eyes. She would doubtless relish another battle with another drunkard. (Claut, maybe, had had a monkey's paw also in that prior demise: Drink too much, monsieur? For a man who has lost three children, what you drink is nothing. Drink more.)

Christian had, before descending the stair, envisaged a grisly fable. The condemned due to be guillotined, and on the way to Madame herself, was informed by his escort that, after all, he was reprieved. Then the scaffold was before them, and the joyful man inquired why he must still kneel and place his head in the niche. "Just a slight weakness," declared the executioner. And as the blade rushed down to sever flesh, bone and windpipe: "I can have a preparation made up for you to soothe the bleeding."

There might be, for the old man's lies, any number of reasons. Mere ignorance of diagnosis, or, more sinister, a desire to profit from false reassurance. The patient had been too astonished to protest. Christian had sat immobile all through a lecture on diet, sleep, wine, this linctus, this compound opiate, disorder of the nerves, the undesirability of laudanum, the tonic properties of the pine trees in the forest. An urge to cry was canceled by an urge to commit violence. But Christian's sluggishness did not abate in time for him to dash at the senile thing and wring its neck.

Now he confronted the three servants who had delivered him to this final reckoning. Not only had they infested the rooms and disturbed his privacy, they had sentenced him to die at the mercy of his illness. The pellet was burned. Blame himself all he would for hesitation, they had given his foolish cowardice the means. To live a few weeks longer, as he would have to live them—

He looked at these three enemies. No desolation was too awful to fit into this scheme, this graveyard of hopes.

They waited for him to thank them for their care. Or to

rave at them. ("You must be careful of your throat, monsieur. No shouting. Speak softly.")

As an ironic salute to that, "Pack what belongs to you," he softly said, smiling at each of them in turn, "and anything besides you'd care to steal. And then leave the chateau." A silence followed. Sarrette bowed his head, Renzo's poppy mouth fell open and tears sprang to his eyes. Madame grew blank and fireless. "There won't be any argument. I've written out a statement for Hamel, and signed it. It's on the table, there. Take it with you when you leave. You'll be recompensed for whatever services you reckon you've done me." He drank the brandy. He closed his eyes, no longer caring about them, or himself. "You'd better," he said gently, "get to the village, or wherever you mean to spend the night, before the sun goes down. There are wolves in the forest, apparently."

"Monsieur," he heard her say, her crisp voice informing him that the erring child should be grateful for the goodness of its elders. "We, or some member of our families, have served this house for more than a hundred years. Much longer, should you consult the records. Periodically, the house has been shut and a caretaker put in. During such times, which now and then happened under your predecessor, we have taken employment elsewhere. But such is our link with the chateau, monsieur, that these situations were never considered as permanent."

"Madame," he said, "consider it permanent, and be damned."

Her skirt rustled as she went. Renzo sniveled. Sarrette marched on parade.

With his eyes still closed, Christian sat down on the ground before the fire.

Chapter 14

───◆◉◆───

The Snow

Loups-gens-aieux.

As the flames died, the scratched inscription under the great cowl of the hearth began to come clear. Perhaps the heat, or a dusting of fresh soot, had emphasized the marks, which before had been illegible.

He watched them emerge, he read them. As an expression of language, they made no sense, an ungrammatical gibberish.

But eventually, when the brandy could no longer keep him warm, in that huge darkening chamber whose air slowly crystallized with cold, a certain intuition made him recognize, in the string of words, a bizarre catch phrase, something on the lines of: "Now we are men, who have been wolves." At last he said the phrase aloud, and heard at once its similarity to the name: *Lagenay.*

As the evening spread through the chateau in a proliferating stain, he set about the business of preparing for siege. The master suite was to be, quite properly, the headquarters of this last, and frankly doomed, stand against winter and eternal night. To that end he now carried up to it the immediacies of survival: logs in their assorted baskets, a few bottles of wine, and those provisions which could be maintained upstairs as adequately as in the larders below. Candles, oil, and matches also made the journey. It would be necessary, from time to time, to lead solitary forays to the major pump in the kitchen, to the cellar and the adjacent woodstore. There might come an hour when all the hoard of logs was used up. Then, in the middle of the wooden forest, he might resort to burning the legs of the chairs and tables. If he could discover an axe, he could break up the piano, a last sonata of smashing, a last nocturne of passionate hate.

With something of this in his mind, he walked into the music room, where no light of any sort was burning.

The vampire rested like a coal-black pool on the air. An umber stillness clung to everything else, thick as curtaining, save for the slot of sky in the window embrasure, narrow as a finger, a mauve and glowing bruise. He sat where the mauveness touched the keys, and played, quiet currents of music, ghostly improvisations, leading to and from the themes of Rachmaninov, Schumann, Debussy. And as the light thickened further he continued to play, blindly now, finding his way by touch alone, as if along a river by night, or over the familiar body of a lover.

When he stopped at last, the room itself pulsed with a cold new improvisation. Snow was falling past the window.

Lying in the canopied bed that faced the tapestry, he dreamed he was in the forest, walking in the thick white snow. As was usual, the dream was vivid and totally real. He smelled the frozen perfume of the trees, felt the crunch of the coarse moist powder underfoot. Heard nothing, for the forest seemed to ring with soundlessness, like an enormous silver bell.

He became aware only very gradually that he wore the black-furred mantle of some lord of the middle ages, aware as retardedly of the slung sword at his side, the trimmed beard along his jaw, the heavily curled hair down his back.

It was a kind of white-blue twilight, neither day nor dark. Where he went in it he had no notion, but he felt a sense of purpose, controlled excitement and complete authority, over both himself and his prospects.

He woke briefly, thrust out of the dream with a dull curse.

And he had the sheer momentary impression of the male line descending from the antique beginnings of the chateau, a male line that continued, undiminished, even through the female, where alien male seed and blood were mingled. An awareness of inheritance, minimized by absence, and by a dead grandfather and a mother who had known only stories to tell her son, the overlay of the sophisticated city, the notes of thirty-odd pianos, disease and disbelief.

Like a young boy glimpsing a hero in the distance, he felt a pang of loss for that man he had been in his sleep.

He rose late the next day, about noon. The snow still poured out of heaven like milk. Beyond the windows, nothing was to be seen. He breakfasted with surprising hunger on the cold meat and bread, and, less amazingly, the wine. Then, succumbing to the habits of civilization, he boiled one of the kitchen's variety of black iron kettles on the fire, washed, and shaved carefully before the cracked mirror. (The bite in his ear was healing in a thin black join. What did it really matter if she had poisoned him? Poison from her subtle mouth. . . . But he did not want to think of them.)

Having dressed fastidiously, he sat before the bedroom fire, reading. Strangely enough, there was no pain in his throat, not even any discomfort, and he seldom coughed. A slight remission, for which he was scornfully ungrateful, having been misled before. He would let himself dwell on nothing at all. He absorbed pages of obscure novels and translations discovered in the library among the Ronsards, Flauberts, Racines and Edouardes.

Dreams, sorcery, lies, he kept these at bay with dreams, sorceries, lies.

He replenished the fire, and his glass, when necessary, and the snow fell hypnotically, its swirlings shimmering on the wall, counterpoint to the shimmer of the flames.

This was an interim, and could hardly continue. Hence his renunciation of thought, which implied prophecy. The ice age when wood and food ran out, the last spasms of the illness, these were not to be considered anymore. His life was reduced to an hour, a minute at a time.

Only the vague presence at his shoulder, swimming like a black fish in the depth of his brain, knew otherwise. Then, do not look. Do not contemplate. Live in the forefront of the consciousness, as you live solely in these five rooms.

He dozed, the invalid's perpetual indulgence. A method, not of harvesting strength, but of avoiding truth.

It became his very first morning at the chateau. Save that no one, now, would break in on him.

At three o'clock, a big valve was turned around in the sky, and the snow dwindled, and then ceased altogether.

Something about the cessation—the motionless quality, like a noise which suddenly falls quiet—alerted him.

He went to the window that faced out over the corner of the topiary garden, but the garden was no more. A white page filled the window, lightly scrawled, though not faithfully, with a suggestion of outlines—of walls, trees, slopes. The horizon of forest was no more than a band of darker white beneath the porcelain sky.

The chateau had become a house of snow on the plains of a snow planet.

Something flashed back in the whiteness. The contrast was so great, it caught his eye like a flash of fire. He searched after it, unable to deduce where it came from. The movement of a bough in the garden, a black crow—he had seen no birds here, save one which was dead—a weakness of his sight.

But there—there it came again.

He looked straight down, and into a corner of the garden. And as he looked, a dust-sheet of snow was shaken suddenly from the shoulder of one of the yews. The bulbous nakedness of the tree appeared, an inkblot on the page; the agency of removal was not apparent.

In that garden he had seen Sarrette, he had seen Sylvie. And, from the music-room window, he had seen a dog.

He did not need to question who was in the garden now.

The undulations of the yew tree had ended. Nothing, no one, emerged. No more snow was dislodged.

What now? He had regained the keys. He could go down and enter the garden, either by way of the ancient well-court, forcing the creeper-snaked wrought-iron gate, or by that other entry he had never discovered, which must connect with the yard beneath the kitchen. If he paused to analyze it, the placing of the garden puzzled him, the eccentric anglings and interpolations of the chateau which always appeared to enclose it, and here revealed one aspect of it, there another, but never everything. An occult garden, then. He turned from the window and the challenge, his heart beating quickly, but he himself intending to do nothing.

Christian seated himself again in the chair, sipped the wine, took up the book of humorous masquerades.

He read three or four sentences, and was forced to reread them. At the fifth sentence, something struck the pane of the window behind him.

He started up, the blood rushing through him, as if in answer to the shot of a gun. The pane was unscathed and empty. Nonsensically, some part of him had anticipated their two faces pressed to the glass, on the assumption they could fly.

One, probably the youth—Luc de Lagenay—had thrown a pebble or a shard of broken urn. Strength and a sure eye would have been needed, nothing else. And now, perhaps in hiding once more, they awaited the return of Christian's white face, peering out from the window.

The wineglass had fallen on the rug, recoloring the oriental patterns of flowers with a pale crimson blush.

They would not leave him in peace. And there were the keys, and somewhere the gun remained.

A second missile hit the window, too swift to see, and he cried out.

Unable to decipher (as once before) what he felt, since (as before) it was not anger, or alarm or even a perverse pleasure, he went into the drawing room, fireless and bleak, its ice age clearly upon it, and picked up the keys.

His astrakhan lay where it had been discarded the previous afternoon. He reached to take it up, then checked, and with a sneer walked out of the suite coatless. Why dress against the chill en route to the scaffold? For that matter, why seek the gun? If they were mad enough, those two children from the forest, to tear him in bits and devour him, let them do it. He strode along the passage, imagining the de Lagenays, in their pelts, conversing with Doctor Claut. Luc: *We can't eat diseased meat, monsieur.* Claut (chittering like a monkey): *There is nothing at all the matter with him. Eat him by all means. He'll nourish you.*

Christian crossed the waste of the chateau. How solid its coldness had become, a veritable weight. Descending, he reached the kitchen, passed through it, walked by the entrances to the larder and the old dairy. The door that led to the outer steps and the courtyard had warped. His hands were strong, and he wrenched it open. Snow carpeted the scrambling little stair. A million knives cut at him, the serrated edges of the atmosphere. Below, beyond the stair and to the right, an arch tunneled through a wall, as if directly through the white paper world.

Christian moved down the steps, with some automatic caution, but already numbed by the freezing static blast of the air. He was very conscious of doing something irrational. And his awareness was emphasized by the difficulty of walking across the yard, his feet sinking at each contact, as if into sponge. As he turned into the arch, a clay utensil or flowerpot under the snow broke beneath his feet, and he remembered treading on the cruciform bones of the forest path in order to crack them.

The tunnel was two meters or so in length, and came out near to a back wall of the disused stables. A white fur gate in a white fur hedge gave access to the stable yard. A salad garden, also composed of white fur, circled a dead fountain choked by ermine. Beyond the salad garden, mysterious snowhills two and a half meters high, the muffled cloisters of the topiary.

There had been a gate here too, but only the hinges remained. A pergola, its vines in lavish snow blossom, had come down, erecting an understudy gate. Someone—sometwo—had flowed through it, snapping only a solitary stem, an isolated strut, to make their passage.

Christian got through at the same spot, but without delicacy. His motions, the striking out of hands and feet, implied foul temper or desperation. He watched himself, rather astonished, for he seemed to feel nothing. Only his heart raced.

The phantasmal artist who had been at work on the village and the graveyard, who had scribbled lines over the page in the window, had also redrawn the topiary garden in the snow. The foot of every tree and hedge was smokily etched, as well as each gap which the snow had failed to penetrate, and all the original designs had been erased. Floured statuary, possessing black armpits, groins and lips, jostled between.

The long windows of the chateau, under their white eyelids, looked over into the garden from almost every angle. He did not bother to identify them. The harsh towers interpolated like massive trunks.

And they? Where were *they*?

The thrown stones had come from the portion of the garden against the bulge of a certain tower. But by now, such creatures could be anywhere. Behind him, even, their glimmering eyes riveted to his shoulder blades.

He did not look around. He walked forward, along the avenues of the topiary.

At any moment, a cascade of snow might plummet from a tree at his side. A ball of snow might fly out at him. Children's games. Yet none of these things occurred.

He reached a crossroads in the yews, a sundial marking the junction. Coming up to it, he saw that the snow on its face had been engraved with a needle, stick or fingernail. *Three paces to your left*, it said. Ah, yes. A game after all. He moved into the left-hand avenue of the cross, took one step, and hesitated. As he did so, there came a weird flutter of the topiary, like a section of scenery shifting on runners over a stage. And there they stood.

He drew in his breath at the sight of them, and gave one irresistible bark of laughter.

Primevally dressed before in the skins of animals, or human nudity, now both were clad in an exemplary sort of holiday "best." Impeccable garments of modernity, cleverly purchased at some date in the provincial town. There they posed, expressionless, as if for a photograph. He in an unbuttoned pigeon-blue topcoat that afforded glimpses of a pigeon-blue regalia beneath, a silk waistcoat the black-red of claret, a collar starched to rigor mortis, a cravat like polished pewter. And she, she the perfect triangle of a fashion plate, a narrow-skirted costume the shade of green olives, topped by a great olive saucer of hat spilling sky-blue plumes. They provided the only splash of color in the landscape. But no movement, until Luc de Lagenay plucked the pearl felt hat off his head and swooped into a ludicrous bow.

Such apparitions were not to be shot at. What was one to do with them? Their incongruousness made them either the more frightful, or yet, possibly, the more touching.

As the young man straightened from his obeisance, he glanced at the woman, at Gabrielle, as if to see what to do next. How exquisite she looked, incandescently pretty, her hair pinned up, her face powdered and rouged, and mascara around those absurd eyes of hers, which today seemed greener than her clothes.

"We didn't think," she said, "you'd reply to ringing at the

doorbell. If it even works. The last occasion we were here, it was broken."

"Really," said Christian automatically.

Involuntarily, he found himself searching for their peculiar nails, the mythical emblem of the werewolf. But the hands of both were encased in immaculate suede.

Abruptly, Luc de Lagenay took a step forward, perhaps a considered movement, slow enough to register as mortal locomotion.

"You're not dressed for the outdoors, monsieur," he said insolently to Christian. "Shouldn't we go inside?" And then one of the suede paws moved too fast to be seen, and a suede finger touched at the healing bitten ear.

Christian's arm flew up in the same moment, and he had the satisfaction of striking the gray-blue hand ferociously away. Luc sprang back, baring his teeth, spontaneously perhaps. After all, they had had all their years in this place to convince themselves they were—what they thought themselves to be.

Christian turned his eyes on Gabrielle.

"What is it you want?"

"Isn't it obvious? We should like to come into the chateau."

"It isn't obvious."

"Well, but I've told you now."

"Not enough."

"We saw the servants leave," she said. "The fearsome Tienne, and the driver and the boy. We've seen a lot of people come and go here. The previous owner, the drunken man, he'd often be away for months at a time, in England, I believe, where he kept his family like a sort of menagerie. The house would be shut up, and a fool of a caretaker installed who was hardly ever on the premises. There were ways to get in. We might have applied them today. We used to play here as children."

The bastard branch of the chateau inheritance. He saw them, a red-haired boy of about five or six, and a golden-haired girl in adolescence, running, yelling, up and down the echoing corridors, setting chestnuts and apples to roast in the embers of impromptu fires, unlawfully kindled in the grates. More their property than his, in fact, theirs by right of frequence.

But his eyes had begun to dazzle from their color on the snow; the cold was like a sickness.

"Wait a while," he said. "In a month I'll be dead. Then everything is yours. Every crumbling brick, every rotten timber. You can wait a month."

She tilted back her head, bordered by the vast halo of hat, in the familiar way, to look at him. She walked very surely in her high-heeled boots, the hobbled skirt, across the snow, right up to him.

"When you speak of your death," she said, "your eyes fill with tears."

"Perhaps I should regret dying."

"Regret nothing," she said, "there's no taste of death on you."

"Ah," he said, but his voice trembled, "you overheard monsieur Doctor Claut."

She smiled secretively. She put her hand gently through his arm.

"You're freezing," she said. "We'll go back into the house."

Her voice, which formerly had spoken of devouring the flesh of a young girl, was soft, caressing, tender as the voice of any Annelise. Her eyes were speculative, he thought.

He drew her hand out of his arm, turned his back on the pair of them and went through the garden, returning the way he had come.

They followed, of course. Not that he heard their steps. He did not hurry. When he reached the kitchen courtyard, he wondered if they would spring forward in order to get in before he could slam the door above. This amused him.

But when he had climbed the stairway to the door, he neither looked around nor waited, but went straight into the house. Nor did he close the door behind him.

Chapter 15

The Visit

The cold house, after the snow garden, was densely shadowed but seemed warm. The blue-glass porthole insisted the chateau lay beneath the sea. The tall windows implied, between their drapes, that: No, it lay at the North Pole. The grande hall itself susurrated as if rushes were scattered on its floor.

Giddily Christian inspected the variety of illusions. He had asked himself where he should lead the two guests who prowled upwards from the kitchen in his wake, and he had decided on the fireless, heatless, inhospitable salon.

He walked into the room and sat down in the chair by the dead hearth to wait for them.

At some point then he became able to listen to them, to their approach, though it was scarcely audible. Two winter leaves, they blew across the grande hall. He pictured them, staring upwards at the blue window, fingering the carved wooden things, the brocades, the silver candlesticks. They would know it all. Their house.

Dimly, the hall chandeliers were ringing. That sourceless draft again disquieting them.

Gabrielle de Lagenay entered the salon first, but Luc was only a pace behind her. You could as little control them or keep them out as two cats.

"Oh," said Luc carelessly, "you see what he's trying to do."

"He doesn't know, himself," said Gabrielle.

"Yes, he does. There's a fire in one of the upper rooms. You could smell it, even outside. But here, no fire."

"This is the correct room for entertaining," she said. "For the English tea, with little cakes and segments of fruit."

Christian watched them, and listened to them. He needed to do nothing else. He did not need to move, not even his hands, or his head. The room was horribly cold after all, but the young man stripped off his gloves and threw them, with his fine hat, idly onto a chair. The auburn nails were not at all ugly, merely disconcerting. Even in the sumptuous top coat, jacket, trousers, he was essentially arboreal. The woman had gone to the mahogany buffet. A bowl of hothouse oranges had been placed there at some time during the preceding day, beside a silver tray with a small vase of Armagnac.

Selecting three of the tiny goblets, she poured some of the treacle-colored drink into them. No longer guest but hostess, she bore one glass to her brother, who accepted it with ironic graciousness. She came to Christian next, extending a glass also to him. When he made no move to take it, she set it down on the table at his side. She returned to the buffet, and raised her own glass, primly, to her lips, lioness, drinking brandy.

Luc lifted an orange from the dish.

Christian stirred. He could not quite resist it.

"Wrong, children. You have made a mistake."

"My God," said Luc. "He spoke to us."

"That doesn't mean," said Gabrielle, "we're forgiven."

"It means," Christian said, smiling at them somberly, "that you've learned your roles improperly."

"Ah, yes?" said Gabrielle.

Luc, taking a silver knife from a drawer of the buffet (familiar also with the cutlery), cut the orange in two neat bleeding halves.

"Wolves," said Christian, "devour flesh. Human where available. Many, many Sylvies. Hares otherwise, birds, fowl, goats, little fleecy lambs. And all in raw chunks."

Luc offered half the orange to Gabrielle. She took it, licking at it meditatively with a pointed tongue. Luc bit savagely into the half he had retained, through pulp and rind together.

"In the stories," said Christian, "the werewolf is discovered when he declines the cooked meat and all the vegetables, and is come on later, gnawing a baby's arm in the scullery."

"How flippant you are," Gabrielle said. "You must still be afraid. Don't you realize we won't harm you?"

"Oh," said Christian, "a million thanks."

"In human form," said Gabrielle, "'we eat human food. Does that seem unreasonable? We also wear human clothes, succumb to human moods and hopes. Perhaps, my seigneur, as forlorn as your own." She put down the piece of orange and the glass and walked across to him again. At the last second, another of those inexplicable swiftnesses of movement, that bodily legerdemain, and she was leaning on the arms of his chair, bowed forward to stare at him, so close he could smell the scent of her powder, the more insidious perfume of her skin and hair. He lay back in the chair, gazing at her, at the reserved eye and the challenging one. "Would it surprise you," she said, "to hear we're also afraid of *you*? No? Yes? Monsieur Silver-Eyes, that scene in our house was pure bravado."

"What else?" he said.

"What else. And so we put on our festive robes and came to beg your pardon."

Again, he could not be sure what he felt. He seemed to be floating in a green dusk; hers. He did not feel the cold. Instead the room glowed with sex, or fever, or both at once. But most of all, he wanted to go to sleep. How strange it was.

The youth had also appeared, leaning on the side of the chair, looking down at him.

"I *could* have killed you," Luc de Lagenay reassured him softly.

His shadow stretched across the chair, the floor. Almost imperceptibly, the shadow lengthened, lengthened. The windows had changed their tones. It must be after four o'clock.

Christian came to his feet suddenly, and, as he had known they would, both creatures sprang aside. Even she, in her stalk of skirt, somehow sprang. They were wary.

"Do what you want here," he said. "I couldn't care less about preventing you."

"Where are you going?" Gabrielle demanded.

"To the room with the fire," said Luc. "The master suite will have been opened."

"Very well," she said. "Let all of us go."

"Oh, I don't think so," Christian said. He had reached the doorway, crossed the threshold, before he thought he could. He turned, nodded to them, seized and slammed the double doors together.

The vision he had had of his actions at the courtyard entrance was to be enacted here. Unplanned, quite unplanned.

He ran across the grande hall. The chandeliers rippled overhead. As he leaped up the initial treads of the curved staircase, he heard the doors of the salon bang open, but did not look about. He remembered running from the dog, the wolf, along the gravel, and an uncontrollable, remote frisson of, perhaps, fear, oddly resembling that of lust, ran with him along his spine.

Two wolves, yet he could outrace them.

His concentration fixed absurdly on the carpeting; he seemed to see each thread of woof and weft, each hair.

And he heard their weightless steps. Their paws.

He laughed, unnerving himself, as he plunged off the gallery into the passageway. He gained the suite, flung himself back against the closing door of the drawing room and locked it. He ran on into the library, having digested that lesson thoroughly. He secured the library door.

Still chuckling rather stupidly, he reeled into the bedroom and let himself fall on the bed.

The bedroom fire had continued to burn, and now celebrated this bizarre victory with torches. Of course, it was all quite senselesss. The room swung to and fro, and he did not resist it, his eyelids slowly lowering themselves, like the blinds of a hotel, closed at the end of the season.

The afternoon, too, was lowering its slow blinds, blooming like a charred flower, into darkness.

Outside the barricade of his current bivouac, in the wilderness of the chateau, they could roam and dismally howl, just as they wanted. They had not even beaten on the door.

His heart throbbed from exertion, and he coughed. He was feverish, and knew, as in the past, the fever would make him appear much younger than he was. He wished he could see himself, had a sudden urgent need to watch himself until the last light faded from everything.

And fix a mirror on the inside of the coffin lid, in case I should wake up and be lonely.

It was true. You did not gaze in the mirror out of vanity,

but merely in order to prove that still you were there, still physically present, alive.

And then he heard the de Lagenays scratching away somewhere in the wall.

He sat up, pulled himself off the bed, catching one of the posts to steady himself.

The scratching, not like that of mice but like that of long claws, repeated itself over and over.

He was afraid, at last, recognizably so, and of a thing so small—yet how terrible it sounded—as a miniature noise behind the plaster.

In God's name, what were they doing?

He knew, in fact. It did not require enormous powers of deduction. He knew. And they, they knew the chateau, far better than he. They had *played* here—

When the tapestry fluttered, the tilting knights seeming each to come momentarily to life, a deadly unsurprise was all he really felt.

A panel had been operated in the wall, one of those devices common to antique houses in romance. The tapestry and the wall gaped, and through both of them, into the dizzy vignette the fading day and his eyes had made for them, walked Gabrielle and Luc.

In that instant, he had expected anything. Or rather, accepted his belief in anything. But they were human, and clad in their human garments. They stood on the brink of the room while the entry yawned behind them.

Well, and am I afraid?

It was the same primordial thing he had felt on the road, more fear than fear, much more.

Their faces looked strangely empty. Their eyes somehow took light, like discs of colored glass. Their mouths were sad.

Fragments of banter came to him, and he let them go. He clung to the post.

The room sank deeper and deeper into shadow. The sun must almost be gone, the sun which, in every case, he had never seen in its own shape in the forest.

There was some final rearrangement of the molecules in the air, some final insubstantial curtain that remained to be pulled over—or away. And then it came, or went. And then.

They were only three or four meters from him when it began to happen, the handsome youth, the pretty woman.

The instigation was faintly astonishing. As if motivated by a wild impulse to bathe or couple, they began, as one, to wrench the clothes from their bodies. They moved in unison, yet independently, at the start hastily unbuttoning, untying, then in a frenzy ripping, struggling to get free. Perhaps a comedy. Yet there was nothing humorous in it. Even her stays were managed with swift tearing gestures. The display of dusk-blurred nakedness did not arouse. It was, by the time it had been achieved, no longer mortal enough to incite. No longer recognizable.

What— What—

What took place? In their flesh, in the atmosphere about them?

It seemed they fell forward, the man first, then the woman, forward and straight down onto the palms of their hands. Yet, as they fell, their arms stiffened, their physiques were condensed. All the vertebrae of the backbone seemed to have pleated together. For a second, the posture resembled that of a frog. But for a second only. The two heads had been thrust outwards, and the jaw of each dropped. The eyes intensified, shriveled into a blaze. There were no longer breasts, limbs, lips or fingers. No faces. There were merely contours and masks. It was so fluent, this transformation, so hideously natural—yes, *natural*. There was no other word for it.

Two wolves stood in the lordly bedroom. Not an illusion at all. Their slender feet were real, their vaulted ribcages, the avalanche of smoking pelt which covered them. And the four eyes burned, so much more brightly than the coals on the hearth.

Otherwise, all light was gone.

PART THREE

LES YEUX DE CEUX QUI M'AIMENT

Chapter 16

———•◉•———

The Delirium

"My apologies, monsieur, but no further credit can be made available to you."

The candlelit room was unclear. He could not be sure of its location, or the events which might normally take place there. But he was aware of a dull rage, and of turning abruptly, walking between curtains of crimson velvet. A lackey, costumed in the satin elongation of the rococo, opened a door for him with contemptuous readiness.

I am my own grandfather?

The night was undiluted summer, blue-black, curdled with random yellow flares. A city street, somewhere, singing. A carriage dashed by, and he noted the aspect of it, like a lantern balanced on wheels, the driver's tricorne hat— No, not the grandfather. Too early for him. Some other forerunner, similar only in the matter of his debts. The flares went out.

A woman, in a tall headdress like the pointed steeple of a church, drifted toward him, down the dark. She looked at him with joy and mistrust.

He stood on a wooden bridge. There were fir trees reflected in the water beneath. It was morning, not long after sunrise, and a man he had killed a few moments before, by thrusting the length of a sword into and through his mouth, sprawled on the bank.

* * *

He sat in an upstairs room with a sloping roof which, even though he was seated, almost touched his skull. An old man was counting money. It was growing dark again, but a great fire burned on the horizon. A plague fire. It was the era of La Mort. The old man spoke. The language was different, accented, and sprinkled with Latin. Christian understood, and answered. Rather, the one he was understood and answered. *He* did not.

The fire sank. It was almost out. It burned on a hearth.

Unquenchable thirst. He had dreamed he had filled cup after cup with water from a deep stone well. But raising the cup and draining it did not appease his thirst.

Awake, he lifted himself on one elbow, reaching for the ewer of water that stood by the bed—

Nothing was there. Of course not. How had he come to think a jug stood in such a spot?

He lay back. He was cold, his teeth chattering together. Too cold to feel thirst.

He turned his head, and saw a large dog, seated bolt upright, not far from the bed.

One of the hounds, perhaps the cream brachet, who would sometimes steal into the bedchamber—

No. There were no hounds, no animals. Only a stone cat with painted eyes which had been brought home from the campaign in Egypt. . . .

The dog continued to watch him. Perhaps it, too, was fashioned of stone. Certainly, it did not move. Even the faintly glowing eyes were quite steady.

He turned onto his face.

A young girl in a yellow silk turban and little else, was dancing on a supper board, stepping daintily between the candlebranches. The male guests leaned back in their chairs, their legs, in pale creased stockings, propped on the table. The girl was a sort of icon, no more, a trademark, if you will, for lust. Once, this bed had been filled with scarlet roses, their thorns torn away, and bunches of the dark red *sang* grapes from the vineyard. And there, in a stifling incense of crushed perfumes and liquors, he and two others had celebrated the birth of his legal son, by another woman, in another bed, and another room.

The dog had moved after all. It stood by the bed. He felt its eyes like two chill drops of mercury forever trickling up and down his skin.

The dogs were running, all of them, full tilt after the quarry. The night hung down close and brilliant with stars; the forest was jeweled with rain. Mud splashed up over the hocks of the horse. Beasts and men alike would go home dirty.

She ran well, the quarry. Given to him, for this purpose. Given to the Lady of Lilies, this lily girl. At first rigid with fright, the draught of wine had brought her to a headstrong, useless courage. Maybe she even had some hope that she might get away. More likely, maddened fear alone drove her to swiftness and to cunning. Yes, they had almost lost her at the river, his clever dogs, but she had not kept long enough to the stream, this foolish demoiselle.

And what year is this, in God's name? Christian rode in the male body astride the horse. The questions asked themselves, with scorn, for his plight filled him with disgust, even while he dreaded it. *Look at the boots, the drape of surcoat, lined with alternating furs. My God, some era even before the Plague.*

He would learn nothing from the girl's garments. On this moist summer night, she would be naked. Naked, and hunted by dogs. The man's expectancy was evident. But the timbre of his brain, the intellectual warp which led him to seek such a diversion, was shut away, inaccessible.

Suddenly the dogs began to bark and bay. They had cornered their deer.

Perforce, Christian rode with the seigneur into the small clearing. The summer pines, slim and young, still seemed to go right up to the spangled black cloth of sky. The ground was a sea of dogs, around one pallid rock. Breakers of dogs cast themselves against this rock, and fell away. But the tide was drawing out to a large restless circle. Well-trained, they had penned but not damaged her.

The seigneur dismounted slowly. The girl trapped in the clearing watched every move he made. Without any preliminary, almost as if some string had been jerked inside her, she started to scream, short thin wails, that sounded quite mindless, that did not even sound really afraid. More as though she must dislodge something from her throat, a sort of mechanical parody of terror. Yet, she was terrified. Every line of face and body revealed so much.

Terror of rape. Yes, terror of that. But of more than that.

He stood on the muddy ground, looking back at her.

Her hair was long and fair, her face absurdly medieval and of its period, though contorted out of all kinship with those expressionless ivory faces seen in tapestries, or chronicles. Abruptly she stopped screaming, and raised both her arms, bending them at the elbows, the juncture of the forearms held stiffly across her throat, and he knew her. Even in the dream, remembering he had dreamed of her before, and in exactly this posture.

And then Christian was cast away, falling like a tear shaken out of the man's eye. The acrobatic though nonphysical exit left him somewhere—curiously everywhere at once, yet nowhere at all.

The reason for the expulsion was not evident. Some exclusive frenzy, maybe, in which humanity was lost, had taken charge of Christian's host, precluding further liaison.

The dogs whined, shrinking away from the center of the clearing, some padding up and down, their tails beating languidly, presumably to propitiate, for it was not in pleasure.

Something, something almost tangible drew Christian backward, and away. His own disinclination, possibly, to watch. Fear, caught from the girl.,

He heard her scream again as the vision dissolved. This final cry was genuine, almost glad.

Sylvie . . . her shrieks sounding orgasmically through the topiary garden and through sleep—

And now, here was a tall pylon, thrust up from the floor of the forest, phallic as was any raised construction of an approximate shape, as even the more slender of the trees were.

Disembodied, Christian hung in everything and nothing, and observed it.

Before, his ancestors had possessed him, or the damnable house, the nearly prehistoric landscape. But this was some other thing, plucking him free of hereditary links, bearing him off alone, like a lost soul, to be shown this stone fetish.

But he knew the thing. Though centuries were youthful, and in another place, it was none other than the monument from the village square.

The carving was quite clear, but very crude in execution, a frieze of ritualistic figures, interspersed with symbols, all entirely meaningless to him. Yet he could now see distinctly the gargoyle creature which craned forward a short distance below the apex.

He perceived it as if only centimeters away, and from every angle at once.

It came out of the stone just above the waist, as though leaning from a window. And it was female, so much was definite, for two full but pendulous breasts hung from the torso. The hands, which rested behind it, lightly gripping the supporting pylon (rather in the manner of some ships' figureheads), had four long fingers, which in turn extended into spatulate claws. The arms, the shoulders, the neck, these had an oddly prepossessing femininity, a delicate roundness . . . the anatomy seemed of a more recent design than the rest of the carving. The representation of hair, too, was ornate, resembling the crimpings and coilings of Roman statuary. But the face—the face belonged to some remoter time. Even here, *its* lines were already worn. As those later cutters had worked on the lumpish surround, bringing out curls, smooth plains of flesh, the elements had sanded down the countenance, which the cutters had left untouched. Despite its decay, and the bluntness of its original formation (which might be contemporaneous with the drawings of the Trois Frères cavern), the visage was, however, unmistakable. It was the face of a wolf.

There was something so terrible about the sight of it that he turned instantly to fly. Not bodily, but mentally, pushing himself away through the layers of his unconsciousness as though between the trunks of the pines.

He came to with a violent start. His relief was illogical and utter.

He could no longer see any glow from the fire, yet he was warm at last, a coverlet pulled over him. Like a child, he was comforted by the presence of two bolsters which lay, one on either side of him, and which gave off a soft heat.

Only very gradually did he become aware of the clean grassy odor of a healthy dog. The smell was neither strong nor unwholesome. As he was becoming accustomed to it, vaguely considering it, the nightmare dying, one of the bolsters, that which lay against his right side, raised its head.

The two eyes, detached, disembodied, hung suspended over his own. He opened his mouth to cry out, but the cry was stillborn. What stopped his throat and his fear together he could not guess. Perhaps only the blatant truth that they had lain by him all this while and had in no way hurt him.

The she-wolf stared down at Christian, into his stupefied gaze. Then she lowered her muzzle again, the tip of her murderer's jaw resting lightly in his black hair. Her eyes went out.

Cautiously, Christian turned his head to see the other. The male lay with his spine along Christian's arm, in the exact posture and slumber of a great lean silvery dog.

Christian imagined a letter sent, via Peton and the train, to Annelise. *My dear cousin and lover, I sport here three in a bed, with two wolves—who have recently devoured the flesh of a young girl. The bed linen need not concern you. We employ a quilt of de-barbed scarlet roses, and blood-red grapes.*

The brief fever had broken, or merely dissipated itself. He felt no unease, simply a slight urge to laugh aloud. But he was not yet in his right mind nor, fortunately, did he regain it before he fell once more asleep.

Chapter 17

◆◦◆

The Morning

In the morning, about nine o'clock, he woke and looked lazily around him, recollecting everything, but in the form of a dream. The delirium, resulting from overstrained nerves, the walk in the frozen garden—several reasons were available—might be responsible for any number of imaginings. Spontaneously, he glanced toward the tapestry; the secret door, if it had existed, was now shut. On the rug beneath, no item of clothing lay discarded, not a stray button, severed by their haste. And on the coverlet, not a hair, not a pine needle. True, the fire still burned a concentrated and intense red. Probably at some point he had risen, gone to the fire and replenished it. That would have been virtually instinctive. That he did not remember doing it did not necessarily mean he had not. Even the two figures in the garden might be part of the delirium: a night dream of the afternoon. (He sat up on the bed, and rested his head on his knees. He felt strengthless, but not unwell. His clothes, in which he had feverishly slept, were crumpled.) Everything could be accounted for. And so long as he remained in the suite, so long as no secret door was operated, so long as darkness did not fall again, he was safe to continue in such pedestrian beliefs. But then. He knew what had happened, every detail, as he had witnessed it, and as he had dreamed it also. For even the dreams had been real. What to do with it then, this situation of impossible actualities? Why, nothing.

As he shaved and dressed himself in fresh garments, taking
the same elaborate care as on the day before (he must have
guessed visitors were to call), the snow began to come down
again, white on white on white.

The snow brought isolation, spiritual as well as physical,
but mostly physical. Though the de Lagenays had walked
quite a distance through it, no doubt barefoot, carrying their
smart town shoes in their gloved forepaws, very few travelers
would venture so far. And soon the snow, falling on and on
as it did, would have built white pillowing mountains against
the doors, the stairways. Already, perhaps, the terrace was
treacherous and impassable, the kitchen courtyard filled up
like a washtub with a solid mound of suds.

There was no escape. Whatever occupied the house with
him, there was not much chance of getting away.

So, you credit the existence of werewolves, do you? he
asked himself in the cracked glass. But what else was he to
credit, when he had seen it? Miracles really happened. Already the strange excitement which he associated with those
two creatures was shimmering subtly about him. Where were
they? Having slept against him, their bellies full of dead raw
hares and God knew what else. Having roused at sunrise, hu-
manly, to remake the fire for him—preposterous.

He pushed the gold pin through his necktie; it was not half
so gaudy as the pin de Lagenay had sported. He ate some of
the chill green fruits he had brought from the kitchen yesterday.

The fever had been nothing, then. No trace remained,
merely a little feeling of weightlessness sometimes, too slight
to be called vertigo. Perhaps no fever at all, but a sorcerous
trance induced by her sharp teeth meeting in the lobe of his
ear.

He went to the tapestry presently, and going behind it, ran
his hand along the wooden paneling; but whatever the knack
was, he could not discover it.

About half past ten, Christian walked out of the suite and
stood looking along the passage at the various doors of the
other unopened rooms. He began to go to them, trying the
knobs desultorily, moving away if they did not respond, or
when the room beyond proved vacant.

It was a sort of lingering inertia that made him do this, for they might have absconded to the lower floors, or made off altogether, since the snow would hardly be a barrier to *them*. But he could not summon the energy as yet to go down and look. Nor, as it turned out, did he need to.

The fifth door to the left—he had absurdly counted them—swung inward to reveal a tall apartment of cobwebbed gilt. Like all those rooms with furniture in them, the effect of an invading winter was heightened by the snowbanks of the dust sheets. But this room was not entirely cold, for a fire smoldered in the grate, regardless of whether the unswept soot in the chimney might be set ablaze. And green and blue clothes lay over the backs and arms of chairs. Their arrogance appealed to him. He had never felt he owned the chateau, they plainly supposed they did. He was the guest, not they.

They were both in the bed on this occasion. He was not unduly surprised. Nor, on going closer, was he amazed to see that their sleeping posture indicated they were intimate in the way of lovers. Their white skins on the tumbled crimson covers—no sheets had been put in—were startling.

He could so easily have killed them. Walked in and fired straight through the quilts and through both their bodies at once. They must have known he would not. Neither woke, both silently and intently asleep. A novel sight.

Incest would not be uncommon in a rural community, and they were enough alike to have proved mutually attractive. Besides, in a wolfpack, what did near relationships matter?

He was quite cool and analytical as he walked out of the room again. He strolled back into the master suite, threw a log on his own fire and sat watching it.

What he felt was a mystery. He continually searched through himself, seeking the familiar responses of anger, lust, perturbation.,

At length, he poured a glass of yesterday's wine, which was dying quickly in its uncorked state. After a few minutes, as if nothing had happened at all, he picked up the book he had been reading when the first pebble had hit the window, and began to read again, this time with a peculiar concentration.

When Gabrielle started to move about the chateau, he heard her only because she sang. He was stimulated instantly, into a kind of dazed alertness. He listened to her voice, that had no strength to it, but was pretty enough, and though not strong, was oddly carrying, float along the passage, and down into the depths of the chateau. (He had an impulse to go after her, but not the physical willingness to proceed.) In any event, after some fifteen minutes, he heard her coming up again, still singing, and still the same strange little song.

> *En forêt noir je vais les soirs,*
> *Les étoiles belles sont au dessus;*
> *Je pense que dans leurs luminères*
> *Je vois—*

Never could he define the last few words. On this, the fourth or fifth repetition, he caught himself idiotically tensed to make them out. But at that very place, she broke off, as if purposely to annoy him. It had had the sound of some traditional ballad; current for years in various versions. And how suitable for her kind: going through the dark forest in the evening, with the beautiful stars overhead. And in their lights she thought she saw precisely what?

And then her white knuckles rapped on the drawing-room door, which he had even left ajar, as though she could not walk through the woodwork just as she chose. The knock itself was comical, too, being irresistibly reminiscent of Madame Tienne.

He did not bother to call out to her, and sure enough, in another moment she had walked noiselessly barefoot into the bedroom.

She had clothed herself in a gray silk drapery, a curtain, no less. The wretch, she must have torn it off its rings for the purpose. But the effect was classical, and left bare her right shoulder, small, square and luminously white. Her hair was a floss, a fizz, of pure light, her unpainted morning face slightly sallow. Her unequal eyes seemed made from the silk itself.

She carried cups and a coffeepot on a tray, feathers of steam rising. Madame Tienne indeed.

"You slept well?" he inquired. "I do so hope you did."

"Very well," she answered, unsmiling. "We've slept in the house before."

"In which guise?"

A flicker of something—it looked mostly like interest—

lifted up through her lips, cheeks and brows, and was gone. She set down the tray on the dressing table.

"Human," she said. "Mostly."

"Ah."

"Ah," she mocked him. "*Ah*, you seem recovered."

"Do I? I dreamed two wolves were lying on the bed."

"They were."

"You knew me then, when you were—not as you are now?"

"Why not? Human memory, some human traits, remain with us as wolves. Just as some characteristics of a wolf remain with us during the hours of daylight."

"I recall. The love bite you awarded me."

"*Love?*" she said. "That was the thing I bit you to prevent."

"I see. You didn't realize the word 'no' would have done as well."

She had begun to pour the coffee, steadily and efficiently. There was something in the method. . . . It reminded him of the gestures of a servant. Yet there was nothing else of a servant anywhere about her. She turned like a dancer, and brought the cup to him.

"It's not general in these parts, monsieur, for a word to be sufficient. And besides, I didn't think you'd know that word."

He took the cup.

"And besides, you already have a partner. Your brother."

"Tut, tut, monsieur," she said. There was a wicked archness on her face which suddenly infuriated him. She moved back to the dressing table and leaned there, drinking her coffee, looking in at herself through the mirror, sometimes smoothing her eyebrows with one finger, whose nail glared like a hot coal.

Eventually, she said, but to her broken image in the glass, "We're the bastard line, the sub-branch of the chateau. Lycanthropy is inherent, though does not always come out in every child. For a hundred and forty years, there was no trace. Then I. Abandoned by my mother, naturally. The warning signs begin around the time of puberty. Not pretty, monsieur, not nice at all, when your little girl in her ribbons and pinafore assumes the nails of a harlot. The hair comes a month later, but only in the night. So the mother discovers her child, covered in long tufts of fur—which vanish at sunrise. The first transformations are very painful. The back-bone—indeed, all the bones—must become extraordinarily elastic. Have you noticed how fluidly we are coordinated? How fast we can move? But then, one screams with the agony, monsieur, rolls about, foams at the lips. Possessed by devils, they say, or has the madness. The priest comes, young and frail, twitching his nose like a tiny mouse brought in to exorcise the cat. Or the doctor comes in his carriage. One is bound to a bed, monsieur. Straps, or ropes, whichever is handiest, and a great deal of laudanum. But in the end, one is strong enough to break out. One would run anyway, but one is sent to the forest, sent there by flung stones."

He drank the coffee, a normal action in the midst of abnormality. How could he believe her? It was ridiculous. Yet, he would have to believe her, for he had seen the results.

"And having borne one lycanthrope," he said glibly, "your mother elected to take the risk again, and duly invented your brother."

"My brother," she said. He saw her entire body rise and sink in the expression of a sigh. She turned again, slowly, and gazed at him. "I'll tell you it all," she said. "Thee must be attending." It was a slip this time, not a mimicry, and she faltered impatiently, then said: "The story goes like this. There was a lord at the chateau, about the time of the crusades, who was also a magician, a shape-changer. One night he took a girl out in the forest, he hunted her down with hounds, and forced her. But not as a man. In the shape of a wolf. She died, but not before she birthed a son. He was a werewolf. This was how the wolf inheritance came about. Tradition has it that the arcane blood, the arcane spirit in the forest, are stirred by a rape, because of that beginning." She put her hand to her face, but she stared beyond him, breathing fast as if she had been running, just like the fair-haired girl in his dream. "Your grandfather, Monsieur Dorse, sold the house, but for some years after, he now and then returned to it, the land, the village. He'd stay at the inn. Here, the seigneur—is the seigneur. He was charged nothing. And being elderly but libidinous . . . there was a woman he fancied whom he raped. She happened to have the bad genes, those that carry the lycanthropous strain. Not that she knew, until I came. Yes, your grandfather's bastard, which will make me thy aunt in half blood. Do you care for our new relationship?"

She had stopped, so he found a phrase to say to her. "Go on."

"Haven't you heard all you would? No? Oh, then, when I was a woman less than a year, less than that one of the wolves' children, the caretaker caught me as I was playing in this house. He was from the town and discounted legends. But the father mattered not at all. The wolf strain, once roused, can go on through the female, and did so with me."

"Luc is your son," Christian said.

"My son. Don't expect any moral embarrassment."

All he could find to say now was the truth.

"You must be a little older than you look."

She laughed soundlessly behind her hand. Her eyes were black and venomous and looked straight at him.

"I was eleven years old when the drunkard's caretaker raped me. Twelve when I sloughed the child."

The feel of the electric current coursing through him was now so vital that he had to get up, and walked, for want of somewhere else, to the fire. His aunt, indeed. He could no more think of her in that way than he had ever been able to accept the fact of his own death. But not only his aunt, his *wolf*-aunt. And the young wolf, her lover, also her son. . . .

"And how old were you," he asked her, satin on his voice, "when you killed the caretaker? I assume you did. Vengeance, combined with a dinner menu. For yourself and the child."

"Yes," she said, "we should never have started that game with you."

"Which game is that?"

"The pretense that we've killed, and eaten, human flesh."

"We can, of course, begin," said a third voice.

Christian looked up, and saw the young wolf, decoratively draped in a Roman toga of coverlet, in turn decoratively draping himself on the doorway.

Christian waited, glancing from one to the other, smiling pleasantly, politely.

Luc de Lagenay slid from the door jamb, advanced on his—his *mother*. He put his arms round her. Both man and woman looked like adolescents, she even the younger of the two, her pale face empty of cosmetics, and of any defense.

Christian smiled more broadly. He was experiencing a ludicrous emotion, insubstantial as the feather of steam from the coffeepot: jealousy. Never before had he observed a perfect unit of any sort, but only those which were imperfect and, as a rule, cried out to him to make them whole. But this. This was Michelangelo's Pietà.

"I thought," he said, after a moment, "that you'd at least begun with Sylvie. According to the folklore of your calling—"

"Why do you listen to gossip?" de Lagenay said. His eyes were almost transparent, very dangerous, very sure.

The grandfather, having sired the girl-child, must have paid some way toward its schooling, before the symptoms of lupine unsociability set in. And she in turn had taught her son, an education somehow more polished in its second-hand application. *Why am I helping them to establish their hysterical history in my mind? Can any of this be accurate? On a premise of hallucination or black magic—*

"Why," de Lagenay said, "assume that, in the form of the wolf, either of us would hunger for human meat? Only consider it another way, my seigneur, and you'll see the sense in what I'm saying. As humans, do we acquire a voracious appetite for the meat of wolves?"

"Quaintly argued," Christian said. "But the evidence is overwhelming." (Oh yes? As if he spoke of politics or the weather. . . .)

"Sylvie?" said Luc. "That was only the joke we played on you in the hut, a trial of strength between us, which you most definitely failed. But we didn't kill her. She'd throw us whole joints from the kitchen window. She was in love with me, with the notion of evil and death she trusted me to represent. It would have been silly to tear out her throat when she was so useful."

Chapter 18

---◦◦◦---

The Test

Once more gorgeously arrayed in pigeon-blue trousers, silk shirt, claret waistcoat, de Lagenay stood shaving himself with Christian's razor before the cracked mirror. The air was still vaguely flavored by the scent of Gabrielle's cigarettes, three of which she had smoked before going out of the suite. Christian sprawled in the chair before the fire. Conversation had been lacking. Luc's fob watch, produced like an actor's prop, had recently informed them all it was midday. Now the wild animals were absurdly washing, dressing, making up and shaving themselves, although, in about four hours' time, metamorphosis would reclaim them. Christian had ceased reacting with any attempt at reason. It was hopeless. But excited—stupidly, yet undeniably—that he had remained.

"How did you crack this mirror?" Luc suddenly inquired.

Christian said: "You presumably know it wasn't cracked before."

"We know most of this house very well."

"Then you probably know just as well how mirrors become cracked."

"Something brown and sticky seems to have adhered to the break. I suppose you threw something at the glass. I wonder why."

"I wonder why you bother with blunting my razor, when in less than four hours you'll be smothered in pelt from crown to heel."

"Form, my dear monsieur," said Luc. He finished with the blade and set it down on the dressing table, rinsed his face and dried it with gentle dandified pats. "In summer," he said lazily, "the day lasts longer, and the human shape with it. Fifteen, sixteen hours or more. Sometimes, in the summer, I've worked in the town. You'd be surprised."

"Would I?"

"Well, maybe not. Let's try you. I was a baker's assistant. A draper's assistant. A clerk—I have a good head for sums, you see. Once, I lived off a very wealthy lady, in the capacity of her—friend. She subsequently threw me out for leaving her every night. You scoundrel, you've been in bed with another woman! Just so, madame, a woman covered in gray hair, out under the stars. Aie—auw!" The wolf's howl, rendered as excellently as a mortal throat could contrive, was startling, even under the circumstances.

"Of course," Christian said briskly. "How else could you buy clothing, books and tobacco. And what did your sister-mother do to support herself? Taught little children their letters, perhaps, eating the odd plump infant on the side."

"That was already explained to you. Our jest. We never harmed, let alone devoured, man, woman or child."

"Sylvie."

"Sylvie, monsieur seigneur, was killed by someone else. A jealous lover, a mad old father, who knows?"

"Who mutilated her? Whole chunks of her were missing."

"How it *does* fascinate you, cher Christian. Tell me, if you lived in a wolf-infested wood, and meant to kill a woman and escape detection, how would *you* set about it?"

Christian stabbed the fire with the poker. This obvious answer—it had been obvious from the first denial, if the denial were to be believed—in no way satisfied him. Or perhaps, despite the details of Sylvie's body, the account of which had literally sickened him, he still wanted to think that here he was, taken hostage by two cannibals. He slung a log on the crackling flames, and lapsed back in the chair. The firewood was diminishing now. But since the two wolves apparently felt the cold in their human form, they might well replenish the wood store.

Ironically, he had found someone to care for him, as someone always had. But never before had there been any like these two.

Luc used Christian's brushes on his long hair, took up the cravat and arranged it, the blue-gray jacket and put it on.

"I am now dressed for luncheon," he said.

"Which luncheon? Does one exist?"

"I at least went hunting early last night. Gabrielle has created a ragout."

"Good God. Stewed babies."

"Good God, I'm sorry to disappoint you. Only rabbits, Monsieur Bloodthirsty. Get up, and come downstairs."

"My thanks. I don't think so."

"Come now. You're our feudal lord. We can't let you starve."

"Why not?"

"Oh, naturally, why waste a good stew. Since you're at the gate of death anyway."

Christian's heart unaccountably turned over at the words. He realized he had not thought about his illness for some while. He should be grateful at forgetfulness, but remembrance filled him with anger and despair. He stood up, walked across to de Lagenay, and slapped him with contemptuous economy, and all the force of his strong pianist's hand, across one neatly shaven cheek.

Luc leapt backwards, that extraordinary action Christian had witnessed before—truly, their bones must *be* elastic. The bright teeth showed in a snarl. But Luc remained human enough to retaliate verbally. "One more blow, is it? The last occasion you struck me, I might have had your guts out on the road."

"But pure aesthetics prevented you."

"We do not kill."

Christian moved forward again, slowly, after Luc. Christian's pulse galloped crazily. He wondered if he looked quite mad.

"Diseased meat," Christian said. "That was why you didn't kill me."

"Actually, misplaced loyalty to your stinking heirship of this land, this house. Which you yourself are too much of an imbecile to understand."

Smiling, Luc raised his face, and Christian hit it again, back and forth and back, and as his hands fell away, Luc sprang once more, but this time for his throat.

The impetus carried both of them into a wild abbreviated

descent. As Christian's skull struck the rug, and the young hard weight landed on top of him, he recollected a similar felling, on the gravel of the road. Now, as then, two demoniacal eyes stared into his; the first pair had been colorless, blazing and without dimension; these were no less terrible for being ostensibly a man's. For there was no mistaking, even now, the spirit of the wolf.

One of the hands had crawled onto his neck and had begun to squeeze, the other punched him two or three times, in short vicious jabs, under the ribs. Yet, there was something almost playful in this attack, as if more lethal methods were being kept in reserve. Luc's face, wide-eyed, open-mouthed, was intent and idiotically beautiful, insultingly so. Christian lashed upward with his own hand to smash the murderous target with a fourth blow. But even as this blow landed, or seemed to land, Luc had jerked sideways, snaked back. Christian found the outer edge of his palm had been caught in his enemy's teeth.

Of course. As with the woman, the youth would fight like a wolf. The pain was thunderous, it poured along Christian's arm like black water. The fingers on his throat had slightly relaxed, he was just able to gauge that. Enjoying the taste of flesh?

What now? The last occasion Christian had fought had been some fourteen years ago, in a frosty exercise yard when school had finished. There had been no requirement since. And his looks had been worth safeguarding. And his hands had been precious. Christ, Christ, his hands—

Christian arched his body up against de Lagenay's and, rather than seek to free himself, rammed the bitten hand more fiercely between these gnawing teeth, into the soft skin inside the mouth, and went on pushing thereafter, as if to force the hand down the wolf's very throat. The teeth presently let go, the dark auburn head went back, and Christian beat his uninjured fist into the vulnerable neck.

The fingers came off his own windpipe simultaneously. De Lagenay choked and started to roll over. Christian, lurching upward from a sort of bow-shot off his own spine, tumbled Luc violently sideways. Now they crashed against the feet of the dressing table and the mirror rocked above them.

De Lagenay's choking had become a steady vociferous growling, which maddened Christian. He had fallen deliberately forward, to pin the creature under him, but the creature had slipped away. Christian slashed out his bleeding hand and caught the immaculate—no longer—cravat. But the material tore. Abruptly, Christian was kneeling, holding a flag of pewter silk ridiculously before him. The boy had swung himself up against the mahogany dressing table. In another second, the long slick blade of the cutthroat razor had been snatched by that red-nailed hand.

Luc coughed. (Odd, how long since Christian had coughed?) De Lagenay's face had ceased to look uninvolved and pristine. Blood smeared his mouth, mostly his own, for the lip had been cut on the teeth. The eyes burned, seeming much paler, for the pupils had shrunk as if in strong light.

Christian dropped the useless bit of cravat, and got to his feet. In that instant Luc de Lagenay darted at him, and the razor cut a white crescent out of the air.

Christian had never moved so fast in his life, or known that he could. As he ducked beneath the blade, he had a feverish mental image of some long-ago duel, a man with a slender sword—but that was centuries in the chateau's past, and could not help him. . . .

The razor swirled over and bit itself back, like some ghastly tongue.

There was no leisure to judge his adversary's expression, whether murderous or merely amazed. The blade moved next so quickly, that Christian saw it not at all; he threw himself aside rather than downward, knowing, by some instinct only, that the angle of this attack had been lower than the previous one. He thudded against a cold and slippery surface—it was the pane of a window—and though he had not felt the blade touch him, he was shocked to see a crimson rosette flower suddenly on his shirt front. In such a moment, you asked yourself if you had been killed.

He heard de Lagenay laugh. It was really no laugh at all.

Christian careered along the icy pane as the blade once more shot forward. The sound it made as it sliced through the drape was unique and horrible. And then it hit the window, although without sufficient strength to shatter it, skidding across the glass with an eerie scream all its own. It was five centimeters, six, still sliding, from his arm. He could knock it away, and the edge could cut his arm to the bone—

He sprang off the window and ran. This blood blossoming

from his shirt—it must be a superficial nick, or how else was he still active? No feet made a noise behind him, which meant nothing. De Lagenay's breathing was just audible. Christian swerved, and dashed the ewer from the dressing table to the ground, jumping over it, catching the momentary skip of de Lagenay's breathing as he, too, jumped to avoid.

Christian reached the fireplace as the wolf came up with him. At the last second, Christian bent double, as if to rush into the fire. Again he sensed that monstrous tongue lick out, scoring the stonework of the wide mantel. He himself had plunged full length, grabbing out as he did so, over the brass fire dogs at the discarded poker. With a bodily revolution that seemed to wrench adrift every joint and tendon under his skin, Christian catapulted himself around and into a sitting position.

De Lagenay was crouching—no—in the act of springing forward, his right arm soaring out to energize the razor, soaring down to hack, to slit, to saw. . . . And Christian jabbed the fire iron, point foremost, directly into de Lagenay's diaphragm. The air went from him in a single labored grunt. Both his arms slapped wide, as if he would fly. Indeed, the poker, which had left Christian's grasp, seemed not only to transfix, but to lift and bear the young man backwards, in an incredible looping dive.

He landed on the oriental rug, soundlessly, and lay motionless. The poker thudded beside him. The razor was still in his hand, but he took no notice of it.

Christian went over. He stepped on Luc's wrist, and as the fingers uncurled, plucked the blade out of them.

He thought initially the telling blow between lungs and belly had knocked his opponent unconscious, but the pale lids slowly came up, and the pale wicked eyes looked out at him. Luc brought his free hand to his collar, ripped it open, and turned his face slightly away into the rug. Christian took it as a move to gain more air. Then, some half-recalled fantastic picture from Christian's father's hotel came idly into his awareness: A defeated gladiator in a Roman circus, stretched on the sand, offering the great vein in his neck to the conqueror's sword.

Christian dropped to one knee. He lowered the razor and held the blade against the throbbing column of throat. This throat that howled: *Aie-auw!*

"I might."

De Lagenay took in breath, and said raggedly: "You—miss the—courtesy—if you do."

Christian laughed quietly. The same unlaugh de Lagenay had uttered a minute or so before, the blade then in his own grip.

"What bloody courtesy?"

"By offering my throat—I demonstrate my—surrender. There's no more need to fight. I accept your victory. I wouldn't—fight you again. Test of skill—you won. I take you—as—whatever you wish. My superior. My seigneur. Cousin, if—you like."

Christian got up and walked away. He flung the razor, still gaping, back on the dressing table. He turned from the mirror's vision of himself, the newly smarting, superficial, profusely bleeding wound. The sight of his own blood nauseated him. He associated it with his death. He leaned on his hands upon the mahogany, resting his forehead on the clammy mirror, and closed his eyes.

Presently he heard Luc rise from the ground. Christian neither looked around nor stirred.

"I think," Luc said, "you've also branded me, in the manner of a true feudal lord. The damned poker was still hot from the fire."

Not opening his eyes, Christian put his hand against his own hand in the glass.

"Get out," he said.

"I'm going. To eat Gabrielle's angelic ragout, if you've left me any stomach to put it into. The fire is alight in the salon. Gabrielle's recipe: rabbits cooked tenderly with oranges and spices."

"Oh, confound you both," Christian said.

The door handle turned. The door whispered to the rug, the door shut. After a moment the door of the drawing room was also shut.

Christian left the mirror. He returned across the rug and retrieved the poker, for some reason thrusting it point downward into the fire.

He began to cry. He did not comprehend why he should at just that instant, he tried to control his crying, walking about the room, his arms wrapped ferociously tightly about himself, as if against extreme cold.

But eventually he sat down in the chair by the fire—the log was burning brightly now about the rigidity of the poker—covered his face with his hands, and toppled forward into bottomless grief.

Chapter 19

The Lovers

Misery is a timeless country. He emerged from it at some point, when the dull white afternoon, so like its predecessors, seemed to have advanced not at all. Like sea spray, the salt of his tears had dried harshly on his skin. He went into the bathroom and with the icy water washed the salt away, thinking foolishly of the stranded liner of the hotel, and the winter surf furling in across the beach below like thin cream.

He had been a child then, his parents' son. Had he ever wept as a child? With toothache, once. Once with anger at some trifle—what was it? He could not remember. And in the later years of his triumph and his arrogance, why had he never heard a rumor of the dreadful voice which promised him: *Your hurt and trouble and despair I save for you. I have them in safe keeping for your future.*

It was probably between two and three o'clock. He stood before the fire and drank the last glass of the dead uncorked wine. He began to decide his doom. He would pack what he needed and could himself carry. Once the snow had thawed or lessened (surely, at some moment, this would occur?), he would walk to the station. He could find Peton. Peton lived close by the station, did he not? Peton would advise him when a train was due. He could put up with Peton until the train arrived. And in the city, he could find some clinic or other. The dribbles of money from the chateau would provide him with necessities. Perhaps better than that. It might be more pleasant to die in luxury. It was just a matter of waiting, for a thaw, a train, a cheque. For death. It had always merely been a matter of waiting. Running away, false heroics, were quite superfluous. He would never, never have had the courage to end his own life. Claut the monkey had at least been correct in that.

The drawing-room door was gently opened.

Damn them. Damn them all. They gave him no *peace*. He could not even lock them out; the drawing-room door, when closed, sent them in through the library door. When that had been closed, there was the secret way in beneath the tapestry. They cast stones at his windows. They used his chateau, his bed, his razor—even to attack him with—there was nothing they would leave him. Not even his sleep, or his dreams. He set down the unfinished wine on the mantel.

As the quiet knocking came on the bedchamber door, he was already striding to it. He wrenched it wide, and cried out in a great and furious voice which shocked him: "Goddamn you, will you leave me alone for once!" And then fell silent, because the woman, Gabrielle, stood before him, clad in her olive-colored costume and her mist of hair, in her cosmetics, her perfume, a tray balanced fantastically on one hand—the stance of some waiter in a suburban café. All this, and the frightful insane tones of his own voice, stunned him.

He took a step back, away from her, and perhaps from himself. He glanced at the tray, the bread, the cheese, the steaming and fragrant ragout—rabbits, their necks bitten through in one swift snap by the teeth of these children of wolves—cooked with spices, herbs, and hothouse oranges.

"What's this?" he said, his voice shaking distressingly. "I thought my servants had gone away."

Her face was blank.

"While you are in this place," she said, "there'll always be found those who will serve you."

"Strange, I never saw you as my cook. And your son. He'll shave me. No doubt, rather carelessly."

She put the tray down on a small table.

"You struck him first. The instigation was yours. He could have ignored you, or fought you. A test of strength, as in the wolfpack. He won't bear any grudge. He accepts that you've won. As in the wolfpack. And you, Monsieur Christian, should accept his acceptance. As in the wolfpack, too. I see the bleeding has stopped."

He had forgotten the narrow wound, and ignored it now.

"Oh, God, because some impossible freak of nature has turned the two of you into monsters, I must join in, must I? To atone for the sins of my wretched grandfather, that I never even met."

"No necessity for you to meet," she said stonily. "You are each other."

"Out," he said. His voice shook, his hands. His heart shook inside him, forcing him to gasp for breath. These were familiar sensations. Before a recital such nervous pangs had beset him often. Not at the beginning, but as his talent and its acclaim grew more vast, so the terror had mounted. Why? Because he must always surpass himself, and might fail? But why think of it now?

He turned his back on Gabrielle, and walked across to the hearth. Noticing the poker sticking up from the center of the burning wood, he reached to take it out, and place it with the other fire irons.

"NO!" the woman's cry was shrill and appalling. The next moment she was by him, with the swiftness especial to them, literally like lightning. And with the same supernatural staccato suddenness, she hit both his hands aside, and up into the air.

He stood there nonplussed, and cursed her, and she said: "You were to take hold of that, you fool—" and she drew the dregs of the wine off the mantel and dashed them across the knob of the poker. A huge hiss and a cloud of steam burst from it, as if from an exploding pod. For the first, he saw that the whole stem of the iron was glowing red. It had been standing in fire about an hour. She seized his hands and raised them to his own eyes, to show him, "How many of the mazurkas of Chopin would you play with such a burn? How much Rachmaninov?" She dropped his hands with some indecipherable little provincial oath that resounded with contempt, almost with hatred. "But that's what you wish, isn't it, monsieur? To die, or to cripple yourself, or to lose your mind. An end to all responsibilities, both to yourself and to what is in you. All fears end when once they come true."

Her words seemed to go through him, as if he had no substance. A terrible pain rose up in him. He did not know what it was, or how it must be dealt with. He pictured his hands, seared to the bone, or cut to the bone, which the razor would have done for them. He felt the raw smart of the slim line which the razor had carved across his chest, and recalled the blood splashing lightly out of his mouth across the piano keys at the conservatoire.

She, in turn, had set her back to him.

She said, "Such suffering. I pity you. What do you know about any sort of pain, of the body, or the soul? My God, my God. You should have been me, or been Luc. You should have been my mother. But *you*." (The disgust with which she said it.) "Wrapped in swansdown from the day of your birth. No wonder the pinprick hurt you. *Oh, the agony*."

"Very well," he said. "If I bow humbly before your chastisement, will you go?"

"Yes. You'd enjoy being alone. To die here. No one to trouble you."

"I can't seem to die," he said. "That's what puzzles me. Or to live, either."

He leaned on the wall. He did not glance at her averted face, her turned shoulder with the shining spray of hair across it. Her hair was not at all like hair of any kind, but like frost, or smoke, or dry water. What a transformation that must be, to change such hair into the pelt of a wolf, perhaps even stranger than the twisting of her bones. . . .

The tears came out of his eyes again, too easily, knowing the way now. He let himself slide down the wall, drew up his knees, and rested his arms on them, his head upon his arms. A minute after, he felt the warmth of her body as she knelt beside him. What scent was that, like dusk in a garden full of flowers—expensive—how curious—

She put her arms about him, and drew him to her. That also was easy, to let her fold him against the softness of her breasts.

"Hush," she said. "There."

Self-pity. He had known as well as she. Known all of it, quite likely. He had had the servant girl about here, on this rug; had her unsuccessfully at that. What a catalog of personal disasters it was becoming.

Far away, he heard himself crying on Gabrielle's breast. He sounded exactly like a child. What a scene, as if from a sixth-rate melodrama.

But—"Hush, my darling," she murmured to him. "Hush, my dear, my dear. Thee will be safe, thee will be happy again."

And—"No," the child wept out. "I never was, I never shall be happy."

And—"Hush, thee shall be happy, and safe with those that love thee."

Somewhere, far away as the child which wept, he beheld Luc, twelve or thirteen years of age, the ghastly agonizing spasm of the physical metamorphosis spent, crying also in her arms for comfort. But Gabrielle—who had rocked and who had comforted *her*?

The child grew tired in a little while. Grew quiet in a while longer.

And still she held him, gently, gently, still rocked him, and soft as whispering she began to lullabye him with that bizarre small song he had heard her sing before, and now he heard it all, even the very last line—

> *En forêt noir je vais les soirs,*
> *Les étoiles belles sont au dessus;*
> *Je pense que dans leurs luminères*
> *Je vois les yeux de ceux qui m'aiment.*

He raised his head and looked at her, and so he saw that she was crying a little, too. Several women had wept because of him, at some harsh word, or because he was going away. But there had never been one who wept at his sorrow. Never, until now. She, who had said: *What do you know about any sort of pain?*

The tears which fell from her two eyes should be of different shapes—

It was the philosopher, Georges Edouarde, who had said: "Lust walks behind despair, as behind the lines of battle, for sadness, like death, is a denial of life, and life, clever wanton that she is, is always ready to announce her presence and renew her claim."

Christian took her face between his hands. The distance between their mouths was very short.

He had wanted her in the hut. That had been nothing to this. She had denied him then. This time she leaned forward,

wrapping her own firm hands about his head, meeting his
mouth with hers.

He caught the green glint of one eye, swimming under its
lashes, not quite closed, watching him also as he kissed her,
but an eye half-drugged, delirious. The dampness of his own
tears lay over her clothes. The center of one breast bloomed
out against his palm and then the other. Lying against the
wall, slipping slowly over onto the oriental rug, the firelight
sifting through her hair, making her hair into firelight, and
her hands passing over him, making patterns on his skin—but
not here, where dead Sylvie had writhed and howled—

He came to his feet suddenly, lifting Gabrielle with him.

The bed was there. The bed of tradition, where roses and
grapes and procreative seed had been scattered together.

They moved toward the bed as one thing, twisting, twining;
somehow arrived there, and fell down on it.

It was not the same with her as with the others. The whole
of her mythology, her very doubtfulness, had resolved into
some extravagant symphony of exquisite feeling and sensation. Great waves seemed to shake her, and yet she was quite
silent, as if to lock the intolerable depth and height of them
inside herself, as if to give nothing away, lose nothing. And
even as she trembled and clung to him, it was undeniably
some caress of hers which hurled him after her, that ultimate
blinding silver nail of crucifixion, driven mercilessly stroke by
stroke, through loins and spine and brain.

"Where's Luc?" he asked her.

"Oh, don't be afraid," and she laughed quietly against his
throat. "There is the wood to be got in."

But presently, when he returned to her, she kissed him, and
said, "Don't you see how dark the light is growing?"

When she went from his arms, and gracefully off the bed,
her baroque body penciled over by the embers of the fire, he
felt a shudder of apprehension at what she must shortly again
become. Not for himself, only for her. But she seemed to
read his response at once.

"Perhaps we can make you understand," she said, taking
up her clothes carelessly. "To begin with, it's vile enough. But
there comes to be joy, too." He yawned, and she said to him,
laughing again, "Go to sleep, my child. There is tomorrow."

She walked to the tapestry, gave some invisible touch, and

the secret wall gaped for her, and closed when she had gone through.

He lay a long time, watching the red gleams of the fire. There was no need to consider, or to think. Though the other might come in and murder him yet. Or the house fall. But in fact only the stew would have congealed, only the fire would go out if he did not attend to it.

He remembered her, and his body drew taut and flared seemingly red and white along every artery. But she would be with him tomorrow.

Two wolves ran through the wood.

They went into the dark forest in the evening, and only the beautiful stars shone overhead. . . .

—And in their lights I think I see the eyes of those that love me.

For what is love, my children, but the name the heart employs when referring to sexual desire, just as the brain will name it "appetite," and the spirit will name it "my reflection."

Long before midnight, he was awake, alert as an animal. He renovated the fire, lit a lamp, then had the impulse to take it and walk again right through the chateau, now looking at everything quite differently. But instead, he confined himself to the suite of rooms. He stayed a considerable time in the freezing library. The lamp explored the cracked and gilded spines.

Everything had subtly altered. The house was changed.

About two or three in the morning, he went down to the cellars, and brought out more wine in cobwebby bottles. The route was no longer unfamiliar. In the bedroom, the plate of ragout had settled into a gray jelly, but the bread and cheese were edible. He opened the wine and drank it.

The night was muttering beyond the windows, branches bending and sighing under their weight of snow. A continuous wind had risen in the forest. He stood at a window and gazed out across those sheets of whiteness. As the wind ran over them, a powdery spume sprayed upward, as if the snow gave off a cold and blowing smoke. . . . The moon burned, the stars emitted a thin high note of light like the wail of a tin whistle. . . . Yes, there would be a fascination in going abroad on such a night—on any night at all—to run through champagne springs, the thick green syrups and tinders of summer, the husks of autumn.

When, much later, eventually the dawn began to come, a heatless pink flame filled up the windows.

Christian pictured Gabrielle and Luc, human or beast, returning to that other room they had selected for themselves, their flesh and their hair dripping the chill rose waters of the sunrise.

He lay on the bed, listening to the birdless, faintly glittering noise of morning. Illumination shivered over the snow, as the wind had, and the whole land gave that same crystalline rippling which would sometimes resonate from the chandeliers of the grande hall.

On the border of sleeping and waking, he was not astounded to find himself lying on his side, watching his own self stretched over Gabrielle a meter away along the width of the large bed.

Initially, he felt only a mild curiosity. Then, as consciousness solidified, the pleasurable sense of illusion faded. He observed the tranced motions of their bodies, the almost motiveless meetings and disconnections of faces, hands, arms. Yet only very gradually did he decide who the lovers were, for the man was not himself.

Disbelieving, he lifted himself onto one elbow. A sense of outrage was swiftly banished by a sense of profane amusement, which as swiftly perished in an onslaught of marveling angry arousal.

Their beautiful faces stared helplessly back at each other, their eyes sometimes closing, their lips parting on small whispers of sound. Were they even aware of him?

Twenty ideas or more passed through his mind as the bright current raced upward with his blood, ideas mostly of violence. But such thoughts were conditional. When her face turned toward him, framed more by the dark red hair than by her own, Christian, too, could only stare back at her, and when her hand glided from the hollows of Luc's body to his, he could only swim toward her.

Her slightly fluttering lids, the rigid tension of her muscles, matched with his own. A fragilely high-strung quivering seemed to pass through the three of them, like the passage of the light across the white body of the landscape outside. As if in a dream, first her mouth, and then her breasts, and suddenly the whole surface of her was pressed against him, as the other man sank aside. There was no hesitation, no clumsiness. It was as if Christian had indeed become Luc. Her hands had knotted across his back, and abruptly he possessed her, and as abruptly seemed to burst through her into the whirlpool, the madness, that thing which was, after all, only a kind of fit, and which so closely resembled one, and yet because of which—because of which. . . . His teeth met through the linen case of the pillow, a fact which would afterwards intrigue him.

They lay relaxed, the three, loosely curled together. The wolf pack.

The room was very still.

For the room had seen all this, on many occasions before.

PART FOUR

FÊTE CHAMPÊTRE

Chapter 20

———◦◉◦———

The Liaison

The winter changed its character; there came a succession
of bone china days. The sky was cloudless, fathoms deep, and
very blue, the sun dazzled with a sharp sheer light—yet it
was so cold that every aspect of the snow had frozen into
ridges and blades of ice and crystal. In the moat, which was
waterless, the snow pretended to be water, and partly reflected things.

The chateau was by now in a state of ultimate isolation,
encircled by snowdrifts as if by high seas.

At night, the blackness was so clear, it seemed possible to
see right through it. . . .The colors of all the stars were visible.

A small, long-dead tree, close to the topiary garden, had
been cut down by Luc and lugged to the kitchen yard. Together, he and Christian had split the tree into logs. The car-
casses of things which had been successfully hunted hung in
the cold larder. Gabrielle had subdued the great black range,
baked bread, brewed kettles of soup. Her provincial train-
ing—her destiny had been surely intended as service, and
most likely to the chateau—showed in her deftness, her
canny use of the large hollow kitchen. But she knew the
kitchen well. Both of them knew every iota of the house, the
estate. They taught Christian by example, as they taught him
the rest of their lives. Gradually the wilderness of stairways,
rooms, passages, became logical, domesticated. Fireplaces

157

were opened and set roaring. Sheets were whirled off furnishings to reveal a sublime and slow and comforting decay. A series of wardrobes were chanced on, yielding extraordinary displays of glamorous skeletal garments left over from ten years before, and pungent with mothballs. In such things she had dressed up and paraded as a child. In such a dress of sequins and butterfly wings she had once been captured and forced. But such horrors no longer mattered, had ceased to exist. Their state was timeless: here and now. Meditation, any form of retrospection, let alone prophecy, were absent from it.

Luc disinterred a black and battered top hat, reminiscent of Sarrette's, and sometimes wore it about the house, tilted at extravagant angles.

Perhaps it was because they had been here as children, sole master and mistress of that shut-up and be-wintered house, that these days came to be imbued with a sense of childhood, for Christian also. Their activities, too, had the spontaneous attitude of childishness—idleness, exploration, interspersed with casual bursts of maintenance; the accumulation of logs, making of fires and food. Even their amorousness was oddly childlike, for it was uncomplicated, asking no questions and devoid of guilt, despite the vigor of its manifestation, the eagerness with which they sought it. The two men shared the woman without rivalry, or without any rivalry that was not offered in the form of theater or a joke—mock sparrings, like those of two young dogs—as unlike the duel with the razor as it was possible to be. Indeed, in their actual physical sharing of her, they were not merely courteous, but sensually fascinated, each of them with the other, as with her. This voyeurism being, however, so open, was in itself a shared thing. She, the courtesan of both, remained obliquely yet essentially in control of both, just as at other times her role was undoubtedly that of sister, or mother, to either of them. Maybe the oldest social condition of the forest, the primeval condition of matriarchy, had reestablished itself among the three of them.

Through the short winter days, then, they would make love, lie asleep or sometimes conversing in the canopied bed. Or they would languish in chairs, reading the books from the library, or they would crouch beside the fires of the house, of the bedroom or the salon, playing long games of chess or ar-

gumentative games of cards—having unearthed the prerequis-
ites from various compartments, or else more bizarre
invented games of adolescence were resurrected, contests of
guesswork or skill—such as tossing small bits of money
against a die to make it roll . . . absurd amusements, like
those indulged in by adults at Christmas. Generally they did
not talk a great deal, or when they did, again in the manner
of children, they reviewed only the present, what they were
doing, or were about to do, or else some incident from the
past was recounted in the form of an anecdote, usually humorous. An interchange of histories was now avoided, save
piecemeal. It was really all too strange to be discussed.

And during the nights—of course, during the nights, they
were gone.

At first, Christian would read, would let the book fall,
passing from brooding into dozing. But an increasing restless-
ness drew him from these sedentary pastimes. He began to
pace about. He would take a lamp and prowl the landscape
of the chateau, just as his companions had taught him to do.
It became increasingly familiar. A carving here, some evidence of collapse there; angles, cast shadows, even the scuf-
fings of the dust, grew known to him, like the language of
some story frequently reread. He was drawn also to the windows, to look into the curious division of the darkness, black
above white. He noticed the moon and its phases, the change-
able position of the stars, the iron and silver planets which
wandered up and down.

At length the magnetism of these insomniac nights guided
him back into the music room. The wildness which the other
two expressed and reveled in, running over the black and
white undulations of the night on the feet of wolves, he pur-
sued along the white and black body of the piano. Initially
this was an undisciplined orgy, which dissatisfaction began to
transmute into a program of exercises—at which point, an
ironic check was applied. Now that he wished once more to
enslave himself to her vampire presence, the piano rejected
him. The cold of the fireless room had reached the delicate
wires. Taunting him with the harshness of her voice, the piano warped entirely out of tune in a matter of hours. He
hated her then, because he could not have her. He fretted
then, because she, not he himself, had said: No. It was a
traumatic volte-face in his life that at any other time would

have driven him inside himself in a predictably disastrous
search for balance. But now, in this place, in their partial
company—more galvanic even in its absence, because of
what its absence implied—he was driven outward rather than
in. Before the long red firelights, he would scribble music on
sheets hastily wrenched from the traveling box, invariably
torn up before sunrise, and pushed into the flames.

And when they presented themselves, hollow-eyed, slinking
into his room like the returning murderers he still partly believed them to be, he would get up sullenly to greet them
with sardonic curses. He never witnessed at that time the reversal of their transformation, from wolf to man or woman.
Nor was he awarded a second view of the metamorphosis of
human to canine. Nor did he ever glimpse their wolfishness
indoors or out, though he had spotted the marks of their feet,
the pads of two wolves, narrow gray slots in the snow ta-
blecloth of the terrace.

They would fight, all three, sporadically with words, come
together and fight soft-handedly in the bed, infantile battles,
resolved in the urgencies of sex.

But, as he paced about now, or sat over the sheets of untidy manuscript, he saw that they withheld from him their
second life, made a secret of it, having revealed it formerly
only as a weapon, a blow against his sanity, a trial of his
strength. They had grown shy, as if of undressing themselves
in front of him, of appearing before him as anything other
than human. Concealing nothing of the facts, by admission,
they now concealed everything from sight.

Alone, excluded from the ritual sorcery, he had only his
own self to fall back on, his self which seemed to have grown
stronger, and by its very strength demanded proofs, demanded employment. If everything that happened was a
dream, an illusion, yet it persisted. Shut out from it, however
briefly, he felt the distant incursion of doubt. In those hours
by himself, a cloudy agnosticism stole over him. Then, and
only then, he came to wonder where such a trio went together, where all of it might end. For surely, they might not
remain forever as they were.

And so, inevitably the night came when he lay in wait for
them at the exit and entrance point they most frequently
used, the chateau's main door, which gave on the terrace.
(What could be more bourgeois than this, that they, who in

the normal course of things must have anticipated the life of servants, relegated to back entries, now as *wolves* made a habit of utilizing the master door?) He had beheld the wooden leaf left ajar through several periods of darkness. Perhaps he had been meant to find it.

As beasts, what reasonableness could he expect from them? Were they even to be judged reasonable in human shape? Or, for that matter, was he?

But he recalled how they had lain against him on the bed, that first time, as if to comfort and warm him. As if, more relevant yet, desirous of contact with him, kindred, lovers, even then.

He stood by the door, meticulously dressed and coated for the outer environs, smoking one of her cigarettes, the ash crumbling on the floor.

When he heard the click of claws, he turned. The she-wolf had appeared, like a smoke-ghost, at the foot of the grand staircase. An incongruous picture.

"I'm going with you," he said. He felt foolish for addressing her, wondering if any atom of her could understand.

But she trotted to him, by him, and through the door. Then, on the terrace, she hesitated, turned and looked back.

As he stepped after her, the male shot past, almost knocking him aside. The move was strangely funny, malevolently capricious, unmistakably Luc's.

Like a man with two dogs running before him, Christian walked away from the house.

The night stung with its frosts and stars. The new high ground of snow had set hard, and by following them, pausing when they momentarily vanished, he discovered his footing to be remarkably secure. That they tamed their adventures to accommodate him, he knew. When they suddenly began to play together, rolling in the snow, feinting, darting up and down the metallic whiteness of the drifts, he suffered an abrupt and terrible pity, a sort of premonition. Where in the world could such an idyll fit, save here? Save here and now.

Contrary to his reckoning, he felt the transience of these moments more keenly, now that the deception was banished. Yet the air exhilarated him, and the novel vitality that had begun to be within himself. He joined in the game, letting them rush at him, their long feet skidding and their wicked eyes like fallen stars.

The forest lay over the edges of the park, the white forest, whispering in its tinsel. The two wolves and he himself would look black against the whiteness. They would protect him, warn him from treacherous ground.

Eventually he was able to stop thinking. They were neither his dogs nor his companions. It was all inexplicable, and needed no excuses.

Yet the aroma of melancholy did not go away. With the logic of his human condition, he foresaw departure, which, all the while he had looked for his death or his escape, had never been so clear to him, so unavoidable as now. He would lose sight of this truth tomorrow, of course—yet, it would remain no less truth for that—some twilit morning, or some steel-still night, walking away over some hill toward the whistle of a train. Because to remain inside a myth was not permissible.

Sometimes the cold smarted in his throat, and he coughed. It meant nothing anymore. He had ceased to credit death as the single easy answer.

Chapter 21

———◆◦◉◦◆———

The Warning

He half woke in the shining net of her hair, the warm human curve of her side under his hand. "What is it?" he said to her, for she was fully awake, her eyes wide, as if she listened—that curious expression, when the eyes seemed stretched to listen, too. It was an hour, perhaps, after dawn, and he dimly noted the light was dull again, no longer blue or gold. "What is it, Gabrielle?" But: "Nothing." she said to him. A vague cloud composed of those previous thoughts of difference and departure was stirred up like sediment from his brain. Did she guess, predict or merely read his mind? He moved, laying his head on her breast, the child's position of trust, and the leaden weights of reason dissolved. He fell asleep again on the wonderful bed of her flesh.

By ten in the morning, there was evidence of a thaw. The color of the sky had altered, the color of the snow followed suit. A yellowish pallor lay on everything, a dying of its purity and brightness. The atmosphere was clammy with a sudden mildness which had no warmth. At midday a slick and stony rain began to come down. The fire in the salon drizzled. The three children stared at it. Christian examined Gabrielle and Luc, examined a mental image of himse̶l̶f̶ it was not only in him, then, this sense of termin̶

Black mud boiled coldly up through the ̶ of snow; such dreadful wounds. A wi̶

163

by some mistaken shift of temperature, barren, dirty and unkind.

The day washed out in rain. Darkness and water trickled together over the chateau. Examining (with no interest) some carvings in one of the old towers, about one or two in the morning, he visualized, with dry amusement, the next day coming on muddy paw-prints all across the carpets. But they would be too careful to deliver such silly idiosyncratic marks. One could not laugh at what they were.

Again and again he pictured what it must be like for them trotting through the mud, and grimaced at the idea of the hunted game the thaw might provide.

Coerced by the climatic change, the piano gave off horrible twangings.

The rain stopped a little before sunrise. Christian stood at one of the high thin windows of the medieval chateau, and watched a transparent wall of palest red come up out of the far-off forest. And he remembered dawn in the city, behind the stairways of roofs, the winged cathedral, the papers of birds blowing over, and down and up again into the thin air. He imagined Gabrielle at one of the little tables in a square, drinking coffee, and Luc strolling along a street with a woman on either arm. But there was also, in his imagining, a phantom cage with a padlock on it, for the hours of night. . . .

Luc, standing in his beautiful, now somewhat rumpled, suit at the edge of the terrace, framed between two cement urns, said noncommittally: "Come and see."

Christian walked out of the chateau's door, and across the gray slush of the terrace.

As he did so, he vaguely thought, *How normal this seems. Less than a month ago, how could I have visualized any of this?*

It was twenty minutes short of noon, the sun a soft white snarling overhead. They stood together, and Luc waved one hand toward the ground below the steps.

The park seemed a sea of mud, its slopes abruptly hard in the distance, its lines of trees sulkily dripping. The moat bridge was like wet newspaper. The gravel road had puddled and darkened and here and there was still patched by a dead snow that refused to rot away. In such a montage, Christian at first detected nothing exceptional.

"I don't see it."

"Oh, what a misfortune to be born blind. Deaf, too. Gabrielle and I would have heard them, if we'd been awake. They must have come visiting in the middle of the morning. I'm sure they wouldn't have dared, by night."

Luc put one hand gently on Christian's neck, and moved his head into a new position. Placing the side of his own face against Christian's, and with the injunction "Follow," Luc drew two interconnecting lines in the air, across the land below. Following this air drawing, as instructed, Christian suddenly beheld the narrow black runnels that had been gouged out of the earth, the snow, and the road alike—each about four meters in length, intersecting each other savagely. They had been formed by dragging some spade-like implement through the mud. The shape was that of the crucifix, or rather, lying crookedly-on to the terraces as they were, the shape of those same lopsided crosses found in the village, that particular brand of *la croix écartée.*

"Apparently," Christian said, "someone's discovered you're here."

"Apparently."

"You know I'm ignorant of your charming local customs. What does it signify?"

"I haven't an idea," Luc said. He leaned weightlessly on Christian, still looking down at the marks of the unwieldy cross. "Our dealings with the village are limited. Meet the inhabitants by day, and they run. By night, one seldom meets them. The occasional girl comes after you. Like Sylvie. Always in a sly scared way, trying to tease, like Sylvie. Gabrielle knows them better. You remember why."

The marks in the mud filled Christian with irritation and foreboding. He resented them, and said inconsequentially: "For such a religious community, they're remarkably careless. I never yet saw one of their damned crosses set straight."

"Nor would you," Gabrielle said behind them. She had come out on the terrace noiselessly. Standing by Christian, and gazing at the lopsided cruciform, she said, "Clearly, you don't know what that mark really is."

"Clearly, I don't. Just some superstitious sign against the two of you?"

"And against *you, monsieur*," she snapped.

"*I*?" Christian smiled. He recalled his excursions to the village, the closed doors, the solitary watching figures, the people who hurried by out of the cemetery. The carved seat in the church.

Luc danced back. "Look," he joined thumb and index finger together in the sideways cross Christian had seen daubed on the post before the inn. "*That's* no holy symbol, my friend."

"Then enlighten me."

Gabrielle glared at him. "You are in the forest with no weapon and no chance of help. A wolf leaps at your throat. Consider, life is more valuable than anything. Your instinct will sacrifice any portion of you in order to retain life, to protect the vital spot. What do you do?"

Very slowly, reconstructing, Christian raised his left arm, and moved it over his neck, pressing as closely as was possible to obscure the windpipe. The gesture was awkward to achieve and to maintain, yet once he had done it.

"Last time," said Luc, "he used the other hand to strike out at me."

"This time," said Gabrielle, "he must forget his bond with the wolves. Forget your instinct, Christian, which told you we wouldn't harm you. You must insert as much of yourself between your life and the teeth of the wolf as you're able."

As slowly as before, Christian raised his right arm and crossed it above the left.

"A difficult stance," he said, "and one which leaves the rest of the body unprotected."

"*Instinct*," she said. "Only that. The beast goes for the throat. You must protect the throat." She nodded with a smug briskness. "The sign you are making now with your arms is the sign you mistook for a cross. The sign they hammer up on the sides of their houses, paint on walls, create with two bones, or their fingers. Not the crucifix. The Lysinthe."

Christian dropped his arms.

"I've heard the name. What does it mean?"

"It means," she said, "they're afraid of wolves. Afraid of the children of wolves, the *Loupsgensaieux*. Afraid of the power that walks invisibly through the forest. Afraid of you, le seigneur, whose ancestor was a shape-changer."

"So I'm to blame."

He smiled again. He saw, as if from a great height, how foolish the scene was becoming. He did not believe in it, though he knew it to be true. Presently they would reenter the house. He would make love to her again. He wanted her all the time. That, and that alone, seemed a true magic.

"Oh, Gabrielle," he said.

His family had conjured the first black curse of lycanthropy, and laid it on hers. What an extraordinary notion.

He put out his hand to caress her face, and Luc said, "Patience, there's someone coming along the road."

The apparition was a long way off, but visible on the curve of the gravel. A horse picked its way diligently, with a small ramshackle dog cart jolting along behind.

Monsieur Doctor Claut did not bother, on this occasion, to negotiate the sodden back way to the stable yard. Having driven over the moat bridge, he left the horse at the foot of the terrace stair, anchored by the trap, and hopped up the slippery steps, grinning.

Christian waited in the door, watching him.

"My dear monsieur," said the grinning Claut, arriving on the terrace and taking Christian by the arm, "standing about in this raw air seems inadvisable for you."

"According to your diagnosis, there's nothing the matter with me."

"Come now, you exaggerate. Nothing remarkable or serious is the matter. No reason to complicate any little weakness you may have."

The yellow monkey's face screwed itself tightly together. The monkey propelled itself off Christian's arm into the chateau's grande hall.

Both hearths were stocked with wood, and alight. All other obvious traces of the presence of the de Lagenays had been removed, save for the cigarette Christian had been smoking, the stub of which he now threw into the nearer fire. Claut took note, nodding affably.

"I'm glad to see you have resumed the habit, Monsieur Dorse. Tobacco, in moderation, is an excellent sedative." He swung his arms nimbly. "How bright you've kept the place. How well you're managing. I've been concerned, since I heard you'd sent your servants away. But surely, you have some girl here still, and Sarrette, perhaps, has come back?"

"Not at all."

"Not at all? Are you sure?"

Christian said nothing, and the monkey began a sidling scamper across the long large room. Although the door had been left unclosed, the chandeliers made no noise, as if holding secrets in.

Claut paused briefly at the foot of the undulating staircase. He went to the door of the salon next. The salon fire was dead, but unremoved ash filled the grate. Claut popped his head into the chamber, and presently out again. He looked at Christian as if entertained. He returned to the foot of the stair, his head raised to look up toward the gallery. Christian considered if the doctor would have the effrontery to skitter up the stair and continue his search above. But, after a minute, Claut minced back to the fireplace where Christian was standing.

"Well, monsieur," said Claut, "if you didn't assure me otherwise, I would swear you had company. Nothing certain, you understand. Simply the feel of the air. An elusive perfume."

"What can I do for you?" Christian inquired.

"There's the matter of my fee, monsieur."

"Damn you, you won't get a sou out of me. You knew that, I thought. I didn't call you in. I didn't require your services. They were forced on me."

"Ah, monsieur. You have all the arrogance of the very rich. Or the very poor." Claut reached over, and grasped Christian's hand, which he then tested with the remembered lascivious thoroughness. "Your health seems much improved," said Claut. "An excellent recovery. Aren't you glad now that I stopped you from doing such a foolish thing to yourself as swallowing a pellet of opium and arsenic?"

Christian withdrew his hand.

"If you insist on this, you'd better present your bill. I might consider paying it to get rid of you."

"Such strong hands," said Claut. "You're a pianist, I believe. A strangler could make good use of such muscular and digital development. Why not strangle me, monsieur? Then bury me on the estate, or in the forest. Or give me to your dogs to eat."

Christian felt a nervous boredom. This deception had been automatic, unplanned. Possibly unnecessary. Definitely useless. He looked into the fire.

"Who told you I keep dogs."

"The entire village knows you do. Didn't you buy a couple of rabbit hounds from the de Lagenays?"

Christian bent to put another log on the hearth. As he did so, a breaker of flame and sparks revealed to him, as it burst on the inside of the cowl, the absence of the inscription he had formerly seen there. He half checked, leaning to the fire, asking himself desultorily if it might have been on the inside of the twin hearth that he had glimpsed those words *Loups-gens-aieux*—those words which Gabrielle had subsequently used not an hour ago. But no, not the other hearth, nor a product of an impending fever. Like the vanishing passage in Hamel's letter, like the sorcerous path through the forest, and the transmogrification itself of human into animal . . . things came and went in this place, like sculptures in sand.

He straightened, faintly perturbed that it troubled him so little. Claut spoke to him, but Christian did not hear, and felt compelled to say, "I beg your pardon?"

"I was remarking, monsieur, that this area of the north is a very interesting situation. We have customs here that might astound you. Or not, as the case may be."

"For example," said Christian, "the Lysinthe."

"And do you know about that? The wolf-cross. Yes indeed. Then you must know about the Lady of Lilies, too. A euphemism, of course, and a sort of pun. For hundreds of years the Virgin Mary was worshiped here under that name, *La Dame aux Lys*."

"That revolting and macabre window in the church," Christian said automatically.

"You thought so? I never go in the church myself. I'm not a godly man, I'm afraid, dear monsieur. What doctor is anymore?" Claut skipped aside. He went to the long table and took up the decanter of cognac. Without a word, he poured two measures in two glasses. There were, naturally, three glasses set on the tray. Gabrielle, in one of her servant's moods, had arranged them so.

Christian took the brandy and swallowed it straight down. He waited.

Claut said, "The Romans were once in these woods, you know. They had a name for her. She was here, even then."

Christian went on waiting.

Claut drank his brandy.

The stuffing had continued to exude from his skin and clothing. He still gabbled, as if amusedly hurrying to tell some joke. His eyes gleamed with a senseless, childlike devilry.

Claut said, "These are only old tales, but the problem is, you'll find, that they're heartily believed. The wolf-goddess was feared and propitiated in this region since pre-Roman times, and the practice has gone on—subconsciously, if you will. The village is full of good Catholics. But examine the Latin of the services and you might, I'm told, notice certain discrepancies. And then, the power exists, doesn't it? The Lycanthropous power and the triad that it forms. The magician and his two acolytes." Claut finished his brandy. "That's the main threat. The triad. The unholy trinity—the mother, the son, and the lord. The lord is the catalyst. What makes them dangerous, gives the Lily Lady in the forest something to work through. Then the village stops propitiating, stops sacrificing. They start consciously fighting her." Claut looked at the empty glass. "You came back at the wrong time; Monsieur Christian. You should have stayed in the city, and played the piano, and coughed blood, and kept away from here."

"All right," said Christian, "that is very educational, but are you coming to any sort of point?"

"Naturally, I've come to advise you. Pack your bags and go. Go to the station. The chateau car is useless. The road is choked with mud and snow still. But my horse is a good horse; I'll drive you. There's a train due in four hours."

This conjuring of Christian's own premonition was unpleasant.

"Why?"

"Because the village has sat out the snow, and now the snow has cleared. They'll shortly be on the road, every man and woman, and every child. They'll come here, monsieur, and they'll set to work on anyone they find here."

"Only I am here."

"The more reason for you not to be."

"You expect me to abandon my property to some sort of mob?"

"Not really a mob. Their intentions are quite disciplined in their own way."

"Intentions?"

"An exorcism."

Chapter 22

---◈---

The Damned

The blue-glass porthole spotted the decanter and the glasses with sapphires, as Christian replenished his brandy. How stupid to notice, only at this moment, those brilliant beads of color in the crystal. The doctor had done something peculiar, sticking his tongue right down inside his glass to ferret out the dregs of cognac. It was a punctuation to the word he had just used: Exorcism.

"The de Lagenays," Christian said, "so far as I've heard, have lived in the forest unmolested for years. The village holds them in abject terror. Because of some fantasy—"

"Come now," broke in Claut, "facts, however extreme, remain facts. The Lagenays have the knack of transformation. An involuntary knack, over which they can exercise no control. We are all actually capable of such tricks, to a greater or lesser extent. The most obvious example being that of the natural accession from child to adult to old man. Has it never occurred to you what a feat of metamorphosis *that* is?"

"You imply the de Lagenays would have been left in peace if I hadn't arrived here."

"Quite so. Fear, and a sort of respect, were given them as their due, just as you mentioned. There were wolves in these forests before."

"And I am a magician. I'm the one they won't put up with, this insane village of yours."

"You or the Lagenays. But you and the Lagenays *to*-

gether. . . . There have been—events—in the past. Or stories of events. They believe stories hereabouts, as I said. Also, monsieur, your hereditary line is capable of sowing the wolf strain. Once you and the woman begin bedding together, who knows where it will end."

"You credit this?"

"I recount it."

"And if I pack my bags and go, what happens?"

"To Gabrielle and her son? Don't concern yourself with that."

"You mean, I think, this damnable medieval magic the village wants to practice will still take place."

"I regret that it will. Whoever they can get hold of will be involved in it. Like any abscess, it has to erupt before it can heal."

"You're all mad," Christian said. He turned toward the stairs. He pictured himself racing into the bedroom, telling the two of them, hustling them into Claut's dog cart—the horse snorting and rearing, as in all the tales a horse did, at the sorcerous aroma of wolf.

"If you are considering an escape for the three of you," said Claut, "I'll assure you now, they would come after, and track you down. The train isn't due for four hours. You alone, it's conceivable, they might permit to escape. They would say, 'What can he do without his minions?' "

"Minions. My God."

"Since Sylvie died," Claut said, "this has been simmering. And before, since Sylvie's death was part of it."

Claut placed his glass, licked quite pristine, on the mantelpiece. He joined his hands and rested his chin on them. He peered at Christian as if leaning over a shelf.

"I will wait ten minutes only, monsieur. If you aren't ready to leave by then, you must make your own way."

Christian drank the second brandy.

"I'm amazed you came here at all. What prompted you to rescue me?" He turned back and looked at Claut. Perhaps this impoverished lecher had hoped for some sort of gratitudinous love scene at the station. The idea was so ridiculous that Christian laughed.

Claut lowered his head until his nose rested on his hands. He looked at the floor, expressionless, and in this abnormal posture he reversed himself and walked toward the house door, and out of it.

Christian sipped a third brandy, leaning on the mantel, counting the seconds, or attempting to, until the ten minutes should be up. Eventually, he heard the wheels of the trap on the gravel, and the neat little crunches of the horse's hooves, going away.

Presently he looked around and saw Gabrielle and Luc on the stairs, she standing, he seated. Luc's pale face was expressive of a controlled, but almost maniacal humor. The look was accentuated by the addition of the battered black top hat, from under which his red hair coiled exotically. Gabrielle's face was a page of distress. She appeared frightened, an old remembered fear, and also very cruel, capable of a horrible revenge for any fresh harm to be inflicted on her. Something twisted in Christian's heart and mind as he saw them. He did not know what it was. It was as if a piece of his skin were being torn away.

"I'm to take it you heard," he said.

"We have sharp ears," Luc said.

Gabrielle said, "We were only just out of the old man's sight. How fortunate the doctor's in love with you, Christian. You might never have had a warning otherwise. What will you do?"

He walked over to the stairs and went up. He put the brandy glass to her mouth, and tilted it to allow her to swallow, as if she were an invalid, or had no hands.

"There's no vestige of law to appeal to," he said, "and no method of contacting the town. Or getting to the train. I suppose we stay here."

"And when they come?" she said.

"Are we sure they will come?"

She gave a melodramatic, terrified giggle. "They will. They will, my dear. Oh yes. They will."

She had been beaten and stoned and raped. She had good cause to be apprehensive.

"There are a few guns in this house," Christian said. "Perhaps they'll pay attention to those."

"They might have guns, too," Luc said. "They'll have used something from the church, probably. Something silver. The blacksmith will have melted it down and made silver bullets. You know about silver bullets, do you, Christian?"

"Confound you. Don't you think ordinary lead can kill you?"

Luc raised his face. His eyes were bleak and pale. The humor had become a grimace. "I don't know."

Christian walked down the stairs again. He shouted at the grande hall, his voice seeming to strike against each prism of the chandeliers.

"What are they afraid of?"

"Of us," Luc said. "The danger of *us*. The unholy trinity. We're celebrities."

"All right," Christian said. He strode to the terrace door, not glancing outside, and slammed it shut. And all the glistening windows throbbed back their grayish lights at him. Three hundred years ago, this place might have been defensible. But now, no longer. He had already learned most of the shutters were unstable. The architect who had brought in the brilliance of day had left a thousand fragile gates as a legacy to the chateau's enemies.

Christian did not truly accept, as yet, that anything would happen, for the outlook was so haphazard, so hopeless if it did. Then again, the hypothetical mob might balk at an ultimate onslaught on the house—chateau property was sacrosanct, was it not? He stared at the closed door and said, "Luc, have you ever used a gun?"

"Never," said Luc. "I've had other means of slaughtering things."

When the dark came, they would be wolves, and might get away as such. But the sunset was some hours off. Would the village, which had waited out the snow, wait also for the descent of day, preferring to confront the manifestation in its bestial guise?

The guns had been replaced in the gun room, amid the racks and velvet cases of dueling pistols.

He himself had hunted them with a gun, and come on Gabrielle in the bed in the shack—

Christian swung around and looked at them. They both stood at the foot of the stairs now, close together, with their hands knotted into each other. Constantly they presented themselves to him as two beautiful children, whom he could not entirely fathom, but with whom his life was precariously bound up. Ties of blood, or sex, or loneliness, or some perverse spell of the forest and the female principle that lurked in it.

He went back to them, and put out his arms to encircle and make contact with them. The painful naturalness of it was almost more dreadful than anything else in that moment. He seemed suddenly to realize the unlikelihood of their physical emotion and completeness. He recognized it, but, as one only recognizes something which is already finished.

Luc removed the clownish hat, as if he were at a funeral. Their three heads lightly touched. None of them spoke.

Almost on the stroke of one o'clock the lowering sky dropped lower and turned very dark. It was the darkness of dusk, long before sunset. It had a theatrical quality. It was unmistakably a backdrop.

Having secured the hall door—rather crazily, they had thrust the long table across it, complete with its silver candlesticks and bowls—they had come upstairs into one of the neglected upper rooms at the front of the chateau. A long window commanded a view of the terrace, the park, the gravel road.

It was cold in the room. They did not light a fire, but went on drinking brandy. Five guns, of assorted appearances and capacities, lay on a sheeted table. They were really no more than a token, a token not even of defiance, more of their understanding that they were threatened.

When the premature dark began, the land was soaked full of it, like bread fallen into wine. The darkness might almost have seemed a further barrier, as the snow had been. Perhaps the villagers would not travel through the darkness. Yet, undeniably, they would.

Christian wondered how the village had known the de Lagenays had entered the chateau. Maybe the servants had suspected such an arrangement when they were sent away, and complained of it. (He had wondered formerly how Gabrielle, the outcast of the village, had heard the rumor that the new lord of the chateau was sick—for she had known, had lashed out at him with the knowledge. Who had informed her? Or did the trees of the forest somehow carry rumors, whispering to each other? Just as words on paper and on stone appeared and vanished.)

At half-past one, Christian retreated from the window.

"All this may be needless caution," he said.

They did not reply. He thought of the Lysinthe, the wolf-cross gouged out of the mud and snow. It was partly visible from this window.

"The concealed passage that comes into the bedroom," he said. "You've never shown me the other entrance. If they get in and want to search the place, you could hide in there." They said nothing. "Could you not?"

"Very well," Gabrielle said tonelessly.

Actually, he had reasoned where the passage terminated or began—the other bedroom they had originally appropriated. Some salacious discreet link with the seigneur's bed.

"This is a most bloody waste of time," Christian observed.

A glitter on or through the pane, from which he had turned away, distracted him, made him glance back.

He saw an amber glare filtering along the road, and for a moment took it for the headlamps of a car, suddenly more incongruous, in this arcane spot, than anything else. And then he recognized the glare for what it was: the unanachronistic light of pitch torches.

Even as he stared, the sheen hitting the glass and his eyes together, he felt a surge of hatred. This biblical advance, as if upon the wreck of Gomorrah . . . and the damnable overcast providing its dramatic mise-en-scène.

"Good God, look at this," he said. But his companions had already looked at it.

"They need the fire, for what they want to do," she said.

"And what's that?"

"Purgation," she said. She darted from the pane, into a corner of the room, and covered her face with her hands. Luc also had backed away. His eyes were wide, and his mouth beginning that almost unavoidable rictus of a snarl.

Christian went after him and seized his shoulders, shaking him. He started to say angry things to Luc, senseless things. Christian's blood was cold.

The rage of the torches gradually ran up the window, an unlovely sunrise. The three in the room began to hear the noise of a multitude of feet, a strange noise of many throats engaged in chanting or prayer. Yes, probably in prayer.

Returning to the window, Christian saw something pouring over the moat bridge and up the gravel; a horde of people— he had never seen so many of them, except perhaps at Sylvie's funeral. But, between flame and gloom, they were a formless entity, some atrocious jelly-like excrescence gliding mindlessly in on the house to devour it whole. They dragged up, too, a thing on a cart in their midst. He was reminded of an army of ants, bearing the corpse of some other insect they have crushed during their unstoppable progress. He could not be sure what this thing was, only that it possessed length, being tilted at an angle across the cart, and it seemed heavy. But in a second more he came to suppose it was a battering ram. Certainly, convention was to be dispensed with. Or vilely resurrected.

Why, why were they so horrifying? It was more than the fact that they converged on him in a mob, more than their fires, their ram, their mere facelessness caused by the erratic hellish light, and by distance.

Yet it was facelessness of a sort.

They had remained, from the very commencement, an amorphous mass; they had never become human. He had met none of them, save for the briefest moments. None of them had revealed anything of themselves or their lives beyond their revulsion of him, and of what he stood for. They had never been *characterized* for him. And now he saw their power, yet he knew nothing about them, only that they were joined, malevolent and immediate.

They had reached the steps to the terrace.

Suddenly, before he was quite ready, he flung up the window. One of the guns was at hand. He snatched it and fired wildly up into the air. The concussion was deafening, and the blast jarred his shoulder, but the swarming monster on the ground collapsed into stillness.

How grotesque it was.

It would be foolish to inquire of it, of them, or to pretend incomprehension.

"Take yourselves off my land," he shouted down to them. "Go this minute." He lowered the gun and leveled it down at them.

"Don't shoot!" someone cried below. "Don't shoot, monsieur."

The voice, which sounded alarmed, seemed amenable therefore to reason, and Christian searched the crowd to find its origin. Abruptly, like deciphering a single word among a thousand that made no sense, Christian beheld the little priest, waving his arms up at the window.

The pale face above the black soutane was imploring, asking only to be trusted.

"Father," Christian called, "I presume you have some authority. Tell your *flock* to move away from the chateau. Or I'll fire into the middle of them. I mean what I say."

And perhaps I do mean it.

"It's necessary," said the priest, "that this thing be done—" He broke frantically into garbled unfamiliar Latin. Christian could not attempt a translation of it, but suddenly the faceless monster surged forward again, a swirl of shapes and flares and shadows rushing up the stairway. Christian's heart leaped in his throat, his brain, and he squeezed the trigger in blind fury and horror. A mindless click resulted. The mechanism had jammed.

Christian flung the gun away from him. He took up another, and leaned half out of the window. He perceived just then a reality in the mob; a woman ran across the muzzle of the gun, and next two children. He was shaking violently, and could no longer control the gun. He managed to pull the trigger with a profound effort, but the bullet only smashed against one of the cement urns flanking the stairway. The urn exploded like a bomb into the crowd, which took no notice, and tumbled on.

The peculiar ram had been unloaded from the cart and was bumping and scraping up the stair. Somewhere a stone was hurled and one of the lower indefensible casements shattered. He saw the flickering spray of glass reflecting the torchlight back across the terrace like a firework.

Christian drew away from the open window. In the corner, the man and the woman were waiting, yes, unmistakably waiting, for disaster. As at the moment of metamorphosis, they did not look mortal, or rather, not intelligent, merely instinctual. Perhaps each of them had recurring nightmares of such a time as this. Where could they live, but in the forest, and what could they hope for except to keep safe by inflicting fear on others, aware all the while of the doubtfulness of their sanctuary. And now the expected retribution had arrived. They had probably pictured it too often to be able to resist.

"Both of you," Christian said, "go into the secret passage."

"You come with us," Luc said.

"No."

Gabrielle ran across the room to Christian. She gazed up into his face, her eyes wetly brilliant.

"It's useless," she said. "Useless. Useless."

"You will hide, and I'll deny that you're here. Someone has to stand in their way," he declared, "or there's nothing to stop them." He was sickly amused by what he had just said. He visualized himself, a hero, facing the faceless thing, defending his hereditary property like some demented medieval prince.

She sneered at him then, as if reading his mind. She began to cry, not noticing, and her eyes blazed with water, the wide eye and the narrow eye, sisters in grief and misery.

"Run away," she said to him, "on foot if you have to. Leave us and go—" She spun aside from him and sped out of the room. She had not worn her shoes, he did not hear her feet on the carpeted floors.

Luc hesitated, his wolf's face turning to the torchlit fluttering at the window, to Christian, to the guns on the dust sheet, to the window again.

"Go with her," Christian said.

"You don't imagine a hiding place can protect us?" Luc's tone was oddly bantering.

A great blow sounded through the chateau: the weird battering ram had met the door below. The floor vibrated faintly, the nerves of the body clenched.

"I'll stay with you," Luc said casually. White with terror as if he bled to death, he idly took up one of the guns. "I'm sure I can manage to inflict some harm on them with one of these. Better than you, perhaps."

"Perhaps. We shouldn't risk it, do you think."

A second blow thundered. Christian sprang at Luc and began to push him toward the corridor beyond the room.

Luc dropped the gun, broke from Christian suddenly and raced ahead. He was gone by the time Christian reached the corridor.

The third blow was unlike the other two. Its effect upon the timbers of the hall door was evident, even though unseen. The house seemed to rock on its foundations.

Christian, gripping the gun he knew he would not use, walked along the corridor to the gallery and the staircase.

The gas was unlit. The fires in the hearths beneath were

low and dull, giving no illumination, save where the table across the door caught an intermittent spark or two on its silver. The table had already shifted somewhat.

As Christian stepped down onto the second stair, the fourth blow of the ram burst the air like cannon fire. With a strange inexplicable surprise, he watched the wood of the door fragment, the metal buckle, and that thing, like the beak of some hideous bird, tear through it all. Only then, mesmerized by this meter of stone thrust into the hall, this rape, did he recognize the ram for what it was.

It was the stone obelisk from the village square.

Chapter 23

———●◉●———

The Rape

Two further windows were broken in the salon before the fifth blow of the obelisk took the door from its hinges, and carried it forward with the impact, two or three meters into the hall. The human mass flooded in behind, over and around it. Some, having clambered in through the smashed windows, scattered in from the salon. Black water at flood tide.

Christian stood on the high ground of the ballerina stairs, and watched the water stop, spontaneously checked and swirling, forty steps below him.

How many times had this happened, For, yes, he could tell it had happened before. And that other seigneur, standing where now Christian stood, gun or sword in his hands, what had *he* been inclined to do?

The village had raised all its manifold heads to him, all those discs of flesh tinged by smoky fire.

But he appeared no less bizarre than they, himself also stage-lit by the torches, this elegant and modern young man, in his immaculate trousers and waistcoat of watered silk, his eyes almost as colorless as his face. He looked afraid, but also oddly remote. He looked extremely dangerous. It was this, perhaps, which had halted the inrush of the crowd. This, and the psychological barrier, the hill of steps which had yet to be scaled.

There ensued a long pause, during which nothing save the

torch flames stirred. Then one man put his foot onto the bottom stair, and Christian slid the gun around to cover him.

"Get back," Christian said loudly and clearly to this spillage from the mass. "Step back off the stair, or you'll be shot."

Intimidated—by gun, or stance, or voice—the man obeyed.

"Where's your wretched priest?" Christian demanded.

There was a sort of whirlpool effect, and the priest, who was like a little mouse, rose out of it and came to the stairfoot. A group of male children washed forward with him. They carried things, mystic things of the church, or the exorcism itself. Behind them, the broken table, the doors, grew visible, resting on the phallus of the obelisk. The doorway was blocked instead by the crowd, the crowding iron afternoon sky.

"How do you explain," Christian said, "this damage to my property? Am I not to be recognized anymore as the seigneur?" A look of drunken exhilaration went across his face.

"You must pardon us," said the priest. "We mean no harm. We're respectful to you, monsieur. But—it's come to this. The Lagenays—it must be seen to. Their devils must be driven out."

"Mine, too?"

The priest averted his eyes.

"There are no devils here," Christian said, "and no Lagenays." He looked from meaningless mask to mask of the crowd. Like an actor dazzled by the flares at the brink of the platform, he could not focus on any of them. "I'd say you're welcome to search my house. But, by Christ, you are *not*."

The priest was hanging his head now, drooping. An inimical sharp and pungent scent came drifting, roused by the indoor heat of fires or bodies, from the boxes the little boys carried.

The monster susurrated to itself.

Christian altered his grasp on the gun. His hands were slippery with sweat, yet icy, almost numb. He recalled, with a lunatic hilarity, his lack of strength, his fear of dying. A high-pitched trembling, like the soprano note double-stopping obtained from a violin, was buzzing through him. He did not feel frightened in any recognizable fashion, and so need not accept the fact that he was, in reality, petrified.

He knew he could not turn them away.

They had not required to break down the door, the shattered windows would have given them sufficient means of entry. But to break in the door was a symbol, just as the implement of ramming was a symbol. As the Lysinthe itself was a symbol. They were attuned to symbols here, they relied on them. And in this bizarre vocabulary, having got so far, there could be no symbol to replace the symbol of the exorcism, no pattern in which they might fit the alternative of retreat.

It was merely a question of time, of nerve. It was the balance of his hereditary rank, his cold histrionic hysteria, and the moot value of the gun, against their demoniacal sense of purpose.

Damn them. Eight hundred years or more had taught them they were right, and that God was on their side.

He had lowered the gun slightly, inadvertently. Or perhaps it was a signal of surrender. For an instant, the tableau continued, and then the invisible ropes gave way. The crowd, without prelude, crashed through. In an enormous wave, they gushed up the stairs. Christian watched them come, unable to move, a wall of water sweeping up to cover him. He shouted unintelligibly, but as he again brought up the weapon—no longer to fire, it had become a primitive club—it was wrenched from his fingers.

The comber of bodies hit him. He was knocked backwards, but he never touched the steps. He had thought they would trample over him, but instead he was seized. Ten fists had hold of him, twenty sets of features leered and yelled and breathed on him, uncountable pressures of limbs and bodies collided with him, and he was borne upward with them.

It was indeed like drowning. He was stifled, could not get a purchase on anything that was still or that would support him or let him stand upright. He had considered that they intended to murder him, but he fought them now from sheer unreasoning panic.

Jigsaw pieces of the chateau—the ceiling, a chandelier, the looping bannister—whirled over and between voids of humanity. He glimpsed the phantom waxwork of a girl, pale and great-eyed, the mouth hugely open; a woman's unbound hair clawed his cheek. Then the race hauled him under. A bent knee struck the side of his throat. A boot with a heel of fire trod squarely on his left hand. The pain was unbelievable, but what did it matter now if his hands were mashed?

But the bones of the hand were undamaged. Somehow, in his frenzy, he had got hold of one man's shoulder, another's dirty neck-cloth. As they hurtled forward, Christian trapped against them, all three stared, panting and screaming curses, into each other's faces. Yet these men, like all the rest, were faceless, or at least, nothing seemed alive behind their facial skin.

Just then, the mob dashed itself and him over the head of the stairs and the gallery. A colossal thrust cast him incredibly aside. They pushed him against the brocaded wall as they rushed by him, and the torches flowed over like the wake of a comet. Even then, something or someone hit him across the lips, an indirect blow, like the others. An old woman, stumbling on him, mouthed toothlessly, her spit stinging in his eyes, before she scrambled on.

Christian sat against the wall, guarded by a thick hedge of humanity. Frequently the contours of the hedge changed, men would take the place of other men. But the depth of the hedge remained constant. They did not propose to let him elude them.

Beyond the hedge, their fellows searched the chateau, violating it with their riot, their clumsiness and spite. The fundamental principle had been dismissed. The house and its lord were no longer privileged.

Sometimes the eyes of the hedge turned inward and gazed at him. Twice a ringing sound came in his head; he started to lose consciousness. Each time, some variation in the din or some encroachment of truth, such as the plushy roughness of the brocade wall against his forehead, brought him back.

They muttered in their dialect. Once, he heard a girl say that he was handsome and he heard also how someone immediately slapped her. He thought that very funny, but had no urge to laugh. He considered vaguely what Annelise would do when she discovered how he had been suffocated and torn in shreds by a mob in the northern forests. Annelise was the only one he could think of who meant anything to him, and then only because she was the last sane woman he had known. Gabrielle, and Luc, being part of this, seemed phantasmagorical. Or else, they were extensions of himself, or he an extension of them.

The supenatural darkness had not cleared. In any event, in less than two hours, it would be sunset.

En forêt noir je vais les soirs.

He became aware quite abruptly that the confused activity all around him had died down.

It was comical. They had searched, but not found.

He looked up as the human hedge altered again, and beheld a woman standing stiffly, poker-spined, in front of him. He reclined on the wall and observed her. Her face had character, of a kind, because it was familiar. He was not amazed to be confronted, in this perverse manner, by Madame Tienne.

"Get up, if you please, monsieur," she said.

"Why? Is the coffee ready at last?"

A man leaned over, and pulled Christian up the wall to his feet. Another of them shambled forward, plucking at Madame's sleeve.

"No," she said, "let him alone. You should not have dared to strike him. It's the devil within you must strike, not the man. Never the lord." And the villager slunk back.

How entertaining that she had some power over them, Madame of the acorn knuckles, the appliquéed lips. Traces of a matriarchy remained.

Christian smiled at her. He had never charmed this one. Neither then, nor now. She had scornfully related the village's superstitions, its provincial ways. She had prevented his suicide. That was one aspect of her. Here was another. The town servant, and the village sybil. *La Dame aux Lys.*

"Well, Madame," he said, "what's your role in this enchanting affair?"

Her irises, like burnished bullets, deflected his gaze. His head swam. He did not need to ask her anything. As if she had pierced his brain and put the knowledge into it, all became plain to him in that moment.

"We'll walk along the passage, monsieur," she said. "If you please."

"I don't please."

"Then you must do it without pleasure, I regret."

She walked, and he walked by her. He missed the clink and clatter of the keys at her apron. She wore a black shawl, now, over her head. She had learned city etiquette, but naturally, she had been born here. Her best camouflage had consisted of decrying what she believed in.

The mob hung at the periphery of Christian's vision, not interfering, as she guided him. They turned into the passage that led to the master suite.

"Ah, sweet revenge," he said. "Would that be it? I mean revenge on my grandfather, who raped you all those years ago. Who got you with child in the tradition of rape hereabouts. A little girl who was a wolf. Gabrielle's your daughter. But you don't love her, either, do you? Except maybe just enough to go to her on my arrival here, to warn her to keep away from me, the sick man dying of a highly infectious disease of the lungs. It *was* you, Madame?"

"You're most astute, monsieur."

"Aren't I? But rather belated, unfortunately."

The gas lamps had been lit in the passage. He noticed this suddenly. He recalled Sylvie, his rape of Sylvie which had not been a rape. And the forest had desired a rape. Through rape, the strain of the wolf children went on—was this why his lust had failed him? Because, without the element of the rape, his seed was reckoned useless? Unless he lay with one who was herself a descendant of the Shape-changer.

The unholy trinity. God help them.

The village had lifted the obelisk of the wolf goddess out of its stone socket in the square. She might have had temples once. Where the church had stood. But elsewhere, too. That heap of stones at the end of the Lagenay path—he had a mental picture of a squat stone building, hardly more elegant than a latrine, yet powerfully visible on its height from between the branches of fir trees in the canyon beyond. And then, there was that other heap of stone in the park of the chateau itself. Lysinthe. And her Roman name . . . Lukanthis—Lycanthia—

"Tell me why Sylvie was killed," he said.

They were alone in the passage, before the door of the master suite, and he halted. La Tienne turned to him, her hands folded upon her nonexistent apron.

"She stole from you, monsieur, and that is considered a crime. She lay with you, which might mean she would bear a demon, as I did. Two good reasons."

"But she was mutilated. As if a wolf had savaged her."

"Yes."

"Then she was a sacrifice to your goddess, wasn't she? Most importantly, a sacrifice. I don't ask which of you did it. It doesn't matter, since consent was general."

"We've learned to propitiate such powers as exist, when we're able, Monsieur Dorse."

"And when you're not able?"

"The exorcism is as old as the worship," she said. "It sets free. She forgives, perhaps." Madame opened the door and walked into the drawing room. Here the gas was not lit. Embers shone like garnets on the hearth. Gabrielle had laid this fire in the hour before Claut drove up to the house. In the hour when the idyll had persisted.

"We assumed you'd be no bother," said La Tienne, as she crossed the drawing room, "that you would die. Monsieur Hamel himself implied it in his letters to me. Suicide, of course, is a sin, and I wished to restrain you from that act. But in the natural way. . . . And then you astound us all. Your illness is a fake. You will live and you will consort with the accursed out of the wood. Almost from the first, you displayed your blood. So like your grandfather. It couldn't be allowed, monsieur."

"You bitch," he said. He walked after her. They passed into the bedroom. The fire was dead here. La Tienne made straight for the tapestry.

"Your life," she said, "can be protected. That is right. You're the seigneur."

"*Sang de seigneur.*"

"Your blood? Only if you're foolish. Alone, you're no threat, provided that you agree to go away."

The dense walnut light in the windows somehow showed everything: the bed, the cracked mirror above the dressing table, the knights at their endless jousting.

"I could break your neck," he said, "Madame."

As soon as he had spoken, a terrific cacophony burst out within the walls. Anguish churned through his belly. He did not need her to say to him, as she presently did: "The other end of the passage has already been opened."

She would know of that secret route, know of its operation. She, of them all, would know. Though he had forced her in that dirty little inn, Christian's grandfather might well have gloated aloud upon other customs of the house. Or pos-

sibly her years of service here had taught her. The house often shut up, the drunkard, who was not then the drunkard,
away in England. Madame, a young woman, coming from
her work in the village, getting in like a thief, prowling the
chateau, as Gabrielle would later prowl it.

A hurricane billowed the tapestry up in the air like a ship's
sail. A fanfare of torches spurted into the room, and just before it, a man and a woman, running out of the space inside
the wall.

If they noted Madame Tienne, or Christian, was unsure.
As they plunged forward into the dark, they were silhouettes,
shadows, only their liquid swiftness marking them for who
they were—yet, even so, they did not seem to move as they
had, mere speed now which had been like quicksilver then.

They reached the door of the bedroom, and unraveled
through it.

A vast roaring came again as they met the second maw of
the crowd beyond the doorway of the master suite.

Men ran from the secret passage. Christian was seized violently by both arms and around the ribs. Torchlight jumped
from bed to canopy, from canopy to mirror, and across the
umber panes of the windows.

Chapter 24

———◦◉◦———

The Festival

"Exorcizo te, creatura aquae, in nomine Dei Patris omnipotenti. . . ."

Under that heavy sky, extinguished as if at a solar eclipse, the priest made passes above the chalice: the blessing of the water.

Half-seen in the crepuscule, the chateau filled the horizon. The ground here was open and reasonably flat. A single lime tree lay over on the air, twisted and disfigured. This area had ceased to be part of the estate. It had become a plane of magic.

The outer circle they had drawn in the mud, and strewn with white lumps of chalk, was a little more than two meters in radius; the inner white-chalk-strewn circle perhaps one meter. A triangle, similarly scattered with bits of yellow chalk was contained by this inner circle. Its apex pointed to the north. The ground within the triangle had been scrawled with signs, religious, astrological, cabalistic, but the mud had difficulty in retaining them. Southeast of the inner circle was a stone block. The ground was disturbed, the stone had been brought here from another place. Northwest of the inner circle a fire of wet wood had been lighted, now spitting and crackling, and sending up a spire of smoke.

". . . .et in nomine Jesu Christi filii ejus Domini nostri . . ."

A black pot rested on the fire, bubbling like a gypsy stew.

There was, this far, only water in the pot. Steam rose with the smoke.

There was fire beyond the outer circle, too. All along the curve of the chalk strewings men had thrust the stems of their pitch torches into the earth.

. . . .ut fias aqua exorcizata. . . ."

The crowd pressed about the outer ring. A forest, which kept most still and silent. But every eye glinted and deadened as the torchlight struck it, an endless succession of lurid winks.

The crackle of the damp wood was very loud.

At four points, east, west, south and north of the outer circle, a man was positioned, more remarkable than the rest because he carried a gun. And in the gun, of course, silver bullets. They had been lucky, there. Though Sylvie, who had tried to steal the silver for them, misunderstanding, had had to die, Christian himself had freely presented them with the means and the material.

". . . . Domini nostri Jesu Christi. Et sancta Domina et mundi domina. Amen."

The priest emptied the blessed water from the chalice into the boiling pot. The hot liquid cooled, seethed and hissed.

The priest clasped his hands in prayer. His mouse's snout fell forward onto his fingers. He was not quite alone in the occult space.

Gabrielle had been stripped to her chemise. She lay inside the southwest corner of the yellow chalk triangle. She could not move, or very little, for her hands were tied, with only centimeters of slack, to a small wooden stake pushed into the ground. Only by inflicting excruciating hurt on her wrists, and by twisting her arms almost from their sockets, could she have faced in another direction, or extended more than the tips of her feet over the edge of the triangle. Her vantage was also limited to the triangle's interior, and mostly to its complementary southeastern corner, where her son, Luc, had been similarly bound. To the woman they had allowed a vestige of consideration and modesty in the makeshift of the chemise. The man they had stripped naked.

Captured, both had briefly resisted. The documentation of this resistance was visible in both cases, in the form of lacerations, welts and bruises which the vagrant lights shockingly displayed over and over again.

They might have been expected to shiver and to cringe in the freezing and funereal gloom, but some insane rigor of fear had apparently put them beyond it. Creatures in abject terror seldom notice anything other than their immediate condition. Not yet transformed by the coming of night, they were nevertheless no more human than the posts to which they had been fastened. They looked scarcely more alive.

This, then, the ceremony accorded to the de Lagenays. For Christian, something else again.

It was with a dreadful sense of déjà vu that he witnessed these preliminaries of the exorcism. Once out of the wall, their prime quarry subdued, the invading horde had returned their attention to the chateau's master. He, too, was bound, not stripped of clothing, though stripped of many less tangible emotional coverings, and herded out into the park.

There, beneath the tortured lime tree, on the slight incline it surmounted, just outside the limit of the greater circle, they had planted the gothic seat from the church. They must have brought it up the road in the cart, as they had brought the obelisk. Now they pressed Christian into the chair, manually. And when he sat there, perforce, they tied him to the wooden back and arms, with coils of rope. He, it seemed, unhampered by the enclosure of the magic drawings, must be more securely fettered than the de Lagenays. It seemed, too, that he must watch.

The villagers were all about him, yet he could see over their heads. He could see Gabrielle, her flesh gleaming through the translucent chemise, through its worn lace, and Luc, crouched against his binding post, slowly panting, a slim thread of blood running along the side of his face.

Yes. Christian must watch. His scrutiny was essential, and his utter helplessness. For he could no more free himself, had no more mobility, than the two in the yellow triangle.

The little boys had reached over the chalk lines and put down their canisters and boxes as close as they were able to the fire and the bubbling pot. Now the priest collected these containers, bore them to the fire, and began to take off the lids.

Did he feel important at this moment, the priest? It seemed likely.

The priest began to paw inside a box. He threw a handful

of granules into the black pot. The pot sizzled dutifully, and the action was repeated.

Like an inventive cook, pleased by initial results, the mouse of a priest began to upend canisters and uncorked vials into the pot.

A stench began to arise, irritant and foul. A smell of spice, of camfre and pepper, of funguses and bad vegetables, and over all, the reek of sulphur.

The priest turned his head quickly and sneezed. As if embarrassed by this lapse, he retreated fom the cauldon. He edged about the inner circle, moving toward the stone in the southeastern portion of the outer ring. Here he dropped to his knees, and assumed a position of prayer.

The crowd began a swaying complementary mutter. The dialect hung thick as the choking fumes that spasmed from the boiling pot.

The stink grew more obnoxious with every second. The crowd coughed and hawked matter-of-factly between the responses of their orison.

The filth of it; how aptly it expressed the soul of what they did, that malodor.

Christian found himself straining, quite automatically, against his bonds, but his urge was merely to run away.

A child vomited from the midst of the crowd.

"Damn you," Christian said to all of them, aloud, and they did not hear him, or care. "If there is a hell, may you fry in it."

The stench of the fumes brought bile into his own throat. In the foremost gusts of its effluvia, he saw them, the man and woman of his blood, curling and writhing like the two halves of something severed.

Sweat ran across Christian's face, neck and shoulders. His stomach crawled. His hands and arms and torso had by now strained so galvanically against the ropes which held him that his skin beneath his shirt had begun to swell up on either side of the bindings. The pain caused by this was intense, yet he could not separate it in any way from his condition, nor could he relax and let the pressure of the ropes ease.

For some reason, he began to hear Rachmaninov inside his head, great gouts of music; piano, orchestra, every instrument audible. He could not identify the work. It made no sense.

He could smell opium, now, in the mixture of the fumes. Poppy seed. And hartshorn. And burned vinegar. . . .

All at once—he did not seem to recall seeing them approach—there were an extra number of figures inside the chalk rim of the outer circle. They had inched through the ring of fires, and others inched through even now, grotesque in their very normalcy, taking care not to be singed.

The priest was getting up again. He walked back around the inner circle to the fire and the pot. Stooping, he took up something from the ground. It looked like a great spoon, or ladle.

The earth *shook*. No. They were lifting the carved chair, and Christian with it. He began to call them by obscene names. As before, no one paid attention. The crowd carried him through a gap in the torch-ring, and his porters were also careful of the flames, both with the chair, which they lifted very high, and of their own clothing. They set him down lightly, a laughable courtesy, just inside the northern apex of the yellow triangle. They themselves did not at any time cross the rim of the inner circle with their feet.

The brew in the cauldron caught his throat, and the internal Rachmaninov died. He began to cough, violently. Through the fit, he heard, instead of disembodied music, the noise of the first lash as it came down.

The smoke must have steadied, or the breeze created by the passage of many bodies might have pushed it another way. Christian managed to gasp in a breath or two of pure cold air. Water ran out of his eyes, and cleared them, and he saw a woman's figure, black on the torches, its arm upraised, ending fantastically in a spray of twigs, as if she changed into a tree.

The twigs reeled down. The blow made a sort of dry splashing sound on Luc's shoulders. It was the fourth or fifth blow, and as yet the marks of each were individual, almost delicately colored in on the pale skin of his back. The woman whirled away. The lash of twigs passed into the hand of another, lifted, dashed down again, and with the same peculiar noise. This time, there was also a nearby echo. Luc slipped forward, the crown of his head diagonally toward Christian, his body sprawled, but as the lash hit him yet once more, his whole frame leaped beneath it. Then the press surged in eagerly, bending over him, obscuring him, striking him now also with their hands. And as he was obscured, so the space about Gabrielle was revealed.

She had pulled herself hard against the post. Her head was lifted at a rigid snake-like angle, her face a white emblem, rent by its eyes and open mouth. Her attention was fixed only on the area where Luc lay, or rather on the milling of the crowd which hid him from her. Her wrists were bleeding, for she worked frantically and uselessly—as Christian did—against the fetters. She might have been snarling, or cursing them, or merely screaming. It was the men who beat her, as it was the women who beat at Luc. The skin across her spine and buttocks had already broken. The little chemise was ripped and stained, as if it bled, not she.

Christian stared at her. Unaware of him, she seemed also unaware of the bundles of vipers which bit into her flesh, though her body too, automatically, danced each time that it was struck.

He could not think why he could not hear her screaming, or hear the cries of Luc. It became important to him to know. A terrible idea came to him, that they had been deprived of their tongues—then, with a foolish sense of relief it occurred to him that the mob was chanting and shrieking itself, loudly, loudly enough to drown those stifled agonized chants of Luc's pain, and Gabrielle's, though not always the dissimilar whippy snapping of the twigs—

He felt something crack and apparently loosen, and looked down, imagining that one of the ropes which held him had given way. But it was the cracking of his muscles under strain, and hot wires ran through him.

The priest had appeared in the mass, with his ladle, which steamed. He had been to the cauldron and returned. The crowd about the inner circle and the triangle gave ground. The chant sank, and Christian listened to the mouse priest shrilling excitedly in the dialect: "I charge thee as thee are Luc, as thee are of Christ. Return to Christ, our son, Luc. Send forth this other which has sovereignty over thee, and let it begone. Oh begone, I charge thee, who is not Luc, but Satanus."

The ladle dazzled as scalding water flew from it. Inside the gut of the crowd, a boy screamed: Luc. This time, audible.

And now the priest turned toward Gabrielle. Gabrielle with her back crimson as if from the petals of roses, her silk hair clotted, her mouth a wolf's. The priest's face caught the torchlight. It shone. It was exultant.

"I charge thee as thee are Gabrielle, as thee are of Christ. Return to Christ, our daughter, Gabrielle. Send forth this other which has sovereignty over thee, and let it begone. Oh begone, I charge thee, who is not Gabrielle, but Satanus!"

He flung the second dose of the ladle across her face and neck and breast.

· She did not call out. She twisted and folded over, her scalded skin pressed into the mud about the post.

As Gabrielle lay there, Madame Tienne seemed to manifest above her. Madame Tienne leaned forward and slashed Gabrielle across the head with her bare hard-knuckled hand. A wealth of maleficence was in her gesture. Her features never relinquished their starch.

"Drive out the Devil!" cried the priest.

The crowd bellowed. They squealed and snorted and growled and stamped, a pack of beasts. The stinging notes of the lashes came again. The drugged stink of the cauldron eddied across this theater of lurching forms.

Christian found himself stumbling out of the chair, but the chair, inexorably attached to him, came with him. He achieved one frenzied insane pace on bent knees, and then the weight of the chair pushed him face down into the slimy frigid soil, and fell on top of him. He kneeled, bowed over and clamped to the mud, buried by the chair, unable to move in any direction, even to tumble to one side, crushed by the fearsome heaviness of the carving, as if a mountain had collapsed on his back. In this position, he was starved of breath, yet he, too, began to scream. He screamed and sobbed, pinned to the pitiless earth, and someone kicked across the triangle at the chair, then another and another, so his prison became also a huge drum.

He could do nothing. He could only cry and listen and feel, and know his impotence, trapped beneath the medieval wood. And the muffled double resonance of the lashes began to resemble the noise of rain. . . .

Exorcism. A process to drive out devils. Incidentally, it would kill the possessed. Incidentally.

His mouth was full of the cold earth. His mind was full of images. He suffocated very slowly.

When small trickles of scarlet began to slip through under

the chair, he supposed them to be blood. The blood of Gabrielle and of Luc, flooding the land, and they would all be drowned in it. He became aware, with a dull and puzzled gradualness, that the rain of blows seemed to have ceased.

With sickening swiftness, they were raising the chair again, pulling it backward, and Christian was pulled up with it. It thudded squarely down on the ground. He found he could breathe. Presently his head fell forward and his eyes closed. He did not care anymore.

A woman wiped the mud from his face. Her touch was brisk yet respectful; unliking, polite. Madame Tienne.

He felt nothing. No longer terror or anguish or a desire to break free. Only a boundless depression, worse than anything, more destructive than fear.

He waited for the exact hands to finish with him, then opened his eyes.

A whole bloody sky spilled into them. The color he had seen was a sunset, for the darkness had been abruptly hurled away from the landscape like a flock of birds. Yet the red was also like a darkness, too deep, too intense, sullen even in its lambency.

Only after considerable effort was he able to bring his eyes down out of that sky, and to look at the earth.

The mud was trampled and churned. The two pale shapes that lay on it seemed similarly trampled, similarly churned, their white surfaces runneled and defaced. Neither moved, though they were no longer bound. Their hands lay helplessly flaccid.

Christian grasped the significance of the unbinding, for now a proof was waited for. If the demon had been driven out, the metamorphosis could not take place. But if both or either of these smashed and mutilated creatures started up a wolf, four men with guns and silver bullets waited.

Chapter 25

———◦◉◦———

The Sky

It was winter.

The reminders of winter were everywhere, the naked umbrellas of trees, the ruined patches of snow, the sheer and stinging stillness of the cold.

But now the winter was scarlet. A geranium winter.

And then this hot color began to cool.

It was extraordinary, as if some massive lamp were being turned down behind the bloody pane of the sky. By degrees, yet quickly, unhesitatingly, the flame faded into clinker. There was not then a single cloud visible, nor was the sun quite gone. Yet the light bled away.

With the new darkness, there came a new silence. Surrounded by a mass of wooden figures, Christian acknowledged this bizarre and sinister quietude to be also within himself. He could not feel the beat of his heart. Inadvertently he leaned forward, and realized, as the ropes slithered away across his knees, that his bindings had been cut from behind the chair. For what it was worth, which was very little, he was now at liberty. At liberty to accomplish what? Like the rest, he gazed up into the deadening sky.

At the last instant, as if conjured, the clouds appeared. Great walls and battlements, furling up out of the horizons of the forest, as if from some concealed bonfire, some colossal torch-ring which had been set to contain the entire estate.

A wind rose. It passed over, first from the north, and then

again, mysteriously, as if returning from the south. In the ultimate flicker of light, Christian beheld the clouds, blown like galleons, rushing toward each other.

The sky went leaden. The wind flattened out over the earth. As those enormous doors of cloud came together overhead, there was a stifled thud all across heaven.

The crowd gave off a spontaneous haphazard murmuring. The voice of the priest pierced through it, thin and urgent. The dialect was all but incomprehensible. It seemed he exhorted them to pray.

Christian stood up. His nerves were tensed for hands to fall brutally upon his arms, but no hands came. Instead, he saw the sky parting across its whole length.

There was a vivid glare. For a second, everything was visible, bleached, gaunt, and completely unreal. As the photographic flare went out, the thunder detonated, directly above.

A ghastly collective wail came from the villagers. It was not merely terror at the storm. It had an uncanny note of recognition, almost of greeting, in it.

Not quite aware of his own actions, Christian had begun to move across the interior of the yellow chalk triangle.

A piece of the air whirled shining past him and landed at his feet with a strange harsh smack. Christian paused. A large pellet of gray-white matter glimmered in the mud. It was as big as an apple.

There came then a series of muffled impacts, incongruous and awesome. A woman screeched. Something hit the side of the black pot, clanging like the tongue in a bell, and jumped into the fire beneath with a fizz and a roar of ejected steam.

Christian irresistibly looked upward, and knew the impulse to throw himself flat on the ground. *Stones were falling from the air*. Just then, the exposure of the lightning came again, and every member of the falling avalanche seemed to blaze and flame.

Christian saw a stone strike the forehead of a man directly across the chalk line. The stone broke in two pieces; the man dropped stiffly forward. The thunder crash behind the lightning drowned his cry.

The villagers milled together and apart. Their feet breached the magic inner ring. They ran in circles like frightened sheep, and in their midst, the priest waved his arms like a windmill.

The hail hit the earth, isolated, appalling fragments, as if of some great masonry that had collapsed overhead. Some pieces of it were the size of coins, some the size of small fruits. But one of these shells of hardened ice smote and bounced away from the wooden post to which Luc had been tied: this stone was the size of a brick.

The panic of the mob was now total. The effect was reasserted of a vast, thoughtless, reflexive and amalgamated creature. A pool of this creature spread and burst against one of the men with the guns. He himself had been turning about on the spot, his free arm wrapped over his head. Now he went down, and the gun went off, firing its silver lozenge of death up in the air, into the cascading sky.

A girl lay in Christian's path. He stepped over her. Hail met the mud, and leaped again upward. The hail flailed into the midst of the heaving, shouting entity of the crowd.

Christian skidded, skated over the mud, and the hail skidded, skated across his feet. Glancing blows, like white-hot buttons, slapped his face and skull and shoulders. He reached Gabrielle, and went down on his knees beside her. In the glittering dark, he put out his hands. The lightning came. Everything was transfixed, crucified. Separated now, the thunder shuddered. His fingers gripped blood and hair—he saw the transformation had recurred. The sun had finally gone down behind a veil of icy bullets.

The she-wolf snarled faintly. The wounds lay like black spilled oil across her back and flanks. It seemed to him, in her pain, she might attack him, and he felt a traitorous horror of her bright fangs. But her head lolled over against his hand, and her demoniac eyes looked blind. How appalling the contortions of metamorphosis must have been, the exchanging of one damaged skin for this other which carried the exact maimings of the first. He was hurt by pity, as if by the thrust of a knife in his side. The hail smashed around them.

He tried to lift the she-wolf a little, but she was heavy with her own laxness, and, as he gained leverage on her body, she whined in agony. He could only think of her as a dog. He could not remember that this was Gabrielle.

He let go of her gently, allowing her to lapse down again into the mud. Christian turned to Luc, or to the animal which Luc would have become. The space by the second post was empty. Then the bomb-blast of the lightning revealed the long low shape of the dog-wolf dragging itself toward him, less than a meter away. Deep in its throat, the beast growled at him. Automatically Christian rose. He stepped back, and watched as the young male wolf pulled itself against the she, and flopped down by her.

Christian took another step in retreat, and half stumbled on a heap of prone human bodies, three or four of those stunned by the icy stones or else injured in the crowd's panic.

Absently, reminded by these casualties, Christian stared about him. The mob had gone away, stampeding through the driven hammer blows of the hail. Here and there, one or two lay immobile, unconscious or dead—he had no particular reason to care. He could not see sufficiently through the storm to judge how far away from him the rest of them had run.

The thunder boomed.

They would think the presence in the forest, their Lysin-the-Lycanthia had sent the hail to chastise them. Or that the magic power of the unholy triad had summoned it.

The earth swung around in a great arc, and he found himself lying full length on the ground.

Almost all the torches had been put out, the fire under the pot of mixture streamed vapor, and occasionally the stones would strike the metal of the pot itself, a weird note, reminiscent of some antique battle or joust. . . .

Digging his fingers into the chill slime, Christian started to haul himself toward the chateau.

When the lightning came again, it was darker. The thunder was more distant. The hailstones went on falling.

He had betrayed them, both of them. He did not know what he should do, so he abandoned them. But, in fact, he had betrayed them long before. As he had lain beside her in the bed, he had thought of going away, pictured it, even if he had made no plans. Like the village, he too was monstrous. Indeed, his contemplation of departure might almost, sorcerously, have precipitated disaster: the warning, the invasion of the mob, the murderous festival of death. For these things had followed upon his fancies. In such a place, electric with elements of the imbecilically supernatural, what could be more likely?

He saw himself now, half crawling, half limping, toward the chateau's broken door. He saw himself with aversion.

What in God's name did he intend? Not truly to leave them? Surely not. Leave them to die in blood and ice and mud. Then, what alternative course?

He was on his feet amid the hail, which had begun to slacken at last. His skin was bruised and gashed, his face numb and frozen, incapable of expression. Miraculously, none of the greater stones had struck him. But of course, *not* miraculously. The goddess in the wood must look out for her own.

He staggered up the steps to the terrace. They were evil and slippery, and once he almost fell. The bowls of the cement urns were piled with the bolts of the hail, like baskets of unnatural eggs. Eggs of the cockatrice, perhaps. He crossed the terrace, walked over the wreckage of the door, and noted, with a curious unease, that the stone pylon had been removed. When and how was not evident. By magic, too, maybe.

The grande hall beyond the doorway was vaguely lit, and he smelled at once the incongruous, slightly fungoid odor of the recently lit gas. And then he perceived Madame Tienne, stationed upright and motionless beside a cold hearth.

It had been, he supposed, idiocy to reckon she would fly with the rest. Or at least, she would fly straight here, this place of habit.

She held a silver tray in her hands, and as he entered, she moved after all, coming to him, to offer him the cognac and the glass that balanced on the tray. He swore at her, striking the tray and its contents out of her grasp. The impact was violent. She did not flinch. Probably she had known what he might do.

"That is a shame," was all she said. "You'd have done well to take something to warm you during the drive."

"Oh, am I driving somewhere?"

"But naturally, Monsieur Dorse. Renzo has packed your bags. Sarrette will bring the car around to the terrace. Sarrette will drive you to the train."

"The train's gone."

"There is another train, monsieur. At ten o'clock. Peton has the authority to prepare a ticket for you."

"The road's muddy. There's still snow on the road. And the hail."

"The road has been adequately cleared, monsieur."

"It's very disturbing, Madame," he said, "this obvious manner in which you're trying to get rid of me."

"It was our bargain, monsieur."

"I don't recall that."

"But you do, monsieur. You weren't to be hurt, providing you would leave here immediately."

"And Gabrielle," Christian said, "Gabrielle and Luc de Lagenay. What about them? Your maniacal village took to its heels before it finished its business."

"The true purpose of the exorcism," she said, "is to kill. I think you understand that. They're too weak to move, to help themselves. Whatever form they occupy, by morning they will be dead."

"Ah, yes," he said. He looked into the ash on the hearth. "What did you think of the hailstorm, Madame?"

"There's freak weather, now and then, at this time of year."

"Rather an interruption."

"If you wish."

"Your side had some casualties, Madame."

"And they're superstitious in the village."

"So they are. I wonder why."

"I would suggest you make what haste you can to leave, monsieur."

Christian shrugged.

"Very well."

He looked carefully around the hall, and for the first time, saw his bags, even the box, piled against a wall ready for the journey.

"Of course," he said, "you have no legal right to do this."

"None at all. But in such a feudal place, monsieur, you could say we have rights that are of the land, the spirit."

"What will you do when I've gone, when the house is closed?" he asked her with idle curiosity. His mind was slowly beginning to wander elsewhere in a fitful impulsive way.

"We shall seek other employment."

"Work at the inn, perhaps? Hardly any fear of a rape now, eh, Madame?"

He strolled toward the stairs. The fine carpets, the wood, were thick with mud the mob had trodden in.

"Where are you going?" she rapped.

"I shall want my coat."

"Renzo will get it."

"Renzo may go to hell, and so, Madame, may you." He went up six steps, turned and looked at her enamel face. "Indulge me," he said. "I'd like to appropriate a sample of the books from my grandfather's library."

"Very well," she said. "But please be as quick as you can."

"Damn it," he said, "there are more than five hours before the train's due."

Near the top, weariness caught him. He rested a moment on the curve of the banister. Last light cannonades of hail smote the indigo porthole, now black. It was a wonder it had not been smashed.

It was a wonder he himself had not been smashed. Or maybe, in some insidious fashion, he had.

He came to the gallery, went along it and into the passage.

The astrakhan coat lay in the drawing room, across a chair, where he had most recently cast it down. As he put it on and fastened it, he walked across into the bedroom. He gazed slowly at everything, surprised to find none of it meant anything to him. He went through into the library and took at random a large book of essays.

Coming away from the master suite, he returned to the gallery, and paused. Madame had vanished from the hall below. Christian crossed quickly over into the corridor which led to the front of the chateau.

In the room where they had watched, the heap of guns had been disturbed by the marauders, but not scattered. There was a pistol in the heap, a pistol with pearl inlay along the handle. He had not thought to use it before, mistrusting its accuracy. Now he took it, inserting it in between the pages of the book. Holding the bulging package close under his arm, Christian went back again to the gallery, and so down into the hall.

Still, no one was there, only the pile of baggage verified the onus of departure.

After a moment, foolishly angered, he strode to the terrace door and flung it open, to confront Renzo on the threshold.

Cherry-cheeked and breathless, the boy gaped at him.

Renzo had all the appearance of a petty criminal, caught in the act of his felony. Christian stood aside dramatically, to let him by.

"Well, get on with it."

Like a scared rabbit, Renzo bolted across the hall toward Christian's bags.

It was the mirror image of his arrival, all in reverse. Even to a reversal of his terror. For he had come here in dread of his own death. He left in terror of the death of others.

The car glided ponderously around the side of the house, its lamps moving ahead of it, and drew up under the terrace.

The hail, when it came, drove in thin hard gusts, lit by the headlamps, its pieces reduced to the size of beans and the heads of pins. The cockatrice eggs were melting in the urns. Sarrette climbed from the car. He wore his top hat. He leaned against the car, folding his arms, waiting.

The road had been cleared, and the hail was melting. They need not turn out, the villagers, to watch Christian driven by on his way to exile. Why should they? Their grisly task was done. Besides, they were afraid. The hail had sent them from their magic before it was quite complete. The hail was the scourge, the mark of the fury of the She-thing in the forest, the thing they murdered young girls to appease. Would they pray to the stone obelisk, or huddle inside the partly Catholic church? For she was there, too, grinning on the window, her wolf lilies foaming over her arms.

Renzo darted up and down the steps, a clever rabbit which had been trained to carry things. The slipperiness did not appear to check him.

Christian went down to the car. Sarrette jerked into alertness. He put his palm on the handle of the car door. Christian considered him.

"What a pity you're going away, monsieur," said Sarrette, "The forests are so good for the health."

Renzo had brought the last bag and secured it. He hesitated, staring at Christian, while Christian looked mercilessly back, his heart galloping through his chest. When Renzo ran away, as run he shortly would, Christian must speak to Sarrette. He did not know how Sarrette would react to the words: I have a pistol which is aimed directly at you. Perhaps Sarrette would not credit the avowal. There might be a struggle, visible from the chateau. Sarrette would overpower him and he could be forced to use the weapon, which would misfire—

"Monsieur," said Renzo painfully, "I'm sorry."

"Are you?" said Christian. What did this peasant's stupid lie matter? Christian desired fervently that the boy should go, and as if aware of it, Renzo moved about and went up the steps, slithering now, and awkward.

Christian adjusted his position, his back to the house, drawing the heavy book from under his arm. His fingers closed on the silken inlay of the little gun between the bent covers.

Sarrette fiddled with the car door, half turned away, not yet cognizant of what went on.

"Sarrette," Christian said, "I have a pistol, which is aimed directly at you."

Chapter 26

———◆◉◆———

The Hut

Sarrette did not, after all, do anything overt; he simply poised, the half-opened door balanced on his hand, his top-hatted head tilted slightly forward. His face had been partially averted and remained so. A silence ensued. Neither man moved. Finally Christian, the aggressor, felt it was incumbent upon him to speak again.

"Did you hear what I said to you, Sarrette?"

"Yes, Monsieur Dorse. I heard you."

"You're probably wondering what we do next."

"No, monsieur."

"Then you should be."

Sarrette continued to lean forward to the door.

"I'd like you to understand, monsieur, I had nothing to do—with what happened earlier. I didn't come with the rest of them. I wasn't born here, monsieur." His voice was quite level, and he did not sound alarmed. He was merely explaining the facts.

"Your father was born here. For God's sake, what does that matter? I'm going to tell you what you have to do."

Sarrette, face averted, waited patiently, and Christian had the conviction that Sarrette would have obeyed him anyway, and that he had not needed to threaten him with the pistol at all. Christian felt suddenly ludicrous, angling the gun out of the book.

"You'll start the car, and we'll get in, you and I. We'll

207

drive over the moat and along the road. There's a diseased lime tree on the higher ground, about a quarter of a kilometer from the house. When we're about that distance along the road, stop the car."

They stood there again in silence. "Don't you want to know what you'll be required to do after that?" Christian said.

Sarrette shook his head. His dumbness was the first sign he gave of possible apprehension.

"Start," Christian said.

He moved around after Sarrette, his back still to the chateau, the pistol still eccentrically protruding from the book. When the car started, Sarrette climbed into the driver's seat. Christian, when he too was seated, let the book fall. He held the gun in the lap of his coat.

They drove over the bridge, along the road. Anyone watching from the house would presumably be satisfied.

He thought, with an indifference too great to be anything save the disguise of some other emotion, that he would never pass over those steps, that moat, that stretch of the gravel again.

Christian could not see the lime tree in the darkness beyond the lamps, only the chaos of kicked mud everywhere.

He glanced behind him. The chateau also had withdrawn into the night, the faintness of its erratic lights invisible. And he would never see it again.

The car pulled up abruptly. A last volley of hail skittered over the roof and was gone.

"Excellent," Christian said. "Now get out." They got out of the car. "Walk toward the tree." Sarrette complied, leaving the car, staring off across the mud. Christian, even now, could not make out the lime. "Do you know where you're going?" Sarrette once more nodded.

Following Sarrette, Christian said softly: "Somewhere hereabouts there are two wolves. Two sick and bloody wolves. We're going to pick them up in our arms, Sarrette, like the good shepherd with his sheep. We're going to carry them to the car. Or I can shoot you immediately."

Sarrette plodded on. His shoulders drooped, and Christian could not tell if he was afraid, revolted, bemused, or if, to Sarrette, just as to Christian himself, this whole event was unrealistic.

In the darkness, it seemed they were advancing through sheets of fine yet barely penetrable wool. The sky, emptied now of hail, emptied of everything, offered neither moon nor starlight. The whole expanse of it was scarcely more pallid than the land. Then the lime tree appeared, crumpled on this dull purple palette.

The situation shot into unpleasing recognition, for the little stakes remained in the ground, the cauldron of the exorcising fluid sat on the folded wood which no longer burned. A smudge or two of whitish chalk glowed as if phosphorescent.

Christian examined the scene, just as he had minutely examined the other scenes, the bedroom, the whole great room of the nocturnal landscape. His heart thudded evenly, like a clock. Luc and Gabrielle were gone.

Christian was distressed, for he realized that his error was no error at all, for surely he had really known all this while that if they lived, they would no more remain here than he could remain at the chateau.

He stooped toward the stakes. He could detect, he thought, the impressions their canine bodies had made. A shuffle of pad marks, however, might be illusory; certainly they were soon lost in the general upheaval of the mud. It seemed to him he could smell their blood, lying in small gelid black pools along the earth. He saw pieces of her torn shift, suddenly, crushed down with the strewn chalk.

He had been gone an hour or more. Of course, why should they stay here? They had seemed too weak to abscond to any place, but the animal strength in them, their instinct. . . . He had believed La Tienne, also, the vision she had given him, of two corpses stiffening, contained inside the magic circles. Could it be she had not known they would drag themselves back into the forest when the crowd had run away? When he had run away?

"Yes, monsieur?" Sarrette questioned, as if Christian had spoken.

"Yes," Christian said. He moved about over the mud, and the pistol hung uselessly from his fingers.

"Come along, monsieur," said Sarrette.

This was how they treated lunatics, was it not? The firm hand beneath the elbow. Sarrette was helping him back across the slime, toward the car.

Christian allowed it. At some point, the gun dropped from his hand into the mud.

"Where are they, Sarrette?" he said.

"You know, monsieur."

The headlamps of the car brought things violently out of the dark. The stone dogs, the pillars of the trees. Presently, the shafts of rain which had started to slant across the night.

I am going away. I shall see none of this again.

"I suppose I do know," he said. "You mean that ramshackle hut in the forest."

He remembered the bed with the embroidered curtaining, and the ugly bath made of metal. The stove. The aroma of Gabrielle's cigarettes. Her body. The hemlock tree. Luc, like a young Dionysos, manifesting by the tree. Something hurt inside Christian, a tiny irritating hurt, some hangnail of the soul.

Sarrette drove carefully along the glacial gravel. All the hailstones had dissolved.

Christian shut his eyes. He was not even aware when they passed through the village. It must have been somber and soundless, smothered as the trees.

Inside the station building, in an odd little afterthought of a room, a fire had been lit. An oil lamp with an ornate greenish carapace stood on a rickety table by a rickety chair.

Peton, the carrier, appeared and began to lug Christian's baggage into the room.

Sarrette sat, unspeaking, in the car, like a cartoon of a man in a top hat, and eventually, when all the bags had been brought up the steps and through into the room beside the platform, Sarrette drove the car away.

Peton hurried about the room. He put bits of wood on the fire. He produced a train ticket, and displayed it, spreading it proudly on the table before Christian. But the man was nervous, and sweated in the cold, and the fine pencil lines of hair unstuck from his scalp, and fluttered about his face, delicate as the wings of moths. He said something to Christian, thickly, in the dialect. He had to repeat it several times before Christian made out the words. "Wine, monsieur. Have wine. I bring thee? I bring thee wine?"

"No."

But Peton went out, and came back swiftly with a gray bottle and a dingy glass, which he placed beside the ticket.

Christian stared at the bottle. Finally he said to Peton, "Why did you show me the path?"

"Pardon, monsieur?"

"The path. To the Lagenay house. The hut. Why?"

"I never have taken thee," said Peton.

"You know you did."

"No."

"Yes."

"Thee made me to take thee," said Peton.

"And how did I do that?" Christian asked. After what seemed only a minute, but might well have been much longer, he glanced up, and Peton had gone away.

Christian sat in the waiting room. The fire sparkled in the grate, making the depression inherent in the room far worse by its cheerfulness. The cold bottle, like Peton, sweated and formed a shallow lake upon the table.

An hour, maybe two hours, drifted through the station, and away. Christian had a premonition that the train, delayed perhaps by unmelted snowdrifts on the line or a landslip due to the thaw, would not arrive.

He walked to the fire, and fed it. He walked about the room, from the left-hand corner nearest the platform door, to the right-hand corner nearest the outer door, which gave onto the steps and the road; from the right-hand corner to the left.

He tried to guess whereabouts Peton actually lived. He tried to imagine Sarrette's conversation, on returning, with Madame Tienne. The servants would remain in the chateau until once again formally dismissed. Even when the house was locked up, they would probably get in. The safest course would be to have the chateau razed. He pictured it on the fire, tall flames groping up through its chimneys, springing from its windows.

He thought about the city. He thought about the soft lamps on the boulevards, ringed by a halo of summer insects, and the orchestras playing in the squares. He thought of Annelise in a vast white ship of a hat in full sail. Of the conservatory of music. Of a song.

> *Je pense que dans leurs luminères*
> *Je vois les yeux de ceux qui m'aiment.*

*　　*　　*

What am I doing here?

He sat down again. He laid his arm along the table, and his head on his arm, like a tired child.

He thought of the hut. Of their blood, their burning, agonized eyes. The eyes of the wolves.

Why had they not trusted him, not waited for him to come back? How dreadfully wise of them to know that he could not be trusted.

His self-hatred rose in him. He would have to endure it.

He was playing at the edge of the sea. Women with parasols strolled up and down. One pointed her parasol at the water and fired it. A dead fish flopped out on the sand. The waves were really piano keys. As he stepped on them, they played, but the tone was poor. Gabrielle held him by the hand. Gabrielle was his mother. His red hair blew in his eyes, and he saw that the nails of his toes and fingers were also red. He struck out at the shot fish, and a bottle rolled off the table and smashed on the floor of the station waiting room.

It was morning, heatless, colorless. The rain had ended and the train had not come.

Christian looked, and saw his bags were still grouped on the boards.

Soon, he went out onto the platform. The passenger marker was up, the signal to the train that it should stop. The moist branches of trees, the wind funneling along the surface of the line, were the only animate things.

If the train had come, surely Peton would by then have been in attendance, would have wakened him and hustled him aboard. No, the train had been delayed.

Obscurely puzzled, Christian walked into the waiting room. He opened the outer door and went down the steps.

The forest, like a bank of fog, lay on the other side of the road.

When he was on the road, he started to run, but long before he approached the village, he moved off the gravel among the trees.

Distant chasms fell away through the towers of the pines; embankments rose. Larches seemed to stare with their boughs. The fluctuations of light and shade were well remembered, hardly disconcerting anymore. He smelled again the sharp resin, the vaguely chocolaty richness of earth and old smoke. The remaining patches of snow were grimy and transparent, a sort of fish skin.

He walked across the village cemetery, and the black shoulders of the graves still had white epaulets.

The forest was no longer unknown country. He seemed to have learned it, as he had learned the geography of the chateau. But what did such a thing signify? Only that he could find his way.

He glimpsed the village through the trunks of the trees. It looked remote, and nothing seemed stirring. Somewhere a sheep bleated, but it might have been on another planet. There was no menace, nothing of importance.

Christian was growing exhausted. The long uphill journey had enervated him, or it might have been apprehension which did so.

Everything was so peculiarly normal. As if the horrible invasion of the chateau, the festival of pagan magic, had never occurred. Even the two crossed bones, when he came to them, looked casual and scarcely more unwelcoming than a signpost.

The ancient untidy gray snow, like the gray glass of Peton's smashed wine bottle, lay in wide scales along the path. The hemlock tree had fared badly, several of its boughs snapped off by the weight of the snow, before the snow itself slipped from those dark spines so like the ragged wings of birds. In the snow, a pale green flower, misled by the thaw, or by the sorcery of the spot, had pushed its way into the world. The cold would kill it, when the cold resettled on the land. Christian stood gazing at the flower, now at last reluctant to go on. Perhaps all of it had been like the flower: premature and strengthless. Easy to destroy.

Chapter 27

The Departure

He saw the break in the forest first, the misty impression of the dip, and the cascading escalation of rock beyond, and the blue-gray fir trees clothing it. And then the heap of stones, as on the previous occasion, the stones which would have been a portion of some temple to the thing known as Lysinthe.

The shack, like the hemlock, seemed to have been mauled by the snow, though in a less easily definable manner. No doubt it had withstood many winters, just as the two who had come back here had withstood many winters of the heart. A string of smoke unfurled from the stove-pipe over the roof.

Stricken, Christian stopped less than a meter from the door. Last time, he had broken in. This time he could bring himself to go no nearer. And as he halted there, adrift in the sea of the forest, the door opened.

Gabrielle came out. She was wrapped about in an assortment of furs, which had a shabbiness in the light, and carried a big terra-cotta jar in one hand—obviously, there must be a well or water source close by. Her hair was knotted up on her head. She looked sallow and unattractive, her lips were dry, but her eyes were gleaming smears of lead, one narrow and one wide. There was a scarlet blister on her left cheek, and he recollected the scalding potion thrown over her. She did not seem amazed to find him there, but when she spoke, it was to a total stranger.

"What do you want, monsieur?"

"Dear God," he said, "you're alive."

"Oh, a small beating," she said. "One recovers."

"Gabrielle—" he said.

"Yes?"

He had never before seen such unreachable hardness in a woman's face that was turned toward him. Hardness which might be softened, yes. Hardness which might be broken in, as the door had once been broken. But this. She watched him from behind a pane of adamant.

"You shouldn't be here," he said. "Why did you come here? Are you mad? Do you think they'll leave you alone now."

"Quite alone, I should think."

She made an involuntary movement, somehow forgetting, and the pain of her beating must have caught her. Her mouth gaped, though no cry emerged, and her face flushed frighteningly. For a moment he supposed she would fall straight forward on it, and he ran to her, and seized her arms to steady her.

At his touch, her eyes cleared. Something even more terrible happened to her face, then. It blanched again, became beautiful, and the lips drew away from her teeth in the wolf snarl which always before had seemed to him laughable, a clownish gesture. But she, as she snarled, convinced him.

"Gabrielle," he insisted, trying to bring her to herself, "you can't stay here."

"And where will thee take me?" she asked mockingly. She clicked the serrated edges of her teeth together. Her eyes had changed color, and were black.

"Luc?" he asked.

"Sicker than I, but alive. Alive, monsieur le seigneur. He'll get better. We both shall get better. Do you not understand how *strong*, how *vital* we must be to undergo the constant transformation of the flesh? The village forgets such things."

"The village will come here after you."

"Where are they?" she said.

He released one of her arms, lifting his hand to smooth her unmarked cheek, and as he did so, she drew back her head and spat in his face.

Repulsed, appalled, he lunged away from her.

She laughed, a brief noise of utter contempt, and moved aside from him around the hut. She went slowly, and as the furs slipped from her a fraction, he perceived her undergarment of dried blood.

Shivering, cursing her, he stepped into the interior of the hut.

The stove had made it warm. Luc lay stretched out, naked, face down on the bed. His hair had been roughly hacked off at the nape of the neck, in order that it should not exacerbate the wounds across his shoulders. He seemed asleep, feverish, tossing in lethargic rhythms, as if on the swells of an ocean.

Christian stood helplessly, looking at him, waiting for the woman to come in again. As he waited, he wiped her venom absently from his skin.

But she did not come back at once, and suddenly, Luc's head turned on the pillow, and the visible eye opened, and looked in return at Christian.

Christian moved forward uncertainly. The eye accommodated his passage. It was sleepy, yet oddly intent.

"She says," Christian said awkwardly, "that you're sick, but will recover."

Luc did not speak. His face was implacable. The face of someone Christian had never met, under any circumstances at all. Deliberately, the eye was shut, as someone would put out the friendly light in a window. Luc dug his face again into the depth of the pillow.

Christian went to the stove, and stood there, resuming his wait for truth or punishment, or simply explanation.

When Gabrielle did come in again, the jar had been filled and she set it down heavily. She too moved toward the stove, and Christian automatically found himself retreating. As if he were invisible, she went past him, and kneeled by the stove. Clearly, she could not sit, or lie, save forwards, as did Luc.

"I ask you again," she said presently to Christian, though she did not glance at him, "what is it you want?"

"To see you safe."

"How would you arrange that?"

"I haven't any idea, Gabrielle."

"Then you're a fool."

"Apparently."

"Go," she said. "That is what you wish."

"Listen to me," he said.

"No," she said, "you listen to *me*." She raised her head,

and he met the awfulness of her eyes a second time. "We're safe. Yes, we are. If you go away, we are safer still. We'll be tolerated, hated, avoided. But secure in that. Just as before.

"How can you say—"

"They have nothing to fear. They know it now."

Luc whispered to himself as he lay over the bed. Gabrielle got up instantly. She went to him, and touched his head, lightly, and took his hand and held it quietly against her. Their russet nails, a perfect match, seemed dipped in spilled blood—their own?

"What you're saying is nonsense," Christian said. In the warm room he was cold, and wrapped his arms about himself."

"I will tell you," she said. "Hear me."

"Very well."

"The village feared the unity of three, the seigneur with the two wolves in the wood. But the village saw, quite frankly, that between the three there's no unity, and no power. They saw you, Christian. They saw that when they came for us, you capitulated. You let them take us. You let them scourge us, and scald us. You would have let them slaughter us."

He retreated from her again, two or three inches.

"That's an exaggeration. I had very little choice."

"Did you?"

"You know I was bound, tied up as you were, but more thoroughly, I suspect."

"Yes," she said. She did not bother to look at him any longer.

"What," he burst out, "was I supposed to do?"

"Oh," she said, "anything but the thing you did, for you did *nothing.*"

The injustice of her accusation filled him with bitterness. Every event rushed through his mind, striving to reach his lips, so that it might be shouted at her: his defense of them with the guns—the first of which had jammed—the human torrent which poured up the stair, overwhelming him; the ropes; the chair falling, burying him; his return across the mud with Sarrette—and yet, he did not say any of it, only, "Whatever I could think to do, I did. I apologize for not being the sorcerer your village supposed me."

She flashed at him one glance. It was like the smiting of a sword. By the glare of it, he realized what he had said, and its impressive significance, and slowly then he comprehended. The dismal, incredible explanation came to him, after all, out of the air.

By the supposition of the village, if he had achieved that mysterious trinity with these two supernatural beings, a power and a sorcery would indeed have come to them, to all three, and especially to him, whose traditional role must be that of the magician. That the power did not come to him, some unimaginable force far greater and more malefic than the minor spasm of the hailstorm, had proved to the village that there was, in fact, nothing to fear. The old stories were not about to be repeated, the legends of triads, of wolves and men, which had held the area in thrall. The villagers' act of hatred, though abbreviated, had established their safety, and thereby the complementary, precarious but acceptable safety of Gabrielle and Luc. One other thing it had established, the thing for which both of them, though not deigning to voice it, condemned and disdained him. Though he had shared so much with them, their moods, their activities, their love, he had not, actually, loved them. He had not actually been capable of oneness with them, or had not been prepared to be. They, also, had been shown proof of him. *Of course*, he had not been meant to protect them by firearms (the jamming of the gun now seemed ominous), or by anything—beyond some huge unholy strength founded, simplistically and stunningly, on his *need* of them. But his needs had not been of the grand order. He had only used them as a stepping stone to regain himself. As with medicine, he had allowed them to cure his pain, but once cured, he had looked beyond them. He had already dreamed of departure before the mob enforced departure on him. While his departure was, he now saw, a mere formality, since the mob knew, by then, he could not harm them. Not because he had not fought, but because he had fought wrongly, and with the wrong weapons.

Christian touched his face, where she had spat at him. She had not blamed him for cowardice, or incompetence, she had only been revolted by his use of her, now made so plain, and in so unique and undeniable a way.

Woodenly he said to her: "I tried to carry you to the house, but you resisted. I came back for you—"

"Another would not have left us," she said. (By another, she meant another Christian, one who had been linked to her, and to Luc, in the true inseparable fusion of the trinity.) "Another would have carried us if he could, though we savaged him in our pain. Or lain down with us. Yes, in the blood and rain and darkness. Lain by us, till he died, if necessary. Oh, I didn't expect it of you. I wasn't disappointed."

As he turned away from them now, from that unassailable pietà, he dimly acknowledged that he was glad to escape the oneness they might, all three, have shared, that glorious and stagnant state worse than vanity, worse than narcissism.

He had avoided the guilt of their deaths, and the lure of magical power—if such power were really possible. (Oh, yes, she would believe in it, and in his failure like a lapse of faith, but must he?) In this modern era of the train, the car, the gas lamp, how should any of them assume a wolf-goddess could reassert her influence. Perhaps he had rejected use of her power, rejected without knowing it, without wanting it. Or perhaps Gabrielle and Luc were in error. Perhaps sorcery, like all ancient things, decayed.

He was almost restored, almost beyond this, now. At the door he paused and announced:

"Despite what you've said and done, I wish you very well."

"I told you to go," she said. "Go away."

"I'll immortalize you," he said acidly, almost threatening her with the notion. "When I write music, which I mean to, which I shall, Gabrielle, you'll be in every note of it."

"Music I'll never hear."

"In the town, perhaps," he said. "After they've played the Rachmaninov, on some long light summer afternoon."

"You," she said softly. "You are the wolf. Feeding on us all to get what you want or think you need. In order to sustain your life, which is the only life you respect. Go, Christian. Go and write your music somewhere far away."

He moved along the path, away from the canyon, the hut, the stones, sluggishly. He had the long walk to the station to do over again. The train might come and be missed, or remain delayed for another week. But no one would attack him now. Probably Peton could be relied on for food, even shelter.

Christian coughed. He thought of the city, and those who would care for him, and he coughed. His heart was already in the city, had never really come away. Strands of melody stole into his mind, floating over and over each other—her song about the forest, that simple ballad, transformed, elaborated, ornamented—variations on a theme. Even the boughs and tines of the trees, the white bruises of the snow, the rills of wind and glaucous sun, became music.

Hurrying now, he stepped across the Lysinthe of bones without seeing them.

DAW presents TANITH LEE

"A brilliant supernova in the firmament of SF"—**Progressef**

To order these titles,
use coupon on the
last page of this book.

10th Year as the SF Leader!

Outstanding science fiction and fantasy

By Brian Stableford

By John Brunner

By Gordon R. Dickson

By M. A. Foster

By Ian Wallace

TO ORDER THESE BOOKS, USE

COUPON ON LAST PAGE.

DAW BOOKS

Presenting JACK VANCE in DAW editions:

If you wish to order these titles,

please see the coupon in

the back of this book.

Presenting ANDRE NORTON in DAW editions:

☐ SPELL OF THE WITCH WORLD (#UJ1645—$1.95)

☐ LORE OF THE WITCH WORLD (#UE1634—$2.25)

☐ GARAN THE ETERNAL (#UW1431—$1.50)

☐ THE CRYSTAL GRYPHON (#UJ1586—$1.95)

☐ HERE ABIDE MONSTERS (#UW1333—$1.50)

☐ MERLIN'S MIRROR (#UE1641—$2.25)

☐ THE BOOK OF ANDRE NORTON (#UE1643—$2.25)

☐ PERILOUS DREAMS (#UE1405—$1.75)

☐ YURTH BURDEN (#UE1400—$1.75)

☐ QUAG KEEP (#UJ1487—$1.95)

☐ HORN CROWN (#UE1635—$2.50)*

* To be published July 1981

THE NEW AMERICAN LIBRARY, INC.,
P.O. Box 999, Bergenfield, New Jersey 07621

Please send me the DAW BOOKS I have checked above. I am enclosing
$_____ (check or money order—no currency or C.O.D.'s).
Please include the list price plus 50¢ per order to cover handling costs.

Name _____

Address _____

City _____ State _____ Zip Code _____
Please allow at least 4 weeks for delivery